Hangma

Gladys Maude Winifred Mitchell – or 'The Great Gladys' as Philip Larkin called her – was born in 1901, in Cowley in Oxfordshire. She graduated in history from University College London and in 1921 began her long career as a teacher. She studied the works of Sigmund Freud and attributed her interest in witchcraft to the influence of her friend, the detective novelist Helen Simpson.

Her first novel, *Speedy Death*, was published in 1929 and introduced readers to Beatrice Adela Lestrange Bradley, the heroine of a further sixty six crime novels. She wrote at least one novel a year throughout her career and was an early member of the Detection Club, alongside Agatha Christie, G.K Chesterton and Dorothy Sayers. In 1961 she retired from teaching and, from her home in Dorset, continued to write, receiving the Crime Writers' Association Silver Dagger in 1976. Gladys Mitchell died in 1983.

VINTAGE MURDER MYSTERIES

With the sign of a human skull upon its back and a melancholy shriek emitted when disturbed, the Death's Head Hawkmoth has for centuries been a bringer of doom and an omen of death - which is why we chose it as the emblem for our Vintage Murder Mysteries.

Some say that its appearance in King George III's bedchamber pushed him into madness. Others believe that should its wings extinguish a candle by night, those nearby will be cursed with blindness. Indeed its very name, *Acherontia atropos*, delves into the most sinister realms of Greek mythology: Acheron, the River of Pain in the underworld, and Atropos, the Fate charged with severing the thread of life.

The perfect companion, then, for our Vintage Murder Mysteries sleuths, for whom sinister occurrences are never far away and murder is always just around the corner ...

GLADYS MITCHELL

Hangman's Curfew

VINTAGE BOOKS
London

Published by Vintage 2014

2 4 6 8 10 9 7 5 3 1

First published in Great Britain by
Michael Joseph Ltd in 1941

Vintage
Random House, 20 Vauxhall Bridge Road,
London SW1V 2SA

www.vintage-books.co.uk

Addresses for companies within The Random House Group Limited
can be found at: www.randomhouse.co.uk/offices.htm

The Random House Group Limited Reg. No. 954009

A CIP catalogue record for this book
is available from the British Library

ISBN 9780099583936

The Random House Group Limited supports The Forest Stewardship
Council® (FSC®), the leading international forest-certification organisation.
Our books carrying the FSC label are printed on FSC®-certified paper.
FSC is the only forest-certification scheme supported by the leading
environmental organisations, including Greenpeace. Our
paper procurement policy can be found at
www.randomhouse.co.uk/environment

Printed and bound in Great Britain by Clays Ltd, St Ives plc

CHAPTER I

" And pleasant is the fairy land
  For those that in it dwell,
But ay at end of seven years
  They pay a teind to hell."

THERE ARE MANY WAYS OF COPING WITH ONE'S BROKEN
heart. The usual alternatives—good works and going
to the devil, the latter journey involving a loveless
marriage to a financier, preferably fat—had been
considered hastily by Gillian before she followed the
more reasonable course of going to visit her grandmother's friend, Mrs. Bradley.

Mrs. Bradley, grinning snake-like upon the guest,
paid the broken heart sympathetic tribute. She
ordered the patient a week's complete rest, the latest
books to read, and a Chinese jacket of surpassing beauty
to wear during the all-too-short and charmingly interesting mornings. These were spent in her room. The
cure included the most luxurious food, and, on the
fifteenth day, when convalescence appeared to be
imminent, a visit from a very expensive hairdresser.
Mrs. Bradley herself kept out of the invalid's way for
almost the whole of the fortnight. This was partly for
the invalid's sake, but largely for her own.

" And now, child," she said, when the hairdresser had
come and gone, " what you really need is a holiday."

" Oh, heavens, Aunt Adela ! " said the sufferer,

speaking reproachfully, turning away from the mirror, and losing immediately the air of seraphic pleasure with which she had been contemplating the new coiffure. " What on earth kind of holiday could I enjoy *now* ? "

" Well, you could borrow the car," said Mrs. Bradley. " And George to drive it," she added heroically.

Gillian, who had begun to cry, looked up, blinked back the more obtrusive of the tears, and squeezed Mrs. Bradley's arm affectionately.

" George wouldn't come. He'd never let you be driven by another chauffeur. I can have Cynthia's sports while she's away. She said I could. Have you got an ordnance map or two ? Oh, and I can send to Lesley. She hikes. She's got wads of maps."

The hotel in York overlooked a little river. At the bottom of the road was the Minster. London, Gerald, the disastrous love-affair and its unhappy ending, all seemed to Gillian very far away. It is a humiliating fact that at nineteen the keenest sorrows have a habit of yielding, with uncanny readiness, to the soothing effects of excitement and a change of scene. It is a sound instinct, after all, which takes the rejected lover to the wilds to shoot hippopotami and lions. Even the female of the species—not of hippopotami and lions— can obtain a considerable amount of balm from driving along the Great North Road at eighty miles an hour. Gillian had no intention of taking a motoring holiday, however. She proposed to make her head quarters at Newcastle, and walk the length of the Roman Wall to Carlisle. Then she was going to cross into Galloway. She would end, she thought, by making a pilgrimage of the Scott country.

Newcastle was a pleasanter town than she had supposed it would be. She enjoyed exploring its streets, spent an hour in the Cathedral, admired the Norman gate and the modern bridge, and saw all that was to be seen of the city walls.

The next day she walked on the Town Moor, met a freeman who had the privilege of grazing two cows there, and was invited to a dance, but refused the invitation. After all, she had to remind herself, it was less than three weeks since she and Gerald (she had cried in bed on the previous night because the hotel orchestra had played his favourite waltz tune) had been dancing at a Thames-side hotel, carefree, and (she had supposed at the time) in love.

The next day the weather was fine, but not warm, and a strong wind was blowing from the south-west. They told her at the hotel that she would find it cold walking westwards, and advised her to drive out as far as Hexham and, when she had seen the Abbey, to continue by car, following the course of the river, to Chollerton or Humshaugh. That would be better than walking, they said, on such a day. They added that later it would rain.

Gillian was set on her walk. She disregarded most of the advice, but drove out of Newcastle at about half-past eight, after an early breakfast, and decided that she would cruise about for a spot which should combine the dual advantages of offering a parking place for the car and a good beginning for a walk.

The wind was cold and very strong. After three-quarters of an hour she began to wish she had accepted the advice of those who obviously knew more about the weather conditions of Northumberland than she did.

In the end, when she had become very chilly indeed, and the prospect of getting out of the car seemed less inviting than she ever remembered it to have done, she decided that a short brisk walk to a castle which was marked on the Ordnance map as being about a mile and a half from where she was, would be quite sufficient exercise for such a day, and that when she had seen it and had walked back to the car honour would have been fully satisfied and she could return to the hotel for lunch.

She had breakfasted well, but even at that hour—it was then barely ten o'clock—lunch seemed to beckon like a beacon. In fact, it was disgusting and humiliating, she found, that food should offer such solace, when her first impression had been that she would probably sink into a decline, in the Victorian manner, and gradually fade away to a flower-decked grave.

She ran the car up a short steep unmade road on to the open moor, left it with its left wheels almost in a gully, and then took a winding pathway, too narrow to be called a road—although it might have been possible to negotiate it in a very small car—in a south-westerly direction across the moor.

It was grand to be out in the bitter air, for the deadly cold was, at first, intensely exhilarating, and Gillian young, strong and athletic.

She leaned forward into the wind and fought her way, enjoying the battle, but comforted, all the same, by the thought that she could end it at any moment she chose, turn her back on the wind, make for home (in her case the hotel) and a good and satisfying lunch. Her interest in food, she had been pensively interested to discover, was not in the least affected by her sorrows.

The road she had chosen followed the course of a burn. Two miles on she came to crossroads, consulted her map, and elected to take the southward branch of the fork, which led to a castle.

Except for the road itself, she might have been in a part of the world uncharted, unheeded and unknown. There was nothing but wind and the heather, the narrow road, and, occasionally, a hovering bird.

She stepped along briskly, still finding the wind very cold. Suddenly she heard, behind her, the sound of footsteps, a confident, masculine stride, on the hard, bare path. She could not forbear to glance behind her. Not more than thirty yards in the rear was a young man in shorts and a lumber-jacket. He carried an ashplant with which he was whacking at the heather.

Gillian's heart sank. Had she not already come so far along the road, she could have found it in her mind to turn back. The last thing she wanted was company, particularly the company of one who was so obviously, like herself, on holiday. The shorts, the lumber-jacket, the ashplant, the pipe (she had seen it, and the slight whiffs of smoke which the wind soon blew away) all filled her with quick irritation. A shepherd, a trapper, gipsies—these would have been, not welcome, but, at least, part of the countryside. The young man on holiday was nothing but an eyesore and a nuisance, particularly considering the circumstances which brought her on this kind of holiday.

She judged, however, that, with a slight quickening of her pace, she could be well away from him in less than a quarter of a mile. She hastened forward, to make sure of leaving him quickly. The young man, however, quickened, too. He was thin and long-limbed. On he came, but he took not the slightest notice of her as he passed her. She might have been a ghost, or the wind whistling by ; nothing more.

" That's all right, then," she thought. " He feels as unsociable as I do." She found that, all the same, she was not too pleased about this, and stared at his thin back resentfully.

On either side the moors stretched, restful and pleasing, to where, further on, the land rose to heights of about twelve hundred feet ; from this again rose hills, another six hundred feet. The burns ran fast, in deep clefts like tiny gorges, and although the streams were narrow, they were treacherous, with deep holes—pot-holes—in the middle, and sudden depths under the banks.

Still following the road, she gained her first sight of the castle which she had decided to make her objective. It was small, square, bold and lonely. She liked the look of it, saw that the young man had passed it by, made for it eagerly, explored it cautiously, and discovered that it was possible to mount to the second floor. To look down from the battlements at this height made her feel slightly giddy, so she sat with her back against the wall, and her feet stretched out towards the interior of the keep, out of the way of the wind. She would have a short rest, she decided, and smoke a cigarette. Twenty minutes she would allow herself, she thought, before she climbed down, and returned, across the moor, for the car.

It was pleasant to get some shelter from the wind. It was pleasant to be alone and to indulge a fit of pleasant melancholy. Her thoughts began to dwell upon her sorrows, and upon the uselessness of further existence, and she was deep in the well of self-pity when the beating of heavy rain upon her retreat caused her to scramble hastily down the staircase and into the ancient guardroom on the ground floor. She wondered how long the rain would last. It was a long way back to the car, and she would be soaked before she got there, unless the heavy shower was over soon.

There was only one corner of the guardroom which was weatherproof, she discovered, but by hugging her feet close under her she found that the rain, as it dripped through the ruined roof, could not reach her. She was congratulating herself upon this fact when she remembered the solitary young man. He must be wet through, she surmised. There had been no shelter, other than the castle, so far as she could remember from the map, for several miles.

She began to feel sorry for the wayfarer. He had had, with his black hair, tall, thin, tough-looking body, brown hands—details which she had noticed as he had passed her—something the look of her elder brother, of whom she was very fond. Then, with a scowl, she remembered that this brother had told her abruptly, with no warning, no self-deprecatory, half-apologetic introduction—in fact with the most distressing and uncalled-for lack of tact—that her Gerald was a snob, a rotter and a cadger—in that order—and that the sooner she gave him up the better it would be for her and for the rest of the family, none of whom had the slightest desire to see her married to a snob, a rotter, a cadger, or (added her brother harshly), a dirty little double-crossing half-Italian. Most unfortunately, this arrière-pensée on the part of her brother proved to be justified by the facts, for, although he had written what her best friend, to whom she showed it, called a perfectly lovely letter, Gerald certainly had double-crossed to the extent that, actually, he had been the one to do the giving up—a fact which she had kept from her family. Nevertheless it remained that she had been jilted and her brother right.

Her thoughts had reached this morbid, indisputable conclusion when she heard sounds. In a few moments there appeared before her the young man who had passed her on the moor. Upon seeing her, he pulled up. Gillian did not want company, but common humanity caused her to exclaim, in kindly tones of encouragement:

"Oh, do sit down. This is the only sheltered spot for miles around."

The young man bowed, and sat down. His face was long and melancholy, but he was not ill-looking.

"Thanks very much. The wind's pretty strong, isn't it?" he said. He paused. "And now this damnable rain," he added, smiling. His smile was not good. It made him look crafty, Gillian thought.

"Yes, I shan't be sorry to turn my back on the wind going back, that's one thing," she agreed.

"I shouldn't be sorry to turn my back on my life," said the young man violently. This remark accorded so perfectly with what Gillian supposed her own views on the future to be, that a feeling of warm understanding took the place of her first desire to be left alone in her solitude. The young man sat with his back against the ancient stones of the keep and his long legs tucked away under him, and produced his pipe, tobacco and matches.

"Do you mind if I smoke?" he asked.

For some minutes after this they sat in silence. Gillian waited for a confidence which she felt was in the air, and smoked her cigarette in the reprehensible way in which young women usually perform this action, and the young man lit his pipe and smoked it sombrely. Sure enough, in about five minutes, the expected confidence came, but when she had heard it she wondered whether she had done well to attempt to invoke it, for the young man's story was a strange one. It took him the best part of an hour and a half to tell it, and Gillian was frozen to the bone, and the rain had ceased, long before he had finished. She did not like to interrupt him, however, and the narrative, although, on the whole, incredible, was interesting and unusual.

"Bewley, then, is not a North-country man?" was Gillian's first remark at the conclusion of the tale, which the young man had told with a spirit and an abundance of detail which she found it impossible to reproduce afterwards for Mrs. Bradley's benefit.

Taking his pipe from his pocket and staring at the bowl, the young man agreed that Bewley was not a North-country man.

"And Mrs. Norris is a wicked old woman, I suppose?" continued Gillian. The young man agreed that Mrs. Norris must be very wicked, and added that, in his opinion, she was ungrateful, too. His uncle had treated her too well, he said, for her to turn round on him in the end and poison him for the few pounds she would get when the old man died.

"What it wants," the young man added, stuffing tobacco into his pipe and getting up, "is for someone who knows a bit about psychology and such things to go along and see into the thing a bit. I'd willingly give up my holiday if I thought I could do any good. As for the police, they're worse than useless. They couldn't see a needle in a seam, let alone find one in a haystack. And the whole thing does approximate to a haystack, you must admit."

"I know someone," Gillian began. . . . "I suppose you are the Joshua Devizes of the story?" she broke off.

"As a matter of fact, no," the young man confessed. "Joshua is my cousin. But I ought perhaps to explain that I've altered the names a bit. Wouldn't do, in case you knew any of the people, to tell you exactly who was who."

Gillian said immediately:

"Then you are the cousin, Mr. Geoffrey, but I suppose that isn't your name?"

He replied that it was, and then added, with a sudden explosion of candour:

"The house is in Yorkshire—well, on the Lincoln-shire border. I've had the story from Joshua, who was, to some extent, in the thick of it, as you gather. I ran along down there at once, as soon as he told me what had been happening, but the old man refused to see me. Sent down a message by the housekeeper to say he wouldn't have me in the house. Her name is not Norris, but my uncle's name really is Lancaster. Any-way, it's a queer tale. You won't hear a queerer one. I wish I knew who to turn to. It wants a psychologist, who is also a private investigator, on the job. I wish I knew of someone I could ask. Money would be no object. And the house is only a few miles from the main-line station at Bournley-in-the-Marshes."

"Really?" said Gillian, who did not know either Lincolnshire or Yorkshire particularly well, but whose head was full of Mrs. Bradley, to whom she was longing to confide the young man's tale.

"I'm not going any farther," the young man said. "Shall we walk back to Humshaugh together? Or I could say good-bye here, if you like. I hope my uncle's death won't be in the morning papers," he added dejectedly.

Gillian concurred in this hope, and added that she had to get back to her car, which was not at Hum-shaugh. She realised, with shock and a feeling of extreme guilt, that she had forgotten Gerald, not only during the telling of the story, but actually after its conclusion. She glanced at her watch.

"Heavens! I shall never be back to lunch, and I'm awfully hungry," she said.

"I say," the young man observed. "I'm afraid

it's all my fault. That's the worst of taking for granted
that everybody else is bound to be interested in the
things that interest oneself. Do you find that, too ?
Perhaps you are not an egoist ? "

This time-honoured beginning to a conversation
between two of the serious-minded young had good
results. By the time they reached Gillian's car, and
she had offered the young man a lift—he, too, was
bound for Newcastle—Gillian not only felt that they
had known one another for a very long time, but had
arranged to meet the young man on the following
morning for a walk along the Wall from Humshaugh.

She spent the whole afternoon, which was wet, in
writing to Mrs. Bradley. The account she gave of
the meeting on the moor and in the guardroom of the
keep was a natural and pleasant one, but Gillian's
stilted paraphrase of the young man's story almost
brought tears to Mrs. Bradley's eyes.

" Dear Aunt Adela," Gillian had begun, " I thought
you might like to know that I arrived safely and that
I like the hotel. I shall probably be here a week, and
then I am going on to Carrick and Galloway. Yesterday, on the moors, I met a man who is, like me, lonely
and disillusioned. He is twenty-four and we had a
long talk, because it rained just as we got to a castle
the name of which I don't know. We talked about all
sorts of things coming home, and I am going out with
him for a walk along the Roman Wall (weather
permitting) to-morrow. There is a dance at his hotel
on Thursday. I don't know whether he likes dancing,
as he seems rather serious, and is, anyway, in very
great trouble. At least, his relations are. It comes to

much the same thing. At any rate, I suppose one ought to think so, and he, apparently, does.

"But what I really want to ask you, Aunt Adela, is whether you would be prepared to undertake a private investigation. He says it must be a psychologist. I suppose that's because the whole affair seems such a tangled skein. Well, I'll tell you the story, as nearly as possible in the way he told it me, except that I had better tell it in the Third Person—oh, is that blasphemous with capital letters?—in case you get muddled. It all seems terrible. I do hope you can do something to help the poor boy. He seems very depressed, and no wonder. Well, here is the story he told me. I had better tell it more like a story in a book. You will get the idea better."

At this point the style of the letter changed.

"It was New Year's Day, at half-past two in the morning. The moon shone on snow, and the three pine trees at the end of the garden sparkled with the glitter of a fairy pantomime," Gillian, after some scratchings-out, had committed poetically to paper. Mrs. Bradley, seated in a deck-chair in her garden at Wandles Parva, grinned and read on.

"In the most luxurious, although not the largest, bedroom in the house, old Mr. Lancaster grunted as he got into bed. His butler and factotum, who valeted him, waited at the bedside until his employer lay still, then he switched off the light near the door— the old gentleman, for reasons known to himself, detested 'cords dangling over the bedhead' as he described them—said good night quietly and, as quietly, closed the door. His own room was one floor higher than Mr. Lancaster's, and as he had already locked up the house, he mounted to the next landing and went to bed.

"The housekeeper, Mrs. Norris, a woman of sixty-four, had a room on the same floor as that on which her employer slept. That evening, in company with old Mr. Lancaster, his niece, Miss Phyllis, his nephew Mr. Joshua, and some half a dozen guests, she had seen the New Year in, and had sung Auld lang syne. Now, having seen her employer go up with the butler, a man who had been in Mr. Lancaster's service almost as many years as she herself had, she began to think kindly of her own bed and of what a comfort it would be to get her stays off and her head on the pillow.

"The household did not keep late hours as a rule, and Mrs. Norris was not used to them. She went to the front door to make certain that it was bolted, went into the drawing-room and put a small fire-guard in front of a still considerable fire, did the same thing in the lounge, picked up a cigarette-end from the polished floor, and mopped up with her handkerchief a tiny pool of spilt whiskey which she noticed on a small table, and 'rubbed up' the dull mark it left with the edge of her black silk apron. This was a garment she always insisted upon wearing whenever she was being treated 'like one of the family.' It was due to her own self-respect, she thought, as well as to her employer, to make this slight gesture recognising the fact that, however kindly she was treated, she was still, as she said, 'in service.' There were rumours that at one time she had tried to hook the old gentleman, but that he had either dodged her or wriggled free.

"Mr. Joshua and Miss Phyllis, the niece and nephew, had gone to bed at twelve-fifty and one-twenty respectively—as soon, in fact, as the last guest had crawled down the drive in the last car. Phyllis and Joshua had quarrelled during the evening, as everyone except the old gentleman seemed to know, but skilled as she was, by long experience, in the reading of signs and portents which affected the family peace, Mrs. Norris had not yet discovered the cause of the quarrel.

"The house was not a particularly large one. It occupied the site of a pre-Elizabethan mansion, but the rooms and even the exterior had been so very much altered that it was difficult to say how much of the original fabric remained. To the eye, there appeared, from the semi-circular gravel drive, a four-story building (counting the attics as a story) with an ornate but not unattractive porch, in the late Elizabethan style, Georgian windows, one Jacobean chimney (the others were of later date) and an exceptionally ugly length of Victorian building which had been added in 1860 to give a schoolroom and a servants' hall. Almost adjoining this extra building, and at right angles to it, were the stables, with their clock and water-butt. Nearer the lodge gates there was a tumbling stream which rushed through the garden into a big lake behind the house.

"The drive in front of the house separated the building from the semi-circular lawn, and there were two sets of gates, only one of which was in ordinary use. Beside this set of gates (on the right as one faced the house) was the small lodge, but no one lived there. It had fallen out of use in 1909, after three of the lodge-keeper's four children had died of scarlet fever. The surviving child was now the old gentleman's groom, and had a room in the servants' wing.

" Mrs. Norris had been promoted from the servants' wing to a bedroom on the first floor some twenty years before the dawn of this particular New Year's Day. She had, even then, been in her employer's service for twenty-four years, and had, at one time, been nurse-maid to the children, all of whom were now either dead or disinherited.

" Mrs. Norris, however, was not thinking of dead children, whether killed in the fire at the house, which had broken out one winter night and had been the direct cause for the erection of an iron fire-escape from one of the attics, or dead of scarlet fever in the lodge. She was merely an elderly woman, tired and short of breath, climbing the back staircase to her bedroom after an evening which had been (even without the distressing evidences of another family quarrel) rather too much for her.

" She had a good room, and it was only her sense of what was fitting which caused her to approach it by way of the back staircase when the front would have been far more convenient. However—as she had a fondness for explaining—she knew her place, none better, and that place was on the back staircase unless she was supervising maids at work on the front one.

" She was a sensible if slightly slow-witted person, and was accustomed, she declared, to believe the evidence of her own eyes. She had to go through a swing door to reach the landing from the back stair-case ; then she had to walk a short way along a corri-

dor, to reach her own door-handle. She reached it,
turned it, and was putting her hand round to switch
on the electric light, when she perceived, standing
perfectly still in the moonlight, a shadowy man.

"In spite of some evidence to the contrary, it is not
really instinctive in women to scream in the face of
the unusual. Mrs. Norris' first thought was 'Burglars!'
Her second was that Mr. Joshua had come to confide
in her. She knew of his quarrel with Miss Phyllis ;
as a little boy he had been rather a weakling—a cry-
baby had been his Amazonian cousin's explicit and
unkind description—and it was not a new idea to Mrs.
Norris that he should bring her his troubles.

"Having given a low croak of dismay upon seeing
that a man was in her room, therefore, the housekeeper
said, in expostulatory tones :

"' This time of night, Mr. Joshua ? Won't it wait
till the morning ? '

"There was no reply from the intruder, and still
he made no movement.

"' Master Joshua ! ' said the housekeeper, reverting
to the title he had borne before he reached the age of
eighteen.

"The only reaction the man by the window made
to the double appeal was to vanish, entirely, completely
and soundlessly, leaving the now stupefied old woman
staring at the moonlit pane against which, a moment
previously, his dark silhouette had been thrown.

"The man, as she described him later, had been
standing with his left side towards the window, so that
she got him in profile. Now, it is an odd but in-
controvertible fact that it is the most difficult matter in

the world to deduce the full-face appearance of a person merely from having caught a glimpse of his or her profile. The full face, which, mercifully for most of us, camouflages the shape of nose and chin, is far less uncompromising, and, too often, repulsive, in nearly everybody, than the stark, unrelieved and, too often, hideous betrayal of selfishness, weakness and general beastliness of which the gaunt outline of the profile is capable.

" In short, even if the man was, in actual fact, a person known to the housekeeper, it is not altogether surprising that she failed to identify him, except by the law of probability, as her employer's nephew. To add to the general uneasiness which the whole affair had caused her was the bewildering vanishing trick brought off by the voiceless visitant. This had been uncanny and disagreeable in the extreme. There was nowhere—no dressing-room, bathroom, or even large cupboard—into which the intruder could have withdrawn, and yet, in an instant, he was gone.

" Mrs. Norris stood still for another whole minute ; then, very shakily, she began to unbutton her bodice. She was accustomed to kneel and pray before she got into her bed, but, making a lame, incoherent, unspoken excuse to God, she scrambled between the bedcoverings, dragged the sheet and the blankets round her ears, and then spent, in listening and waiting, as terror-stricken an hour as she had passed since early childhood.

" Next morning the household, so far as it would

have appeared to an unprejudiced and non-suggestible observer, conducted itself as usual.

" Mrs. Norris was the first, apart from the servants, to come into the breakfast-room. Here, as was her invariable custom, she made coffee for the old gentleman in a special percolator.

" At half-past eight Mr. Joshua, who proposed to spend a morning in overhauling his uncle's collection of stamps, joined Mrs. Norris in the breakfast-room and observed that she looked pale.

" ' Morning after the night before, Betsy ? ' was his query. Mrs. Norris assented to what she privately considered an outrageous suggestion, although, had Mr. Geoffrey (another nephew but one who had not been invited to take part in the New Year festivities) made the same point, Mrs. Norris' response would have been more cordial and her reaction the satisfactory one of threatening to box his ears.

[*He says*, Gillian had interpolated at this point, *that the housekeeper had always liked him ever so much better than Joshua.*]

" Nothing more was heard of the Disappearing Man, and things continued as usual for several months. In the summer [*that means this summer*, Gillian had interpolated] Mr. Joshua came down from London again, and, on the second morning of his stay, Miss Phyllis had breakfast with her uncle, and, a very special mark of the old gentleman's favour, received two cups of the special coffee made for him by Mrs. Norris. Mr. Joshua had already breakfasted, and was walking round the estate

" ' Mr. Joshua was talking about the stamps,'

said the housekeeper, in reply to a bark from her
employer.

" ' Stamps ? Oh, yes, stamps,' said the old gentleman. ' I said he could go through them if he liked.'

" ' You're not going to let Joshua look through your
stamp collection, Uncle ? ' said Phyllis.

" ' Why not ? '

" ' Well, I wouldn't trust him, especially this morning. I think he's probably feeling rather bad-tempered.'

" ' Now what do you mean by that ? '

" ' Nothing.'

" ' Have you and Joshua quarrelled ? '

" ' No, of course not, Uncle. That is to say——'

" ' You've not broken off your engagement ? Where's
your ring ? '

" He picked up her left hand, sorted out the ring
finger, and held it up in front of her somewhat in the
manner that the owner of a puppy might adopt to
impress some small misdemeanour upon the animal's
mind. Phyllis flushed, but said nothing, except that
she did not want to talk about it.

" ' Mulish, eh ? ' said her uncle, dropping the hand,
his table napkin and any semblance of interest, all in
the same instant. ' Well, I must go. I'm late.'

" He still liked to think that he conducted his
business personally. He had never liked motor cars,
and used to drive himself to the station, four miles off, in
a trap, each morning. The groom who accompanied
him brought the trap back, and returned to the station
with it in the evening so that his employer could drive
himself home. The town in which the old gentleman's
business flourished was about twenty-five miles off.

" This routine was scarcely ever broken from one year's end to the next, but after the beginning of Mr. Joshua's summer visit something occurred each morning to upset it, with the consequence that it was not until some days after the end of that first week that the old gentleman went into the town again at all.

" The contretemps which started the run of ill-luck was extremely trivial. The old gentleman had a favourite whip—not that he ever used it on the mare—and, on the morning under discussion, when he left a rather pink-faced Miss Phyllis still seated at the table in the breakfast-room, this whip was not to be found.

" Old Mr. Lancaster cursed the groom, and even went so far, in his exasperation, as to give the man a kick on the behind. It was not a vicious kick nor a heavy one, and, physically, there can be very little doubt that it must have upset the old gentleman, who had some difficulty in regaining his balance, considerably more than it did the recipient, for he clutched at the toe of his boot, after he had staggered backward and clutched the back of an arm-chair, and demanded irascibly whether the groom's one-syllable posterior was made of iron. The groom muttered darkly, and his face (according to the somewhat hysterical evidence given, later on, by the housemaid, who, for reasons best known to herself, was in the yard at the time) was ' livid with dreadful fury.'

" He then called his master (according to the same witness, who insisted upon indicating the adjective and substantive by their initial letters only) a b old f, and told him he had probably swallowed the b whip and that he wished it had b well choked him.

" This speech seems to have calmed Mr. Lancaster, for he gave the man a florin and said that he had, anyway, missed the train, and should not trouble to go into the town that day.

" By the next morning the whip had reappeared. It had been found lying on the further side of the wicket gate which led from a small orchard into a very small paddock. It was an extraordinary place in which to find the whip, since the paddock was in no sort of proximity at all to the stables and coach-house, and there seemed no reason why old Mr. Lancaster, or anybody else, should have walked that way carrying the whip, let alone dropped it without realising the fact.

" In view of later developments it seemed likely that the dropping of the whip there was deliberate, and had been done with the intention of hiding it, but, at the time, the circumstance was inexplicable.

" It was the niece who found the whip. She was going into the paddock (she said) to do her early morning exercises. As she was given to extraordinary crazes in athletics and dietetics, this reason was accepted at the time, although later on it was treated with what politicians call ' reserve.' Her explanation was that she fell over the whip, hurting, she explained, her bare toes. This was on the second of July. Recognising the whip as the one which her uncle had missed on the previous day, she took it back with her when she returned to the house.

" Unfortunately, the restoration of his favourite whip was not in itself sufficient to allow old Mr. Lancaster to go to business that morning. The mare had gone lame, and Mr. Joshua (explained the groom, warily eyeing his master's boot) had gone out riding on the only other horse which could be put between shafts—for Polly, as Mr. Lancaster knew well, would kick the trap to bits sooner than look at it, and Rollo had 'no force in him for the hill and would die this minute' if asked to attempt it. The groom was an Irishman. Mr. Lancaster, regarding him with Yorkshire dourness and a certain amount of Yorkshire humour, wriggled his toes inside his boot and grunted. His business did not see him that day. Strangely enough, the mare recovered sufficiently in the early afternoon to take the niece to the vicarage, a distance of nearly three miles, for toasted tea-cake and village gossip, but this surprising circumstance was 'of itself, itself,' said the groom, with the dark philosophy of his race and kind.

" On the two following days, July third and fourth, matters became more serious. On Friday, the third, the nephew, Mr. Joshua, returned to his London flat. The niece stayed on. There had been some talk that she might make her home with her uncle, and although neither party to it was particularly enthusiastic about the arrangement, there were reasons, notably the indigence of the niece and the loneliness of the uncle, which made it desirable that they should pool their resources.

" The nephew drove to the station very early. This was by the old gentleman's wish, for the mare, he said, would be needed later in the morning. By half-past seven, therefore, Mr. Joshua had breakfasted, tipped the servants, given Mrs. Norris a pound of a particularly delicious tea—his customary parting gift to her—and was bowling along, in a wind that almost flayed his face, towards the little station.

"At a quarter to eight the butler-valet called the old gentleman, and, in the words of the household generally, 'got him up.' At half-past eight Mrs. Norris was pouring out his coffee, and at eight-thirty-three he was complaining, with Shakespearian 'strange oaths,' that the coffee tasted salt. He ordered her to pour it away and to make some more.

"It was the first time in three years that Mr. Lancaster had complained about the coffee, and Mrs. Norris, 'what with his language,' she said, and her own distress that the coffee should prove undrinkable, burst into tears. This delayed the making of fresh coffee a matter of ten or twelve minutes. However, after she had taken the offending beverage away the housekeeper tasted it, and was compelled to admit that it had a peculiar flavour. She said this to the cook, the kitchenmaid, the solicitous butler and the groom. The last had no business in the kitchen at that time in the morning, but had come in, he explained, for the sake of his sins and his soul, to thaw the devil out of himself, for it was so cold, although it was July, that the mare herself was standing in the drive 'dancing the cramps out of her.' He also tasted the coffee. He spat it out again. At this the housekeeper remarked that, in her opinion, it could have been drunk and no harm done, but that that was neither here nor there, and she supposed Mr. Lancaster had the right to complain if he liked, and that time would show whether it was the grounds or the sugar that was wrong.

" By the time the fresh coffee was made, the old gentleman, once again, had missed his train. Contrary to the anticipations of the household, he neither fumed nor fretted, but merely walked out to the stables and told the groom to take the trap in himself to a chemist's shop, and buy some strychnine for the rats. He also ordered him to get plenty, for the magpies would be a trouble later on, and he was not going to be plagued with them the way it had happened last year. The groom called down heaven's malediction on the magpies, and master and man parted.

" Their conversation had been heard by the housekeeper, the butler and the housemaid, for the old gentleman had a good carrying voice, and the groom a distinctive brogue.

" The groom returned at about a quarter past eleven and went straight to the library with his purchases. Nobody heard what passed between him and his employer, but there was evidence from the kitchen staff that he came out looking extremely pleased, and said that Mr. Lancaster had paid him a couple of pounds which had been owing for nearly three years.

" Nobody could make anything of this statement, for nothing could have been further from the old gentleman's habits than to owe back wages to his servants. Mrs. Norris, when the news came to her ears, reported to Miss Phyllis. Miss Phyllis thought it rather strange, but added that Rafferty was a strange man, and that no notice need be taken of his remarks.

It was not, she said, as though he had a cause of grievance. The opposite was the case ; and, if he was pleased, that might be allowed, she thought, to be the end of the affair. She then added that it was probably his Irish sense of humour coming out.

"The next day, Saturday, the coffee again tasted salt, or so the old gentleman said. Miss Phyllis was breakfasting with him—an unusual occurrence, for he liked to breakfast alone, except for Mrs. Norris, whose function it was to make and pour out the coffee. He had, Miss Phyllis said later, particularly requested her, the night before, to come down early to breakfast on the Saturday and to have it with him, and had mentioned, casually, and interrupting himself to throw a piece of the supper bread at the cat, that he wanted to talk to her about his will.

" It appeared that she did not think it at all strange that her uncle should choose such an inconvenient time for such a subject, although she admitted that she had communed with herself to the effect that it either meant it would all go to charity, or that she and Joshua would have most of it between them, because the breakfast-time the old gentleman allowed himself was too short to allow of the discussion of any complicated testamentary deposition, and she did not, she stated frankly, suppose ' that poor old Geoff would get anything.'

" The coffee was made by Mrs. Norris as usual, and when it was poured out the old gentleman tasted his, declared it salt, and then suggested that she should try hers and tell him what she thought of the flavour. She sipped, twisted her mouth, sipped again and then took a brave gulp. She was obliged to admit that the coffee did taste very queer indeed. The old gentleman, remarking again that it was salt, shot his cupful into the bushes outside the french windows, spat and spluttered, and then commanded Mrs. Norris to explain what she meant by it.

"Apart from weeping again and exclaiming that she 'meant nothing and never had,' the housekeeper made no valuable contribution except to supply some more coffee. The old gentleman and his niece resumed their breakfast, and then, the trap having been brought round, Mr. Lancaster, assisted by Rafferty, climbed up, and, for the first time in several days, looked as though he might be going to catch his train.

"He was fated, it seemed. The drive to the station took about half an hour. As he climbed down and was glancing at the church clock, which could be seen from the station approach, the station-master, who had known him for thirty years, came out from the booking office entry and said, red-faced with importance:

"'Mr. Lancaster, sir, there be a message on telephone telling thee to get back home fast as the mare can shift, sir, Miss Lancaster, thy niece, be took very bad and they want thee to pick up doctor and take him back with thee.'

"So the mare was turned round and off fled the trap, stopping only to pick up Doctor Moffat. By tea-time the dreadful nausea and the agonising cramps and pains, from which Miss Phyllis had been suffering, died away, and by eight o'clock in the evening she was almost herself again.

" *One other incident needs recording, I think,*" said Gillian. " *In the afternoon the groom was sent to the chemist's shop in the town to get more strychnine for the rats, but the chemist (he declared) would not serve him.*

" The next day was Sunday, and therefore the question of old Mr. Lancaster's setting out for the station did not arise. Nevertheless, the day did not pass without its upsetting incidents, and the most picturesque, odd and generally interesting of these occurred, not to the old gentleman himself (although he too was subjected to some annoyances), or even to his niece, but to the housekeeper.

" Briefly, the church ghost, which had been a parish legend for a couple of centuries, decided to manifest itself to the unfortunate Mrs. Norris whilst she was performing the voluntary service of restoring all the hassocks to their little brass hooks on the backs of the strong wooden chairs at the conclusion of Evensong.

" Why Mrs. Norris had undertaken this task nobody had ever discovered. She had accomplished it for more years than most people in the parish could remember, and, by the time she was sixty-four, both they and she would have considered Sunday incomplete if she had not stayed behind when everyone else had gone, and, tiptoeing up and down the aisles, had not ' tidied up ' as she expressed it, before she returned to the cold beef, pickles and potatoes (boiled in their jackets, if new, or fried in chunky strips if old) of her Sunday evening supper.

" She was walking down the north aisle, her task completed, and was expecting to hear the footsteps of the vicar who always made it his duty to put out the lights and lock up, when she received a sharp blow on the back.

" Startled, she turned round, but could not see anyone there. She was feeling decidedly shaken, but was trying to persuade herself that she had imagined the blow when she felt another, this time between her shoulders. She experienced a feeling of considerable alarm, but called out to her invisible assailant to ' Go home, you stupid boy, and don't play silly jokes.' All the same, she could not believe that a village boy or youth would be impudent enough to tease her in this way, particularly inside the church. As she turned towards the door again, however, a third blow struck her, this time with sufficient force to send her staggering forward.

" She cried out in terror, and was running towards the door when she heard the vicar's footsteps. He wished her good night as she passed out of the church, but she did not respond, and reached the house in such a ' sweat and a flurry," according to the housemaid (that mine of information upon all aspects of the matter), that she would not sit down to her supper but went straight upstairs to her room, and, she said afterwards, to bed, where she remained all the following day. Miss Phyllis, who had recovered sufficiently to do so, made old Mr. Lancaster's coffee in the morning. It was pronounced to be ' only medium ' by the old gentleman, but he drank it and seemed none the worse. After breakfast he remarked to his niece that he should have to tell Rafferty to get some more strychnine, as he did not think the supply was sufficient, and that if one chemist would not supply it, another must be visited. Miss Phyllis replied that she did not see why ' that dreadful stuff ' was necessary, and that she thought a more humane method of killing the rats might be adopted. A sensible, penniless girl, however, she did not press this point, as it appeared to be received impatiently by her uncle.

" Rafferty bought the extra strychnine and handed it to his employer when the latter returned from town. Next morning there was a repetition of the ' salt coffee ' incidents, and Mrs. Norris, who, in obedience to a testy order from the old gentleman, tasted the coffee, was sick afterwards. The kitchenmaid, who also drank some, was in such pain that she had to be helped up to bed, and Rafferty, instructed by Mrs. Norris, went for the doctor. This happened a short time after the groom had returned from driving Mr. Lancaster to the station.

" When Mr. Lancaster returned in the late afternoon, he was given a note which the doctor had left for him. Nobody saw the note, but it put the old gentleman in such a passion that, after swearing at the doctor and stamping on the letter, he ordered that his nephew Joshua should be sent for immediately, and also required his solicitor to be summoned.

"Mr. Joshua arrived two days later by the two o'clock train, but there appeared to have been some hitch or delay in sending for the solicitor, who did not appear. Two notable incidents occurred during Mr. Joshua's first evening and morning at his uncle's house upon this second visit. One was that when he was dressing for dinner he dropped his collar stud. Knowing that there was another one in the small drawer of the dressing-table in his room—for he himself had left it there upon his previous visit—he pulled at the handle of the drawer but found that it was stuck. He pulled harder, and then had to dislodge a piece of stiff paper which had become wedged and was preventing him from opening the drawer. When at last the drawer did come out, he discovered his stud and also that the stiff paper was the wrapping on a packet labelled ' Rat Poison.'

" Mr. Joshua, holding it none of his business to remark upon what his uncle chose to keep in the drawers, said nothing about this small discovery, and left the packet where it was. Oddly enough, the package was not there when he looked in the drawer after dinner.

" After breakfast on the following morning he asked his uncle when he would find it convenient to discuss with him the business on which he had been called down from London, and mentioned that he ought to return on the following afternoon at the latest. His uncle, however, disregarded both the request and the statement, tossed his table napkin on to the seat of his chair when he got up, and announced his intention of going to business as usual. He ordered Joshua not to return to London until he was told.

" Knowing that it was of no use to argue with the old gentleman, Mr. Joshua accompanied him out on to the drive and watched him drive away with Rafferty. As it was a fine clear morning, he decided to take a

walk across the park to the woods. Half-way across
the field that lay beyond the park he was met by the
gamekeeper Bewley. They greeted one another, and
Bewley enquired whether Mr. Lancaster had gone in
to town or not that morning. Upon being informed
that he had gone in as usual, Bewley remarked :

" ' There be funny goings-on, by what I hear.' He
then requested Mr. Joshua to go back with him to his
hut. Tucked away among the thatch was an empty
bottle, coloured green. A lurcher, which was tied up
near the hut, strained and barked as soon as Mr.
Joshua appeared. The gamekeeper growled at the
dog, and then said :

" ' Ah, but he never barked at whoever pushed that
poison bottle into my thatch.'

" Perceiving that the man was telling him that he
knew the name of this person, Mr. Joshua invited a
fuller expression of the confidence by asking :

" ' And whom wouldn't he bark at ? '

" ' He doesn't never make no sign or sound for
Rafferty, the groom,' replied Bewley, 'giving me,'
said Mr. Joshua later, ' a peculiar look, which, in view
of my uncle's very serious illness, I could not help
recollecting later on.'

" For Mr. Lancaster, it appeared, had been taken
desperately ill in the trap just as they sighted the
station—in fact, while Joshua was still in conversation
with the gamekeeper. This time the doctor left no
private correspondence on the subject. He rang up
the police, on his own responsibility, and ordered the
servants not to wash cups, plates and glasses.

" Well that," concluded Gillian, in her earlier, and,

in Mrs. Bradley's opinion, preferable epistolary style, " is about what it all amounted to. I don't think I've left out any bits, and I've tried to remember everything in its exact order as he told it me.

" Do please write soon, and let me know what you think. I hate to say so, because it sounds frightfully pooh-bah, but he says that money's no object. Please forgive me for mentioning it, I expect it's in bad taste.

" Well, good-bye for the present, dearest Aunt Adela. It's funny, really, that he should have said it needed a psychologist who is also a private investigator, because it just sounded like you right from the very beginning. Do you think anybody really is trying to murder the poor old man for his money ? Do let me know what you do think. I am sure that Geoffrey—I call him that to myself, although not, of course, to his face—believes the housekeeper is doing it. But why, after all these years ?

" Oh, well, you'll know, I expect.

" Love from

" GILLIAN."

Mrs. Bradley, grinning, put the letter in its envelope, glanced at the postage stamps on the outside, went to the telephone and rang up the Assistant Commissioner.

His comments were terse and ribald. Mrs. Bradley, still grinning, this time with great satisfaction, picked up a book of modern American verse, and read it until the telephone rang.

" No," said the Assistant Commissioner (adding what seemed to him suitable and picturesque comment), " neither the Lincolnshire nor the Yorkshire police know anything of your Mr. Lancaster. But I am able to verify the address. Anyhow, keep your loonies. Haven't you heard of the East Bierley mystery of 1910? Some funny person has wished it on you again. Perverted sense of humour, that's all, I should suppose. Good hunting—but I fancy you're losing your grip."

"I thought you'd say that," said Mrs. Bradley. "Is there a rumour of strychnine in Yorkshire or Lincolnshire?" She chuckled into the receiver at the sound of the harsh words which came from Scotland Yard, and then rang for her maid to pack a bag.

CHAPTER II

"'What became of your bloodhounds, Lord Randal, my son?
What became of your bloodhounds, my handsome young man?'——
'O they swell'd and they died; mother, make my bed soon,
For I'm weary wi' hunting, and fain would lie down.'"

CURIOSITY, MRS. BRADLEY REFLECTED, AS, GAZING AT herself in the mirror of a first-class compartment, she straightened her veil before getting out at the station, is said to have killed the cat. Nothing but curiosity had brought her on this tedious journey, or had caused her to embark upon an enterprise which her judgment persuaded her was foolish.

She had dismissed Gillian's appeal in a letter, by return of post, which consisted chiefly of soothing words, no promises, and a prescription; all the same, she had sent immediately to the library with some explicit instructions, and had set to work to make a précis of Gillian's version of Mr. Geoffrey's long and elaborate story.

The headings she used might have interested and startled the young man could he have read them. They were as follows :

(1) Facts from the East Bierley murder of 1910.
(2) Interpolations from other true stories.
(3) New material, i.e., facts whose origin I cannot, at present, trace. (It was surprising how many of these there were, when she came to analyse the story.)

Under the first heading she wrote a concise account of the true story of the death by strychnine poisoning of a certain Yorkshire manufacturer named Mr. Joe Scott, who had purchased a shooting estate, and a residence called Copley House. On February 9th, 1910,* this gentleman had died suddenly, and in very great agony, on his way to business. An inquest had been ordered, the police had made some enquiries, and one of the most important witnesses at the inquest was the housekeeper who had made the coffee.

There were a groom, a housemaid, a niece, and a gamekeeper in the East Bierley story. All of these gave evidence at the inquest. The mystery of Mr. Scott's death was never solved. The verdict was worded : Death by strychnine poisoning. The jury had added that there was not sufficient evidence to show who had administered the dose.

A good deal of the evidence was contradictory, and some of the witnesses were illiterate. Difficulty was caused by the fact that there seemed to be no motive for the crime, and yet there was nothing to suggest suicide. Mrs. Bradley, in a neat, indecipherable hand, noted these facts and compared them with Gillian's version of Mr. Geoffrey's tale.

" Poor fellow," she said aloud, ringing the bell. To the smart and very pretty maid who responded, she indicated that the books might be returned. Rather less than twenty-four hours after the pitying ejaculation had come tartly off her tongue, she was stepping from

---

* *Poison Mysteries Unsolved,* by C. J. S. Thompson, M.B.E., Ph.D., published Hutchinson & Co. 1937.

her railway compartment on to the platform of a small country station in one of the marshier portions of England, and was directing a porter to place her luggage on a taxi. After a good deal of work upon maps, she had decided that perhaps the border between Yorkshire and Lincolnshire was not the only part of our island which fitted the story. Rude comment from Scotland Yard did not dispel this theory.

The round-faced boy declared that there was nowhere to go in a taxi.

" I want the inn," said Mrs. Bradley firmly.

" What, the *Rising Sun*, like ? "

" Is that the only inn ? "

The youth admitted that it was not the only inn, but added that it was the only inn at which a lady could stay if she were going to stay at all.

" How far is the *Rising Sun* from here ? " Mrs. Bradley then demanded.

The youth first shaded his eyes to watch the departing train.

" Eh ? " he said, swivelling round again, as though he had lost the thread of the conversation. He then informed her that it was " over the way," and that he was prepared to take her baggage across to it himself, so long as the man in the signal-box did not want him to take over the signals while he had his bit of dinner.

He raised his voice in a kind of yodel. A similar call came floating down from the signal-box.

Mrs. Bradley, unversed in the local dialect, could interpret neither the question nor the reply, but apparently the latter was satisfactory, for the porter picked up the suit-cases and made for the small dim booking-hall. The road outside the station was little more than a lane. Half a mile away was the village, straggling between two streams. Set back from the road on the opposite side, and about sixty yards from the station, was a respectable public-house. The porter set the bags down in the side entrance to the garden, wiped his palms down his trousers and suggested that perhaps Mrs. Bradley had a railway ticket. He said this diffidently, as though he half suspected—and was prepared to accept the fact—that she had travelled as a stowaway on the train. Mrs. Bradley produced the ticket and a tip, and the youth, with a grin and a country courtesy, shambled across the road in a long slant, and was gone perhaps seven or eight minutes.

He returned, observed :

" Her never answer, but her'll have thee, that I *do* know," and then picked up the bags again, and set them down outside the door of the inn.

Mrs. Bradley had not followed him, but now she advanced, pushed open the garden gate, walked up to the door, and knocked. A head popped out of a window. The youth, with a grin, disappeared.

" Not till Hours, I tell thee ! No good thee worritin' theer ! " said a plaintive voice with mild but motherly firmness.

The window, which had been flung up, closed down again. The house resumed its tranquillity. Mrs.

Bradley, who had not lost hers, went over and rapped, with some sharpness, upon the glass. The window was flung up. The same head, that of a middle-aged woman, shot out again, but, confronted, this time, by Mrs. Bradley's yellow face and sharp black eyes, it enquired, in a civil tone :

"I'm sorry I can't serve thee, but that want ten minutes, and they do get so airy impatient."

Anxious as she was to know the exact local meaning attached to the adverb "airy," Mrs. Bradley adhered to the point at issue, and observed :

"I am sorry to have disturbed you, too, but can you let me have a room here ? I do not require, at the moment, to be served with anything to drink."

"Room ? Hast thee luggage, my dear ? "

Mrs. Bradley meekly displayed her suit-cases.

"And brass ? "

Mrs. Bradley, noting the Yorkshire substantive although she was not in Yorkshire, meekly produced her note-case and a cheque-book, displayed a jewelled watch, and indicated a diamond brooch and her rings.

"Happen thee's all right," admitted the woman, nodding, "but, with all this I.R.A., 'tis foolish taking any chances. I'll come down and let thee come in. That do get real tiring, riding on they old trains."

Mrs. Bradley restored her note-case and cheque-book to her handbag, and, by the time she had fastened it, the side door was open, and the woman, with a smile, was holding it back against the wall.

"Happen thee's had thy tucker ? " she suggested.

Mrs. Bradley agreed that she had had some food on the train.

The inn was old and interesting. Part of it, Mrs. Bradley thought, could not have been built much later than 1340. Exploring it, she demanded a bedroom in this part of the house.

" Thee might as well sleep in the barn," protested the hostess, who, by supper-time, had taken a fancy to the guest.

Crop-haired children and a shy and clumsy boy, the son of the house, stared at her solemnly as she ate, and by lunch-time the next day Mrs. Bradley had made several discreet and tactful enquiries, and was in possession of certain facts which she found interesting. The name of the owner of the second biggest house was Frere. He was, in every village sense of the word, a Dark Gentleman ; that is, he was of mixed blood, was credited with Satanic attributes, and was, in most of his utterances, tastes and dealings, a mystery to his neighbours.

About five miles across the marshes, in the Big House, lived old Mr. Lancaster. He had a niece and a nephew, who had stayed at the house at Christmas, and there was another nephew, it was thought. The house was said to be haunted. . . .

" But, then," said her chief informant, the landlady's son, " happen so be every third or fourth big house in these parts. 'Tis in the nature of the place."

With this Mrs. Bradley could agree. The country was flat and marshy. Slow rivers, in parts almost silted up, pushed sluggishly between soft banks overgrown in summer with reeds. There were few trees, and the views extended for miles—or, rather, would do so, Mrs. Bradley surmised, when the heavy mist, which lay like a blanket on the land, should lift with the approach of sunny weather, for the sky was overcast with heavy cloud. The prospect was desolate without being dreary, and in walking the long miles over causeways beside the brownish sedge and the crawling water she soon found a peaceful pleasure. It amused her to think that, in persuading Gillian to take a holiday, she had also secured one for herself.

Mr. Lancaster's house, which she went to see on her fourth day, lay back, forty yards or less, from the road, and corresponded, so far as she could tell, to the description Mr. Geoffrey had given of it to Gillian. She soon realised, however, that there had been one detail, at least, in his story, which did not tally with fact. He had mentioned that the drive to the station was uphill. She had the words in Gillian's letter, which she consulted as she stood before the gates.

". . . for Polly," the groom was reported to have said, " would kick the trap to bits sooner than look at it, and Rollo had *no force in him for the hill*. . . ."

Mrs. Bradley nodded. She could not imagine that Gillian had invented that remark. But, because she was methodical and painstaking, she walked the long miles to the station. The road, assisted by culverts, shorings-up of stones, little bridges and the ancient foundation of a causeway built up on the marshy soil, went in a series of shallow loops (finding the easiest way across the rivers and avoiding a dangerous bog), to where the little station stood almost opposite the inn of the *Rising Sun* where she was lodging.

"No hill," said Mrs. Bradley, shaking her head. The landlady's son, who overheard her, grinned and asked :

"What would thee want with hills, like ? "

"Nothing, child. Hills—even one hill—would make the landscape so uninteresting that I should go north to-morrow."

"But there's mountainy hills in the north," the boy protested. "Thee want to see a long way, on the flat, like, come along here."

"Tom," said Mrs. Bradley, "if you knew that someone was in great danger hereabouts——"

"Oh," said the boy, "if thee mean old Mr. Lancaster, make thy mind easy on that. That been giving out these five or six years—ever since he retired from business, like—as somebody was trying to murder him for his brass. Cut all the nieces and nevvies out of his will, so they do say, to give them no cause to poison him. Thee don't want to take notice of poor old fool like that. Daft, that do be, daft."

"Oh ? " said Mrs. Bradley, thoughtfully. She gazed upon the boy, and then said suddenly : "Tom, do you go to church ? "

"Parson do be temperance," said Tom. "Preached upon, Mother have been, like."

"Unreasonable," Mrs. Bradley agreed.

"And us do be foreigners here," the lad continued. "But if thee want to go, like, there do be a church over by old Mr. Lancaster's, near by where thee took thyself this morning."

Slightly startled to learn that her movements had been such a source of interest that the boy had followed them, Mrs. Bradley said, grinning :

" Your mother's cause shall be mine while I stay in her house. But I want to speak to the vicar, so I shall get there after the service."

" Name of Dodd. And Mr. Lancaster's house-keeper's name be Bertram," Tom volunteered.

" Bless you for an intelligent boy," said Mrs. Bradley. " And now, come and lean on the pump-handle while I wash."

The evening meal at the *Rising Sun* was supper, not dinner. Mrs. Bradley ate cold beef, pickles, cheese, a salad, tipsy-cake, and stewed raspberries, and per-fected a plan of action for getting into the house of old Mr. Lancaster.

The simplest method of achieving the main object of her visit was to make friends with the church-going housekeeper, she thought, so on the following Sunday evening she waited until Evensong was concluded and then walked into the church.

True to the story, so far, an elderly, but not old, woman was restoring hassocks to their little brass hooks. The church was a fine, large, perpendicular building, with a nave almost as high as that of a small cathedral and an immense square tower, probably built by the friars.

D

Mrs. Bradley walked up and down the nave admiring the impressive architecture of the building, and then waited beside the font until the woman had finished her task.

" I believe," she said, " that I am addressing Mr. Lancaster's housekeeper ? "

The woman, a short, stout, round-faced person in about the middle sixties, white-haired, black-clad and not, Mrs. Bradley deduced, deficient in brains, smiled shyly and admitted that she was.

" And if you've come to take Annie's house," she added, " I'm sorry to say I let it on Monday afternoon. Come a mort of people after it, once the advertisement was in."

Mrs. Bradley said that she supposed so, and that it was not for herself that she wanted a house, but a friend had asked her to take a look at it.

" Take a look at it you can, with pleasure," said the housekeeper, " and until Mr. Geoffrey suggested advertising, I thought I should have it on my hands till the day of my death, really and truly I did, and little Malcolm to educate, too. I'm really grateful to Mr. Geoffrey, I can tell you, although them I could mention don't like him. And he paid for the advertisement, too, like a thorough gentleman."

" Very handsome. I almost feel I know Mr. Geoffrey," said Mrs. Bradley. She added : " A young friend of mine met him on holiday."

" Did he so ? "

Mrs. Bradley did not alter the impression that her young friend was a boy, not a girl, and they came out of the church and walked side by side across the church-yard to a curious gate with a stile.

" Used to be a right of way across here," explained the housekeeper. " Then Mr. Bracknell, back in 1860, he thought courting couples shouldn't carry on under God's windows, so blocked up path, and carried church gate to other corner. Then Mr. Griscott, he thought shame to take any village privilege, and told us all God loved lovers, and had stile put for they young folks to sit on. Not as they ever do."

" Why not ? " enquired Mrs. Bradley, greatly intrigued by this insight into the psychological reactions of vicars to love and the rights of the people.

" Too public. Highroad runs by, you see, since they took off the toll-gate back to Leverbottom."

Unable to follow this divergence into local history, Mrs. Bradley reluctantly abandoned the conversational bypath, and asked where the house was situated.

" I'm taking thee right to where it is," the house-keeper assured her. " 'Tisn't far, and not too mucky for thy Sunday shoes."

The house was really two cottages knocked into one. It was pretty, and Mrs. Bradley expressed regret that she had not been able to get there in time to secure it. They discussed its possibilities, and then the house-keeper suggested that Mrs. Bradley might care to come back to the house for a cup of cocoa and a biscuit before beginning her long walk back to the *Rising Sun.*

On the way—perhaps half a mile—to Mr. Lan-caster's house, Mrs. Bradley touched on the subject of ghosts. To her surprise, the housekeeper immediately

repeated the story of her own visitations, much as
Gillian had had them from Mr. Geoffrey.

"But such happenings are supposed to foretell
disaster, are they not?" Mrs. Bradley suggested.

"Disaster enough!" exclaimed the housekeeper.
"Why, not so long after, we thought Mr. Lancaster
was gone from us for good and all."

"I heard he was just a little . . ." Mrs. Bradley
began.

"Oh, he isn't quite right in the head, if that's what
you mean," said the housekeeper, with startling—in
fact, incredible—candour. "But you can't get past
poisoning by strychnine. And in his coffee, too, the
poor old gentleman."

"But I understand," Mrs. Bradley said, persevering,
"that he was given to making wild statements about
his relations, and that for years he had said he expected
one of them to murder him."

"Not that I know of," said the housekeeper. "But
some people will say anything."

She led the way in through a small gate beside the
lodge, and, to Mrs. Bradley's surprise, they went to the
housekeeper's room by way of the great front door.
As it opened, carved Tudor bannisters met the
eye, and the grand staircase, short and broad on
its first flight, rose to a coloured window on the
landing.

At what would have been the picture-rail level in a
modern house were various small coats of arms with
quarterings, and on either side of the entrance hall
were dark, wide doors. The housekeeper opened the
one to the right and led the way through what seemed

to be the dining-room, to the servants' part of the house.

Here the rooms were small, ugly and mid-Victorian in fittings and furniture. The housekeeper's own room was next to the kitchen. It contained one comfortable chair, three Windsor chairs (one with arms), a footstool, two engravings of Canterbury Cathedral, a lithograph of a stag at bay, and the usual picture of the Infant Samuel in a nightgown. The housekeeper indicated the comfortable chair, and invited Mrs. Bradley to sit down. Then she removed her black hat, gloves and scarf, and rang a bell. A sharp-eyed girl in a green-striped dress appeared.

" Where's your cap, Ethel ? " said the housekeeper. " Put on the milk for the cocoa. And mind you don't water it this time. *Is* there any milk ? "

" Oh, yes, Mrs. Bertram. And I've only just got back from Chapel," said the girl, half cheeky and half on the defensive. The housekeeper went to a small mahogany cabinet, brought out two large, rose-decorated cups, one of them a moustache cup, and placed them on a small black lacquered tray. She then placed granulated sugar and a biscuit tin beside them. The tin had pictures of Queen Victoria's Jubilee on it, and was the kind which can be used as a tea-caddy when it is not required for biscuits or when its first cargo of biscuits has been eaten.

" In my childhood," said Mrs. Bradley, " we had a tea-caddy with the Battle of Trafalgar on it, and the date. It had also a picture of Nelson and Lady Hamilton on the side, which I hardly thought quite suitable."

"Really?" said the housekeeper. "I have never seen one like that."

Mrs. Bradley, who had not seen one like it, either, and had just invented it for conversational purposes, proceeded to describe the imaginary box in more detail.

"Moreover," she proceeded, "it was said by one of my aunts, but with how much truth I do not know, that such boxes contained a secret panel behind which were three hairs from Nelson's wig."

"Genuine?" enquired Mrs. Bertram, who obviously did not believe a word of the story. She cascaded a heaped spoonful of sugar into the moustache cup.

"No sugar for me," said Mrs. Bradley. "My doctor has forbidden it."

"You poor thing. Diabetes, I suppose?" observed the housekeeper; and in the pleasant channel of illnesses past, present and to come, the conversation continued until the girl came in with the cocoa.

"Now, then," Mrs. Bertram continued. She poured out the cocoa from its jug. "*All* milk, Ethel?"

"Oh, yes, Mrs. Bertram. Just brought to the boil, like you said."

She winked impudently at Mrs. Bradley, and the housekeeper handed biscuits. When it seemed cool enough for the purpose, Mrs. Bradley delicately sipped the cocoa, was taken with an explosive, mannerless, untimely fit of coughing, and contrived, with some skill, to get rid of the mouthful into a very large handkerchief. In returning the handkerchief to her pocket she caught her cup with her elbow, and in a second the muddy liquid was streaming off the table on to the floor.

"Never mind!" said the housekeeper kindly, to silence her protesting apologies. "Have my cup. I haven't touched it. Ethel can soon make some more."

Mrs. Bradley, still, it appeared, on the verge of asphyxiation, shook her head in a helpless way, and, holding a hand to her chest, began to make for the open air.

"Oh, dear, oh, dear!" said the housekeeper, fluttering about her. "Oh, dear, I *am* so sorry. Went down the wrong way, did it? Isn't that just too bad!"

"Mother and me, us give thee up," said Tom, "so long thee been coming back from church."

"You may well have given me up," said Mrs. Bradley. She was anxious to meet Gillian's Mr. Geoffrey. On the other hand, it was a great temptation to remain for a bit at the *Rising Sun*, if only to find out why there was this conspiracy to keep her interested in Mr. Lancaster and his house. She began to have some kind of glimmering idea of the method behind the madness, but further investigation was imperative. There had certainly been strychnine in the cocoa, although not, she thought, very much.

Again, the very fact that this was so, made her all the more inclined to seek, first, the explanation of the trap which seemed to have been baited for her.

She sent a telegram to Gillian :

Keep Geoffrey handy with you Wednesday Bradley.

Tom said :

" What, going to clean thy teeth, like, afore thee have thy supper ? "

To what extent Mrs. Bertram suspected that Mrs. Bradley had detected the strychnine in the cocoa was not at all clear next morning, when Mrs. Bradley called to apologise for spoiling the cloth, the chat and the housekeeper's Sunday evening.

She went to the back door to knock, and Ethel opened it.

" Mrs. Bertram ? " she said. " Come in. She'll be down in a minute. We've had the usual upset with the master. He's making believe he's poisoned once again. Mrs. Bertram sent Perkins for the doctor, but it's only a bit more of his old buck."

" Take me to him at once," said Mrs. Bradley. The girl, astonished, was about to refuse, it seemed, when she caught Mrs. Bradley's eye. Black, bright, implacable and commanding, it compelled an obedience which the girl was plainly loth to give, for she began to finger her apron and tried to avoid the glance.

" Which way ? " said Mrs. Bradley.

" Mrs. Bertram's with him. You couldn't see him now," implored the girl, obviously thoroughly alarmed. Mrs. Bradley paid no attention, and the girl, dubious about, and resistant of, these unorthodox and question-

HANGMAN'S CURFEW 57

able proceedings, sulkily showed her through to the front staircase and even went so far as to tap at the door to the left of the staircase window when they reached the first broad landing.

The housekeeper opened the door. She affected surprise and received Mrs. Bradley pleasantly.

" So you got home all right, then ? " she said.

" I've come to apologise for making myself such a nuisance," said Mrs. Bradley.

" You're just in time to see the master in one of what I call his real fal-de-lals," said the housekeeper, in so light a whisper that only a person with first-rate hearing could have caught it. Mrs. Bradley, who was filled with the blackest suspicion of the house and everybody in it, affected not to hear the whispered words. Thereupon, as she inclined her ear, the house-keeper, instead of repeating what she had said, drew her inside the room, and she had her first glimpse of the patient. The housekeeper encouragingly pushed her a step or two nearer the bed.

" He's been making himself into the shape of a half-hoop until ten minutes or so ago," the housekeeper whispered. " But we gave him his usual permanganate —very weak, of course—that he says is his cure, and he's been all on at me for chloral. But, as I tell him "—her voice grew gradually louder—" that's the doctor's job."

" I see," said Mrs. Bradley. She moved round by the foot of the bed and went to the further side of it, so that she faced the housekeeper and the maid. The patient was lying flat on his back. His arms were spread wide, and his mouth was slightly open. He

snored a little as he breathed.   Mrs. Bradley bent over
and delicately pulled back his eyelids.

"That's what the doctor always does," said the
housekeeper softly.   "Of course, the poor old gentleman ought to be in a home, although I say it.   There
isn't any doubt about that."

"Hysterical subject, you think?" said Mrs. Bradley.
She watched the old man intently for another full
minute, and then walked to the door of the room.
The housekeeper followed her out.

"I'm glad you've seen him," she said.   "The way
he goes on, you'd really think someone was trying to
poison him off if you didn't know him.   The doctor
will be here soon.   We always send for him, although
it's only just a lot of nonsense.   One thing I *will* say.
He's always very nice to poor old Mr. Lancaster, even
when the old gentleman calls him names, which he
does more often than not."

The doctor's car was in the drive, and the young
doctor was getting out of it with his bag whilst Mrs.
Bradley took her leave after referring again to the
incident of the spilt cocoa.   She did not go far, however, for when she was clear of the house and away from
scrutiny—the house was blind on the east side, owing,
she supposed, to a former tax on windows—she worked
her way round to the little wood and so to the gamekeeper's hut.

The wood was a newish plantation, and the gamekeeper seemed unnecessary.   However, he had his
thatched hut, and he had hung out a few moleskins (to
give verisimilitude, Mrs. Bradley supposed, to a bald
and improbable tale) and he himself was lounging, gun

on arm, like a gamekeeper on a stage, or in a novel of the 'nineties.

"Good morning," said Mrs. Bradley. The gamekeeper touched a deerstalker cap which Sherlock Holmes might have envied, and informed her that she was trespassing. Mrs. Bradley apologised, and explained that she was trying to find a short cut back to the station. She explained that she had come from the house. The gamekeeper briefly directed her, and called up his dog, a lurcher by the name of Husker.

"Go with her, Husker," said the man. The dog politely and firmly escorted Mrs. Bradley from the wood and on to the road.

"Good-bye, Husker," said Mrs. Bradley. "Will you know me again when you see me?"

The dog gave a light, suspicious growl when she began to speak. She noticed how thin he was; much too thin for a gamekeeper's dog, or even for a watch-dog, she thought.

"The way to a gentleman's heart is through his stomach," Mrs. Bradley pronounced, looking thoughtfully at the animal. Husker slightly twitched his tail, then thought better of the gesture, and, having grumbled at her once more, sloped away through the plantation.

Mrs. Bradley was not yet bound for home. She looked at her watch, walked a quarter of a mile down the road, and then signalled the doctor's car as it came along. She had had a good look at it in the drive. The young doctor pulled up.

"How is Mr. Lancaster?" demanded Mrs. Bradley, putting in her head at the right-hand window. The doctor, completely taken aback at being confronted, at such very close quarters, by an old woman who looked like a witch and behaved like a lunatic, asked her who she was.

" Thine evil spirit, Brutus," she replied. " And you take care, young man, that the patient doesn't die on you one of these days."

" I expect he will," said the doctor, irritably. " And now, if you really wouldn't mind——"

" Of strychnine poisoning, I mean," said Mrs. Bradley. " And now will you give me a lift as far as the station ? I want to talk to you."

The doctor opened the left-side door and round she went and got in. He drove for about two miles without saying a word. Then suddenly he observed :

" Have you anything to go on, in what you say ? "

" How long have you been in practice here ? " retorted Mrs. Bradley.

" Seven months, I think it is. Why ? "

" I wondered. How often do these attacks come on ? Of old Mr. Lancaster's, I mean."

" Look here, I can't discuss my patient's affairs."

" Oh, yes, you can." She produced her card. " Didn't you come to my Short Course on the Psychopathology of Manipulative Surgery ? "

The young man laughed, and the car lurched dangerously ditchwards.

" I'm quite certain I should have done, if you'd ever given such a course. But, look here, Doctor, what are you doing down here at old Lancaster's place ? He's nothing but a harmless old loony, who gets these ideas occasionally that his relations are dosing him with strychnine to do him in and get hold of his money, you know. Why, even the police know all about him. They took him seriously the first three or four times, I understand, but they certainly fight shy of him now.

"The funny thing is that the silly old devil knows all the symptoms, and makes himself sick with the handle of his tooth-brush, and bends himself into all the strychnine shapes, and positively yells with pain. It's one of the most interesting cases of hysteria I've ever encountered. All I have to do is give him a nice drink of water which I swear is permanganate of potash, and he's perfectly happy, and thanks me with tears in his eyes for his marvellous recovery. Trouble is, he's started sending me extra cheques which, of course, I have to send back. He don't like that. And neither do I, very much," he concluded ruefully. "The last was for a hundred pounds. I could have done with it nicely."

"What a gift he might be to a parcel of really unscrupulous people," said Mrs. Bradley, almost in a whisper. "When did you first see him?"

"A month after I came here. Why?"

"Nothing, child. Drop me at the Inn of the Rising Sun. And mark my words."

"Which ones?"

"You'll know which ones soon enough, if you're not very careful," said Mrs. Bradley, grinning.

"No, I say, you don't really think?——"

"I think the poor old man is . . ."

"Pennies from heaven, so long as I can be called on to give a death certificate which *doesn't* say strychnine poisoning," said the doctor. "Yes, I see. But, then,

I *should* say strychnine, if it was. It isn't like arsenic,
you know, where the prejudiced and cocksure medico
airily writes it off as gastritis or something." He
grinned. "And at that I should Giaconda-smile,"
he added unpardonably.

CHAPTER III

" ' In behint yon auld fail dyke
   I wot there lies a new-slain knight ;
   And naebody kens that he lies there
   But his hawk, his hound, and his lady fair.' "

"THEE'S WANTED ON TELEPHONE, LIKE," SAID YOUNG
Tom, after lunch that same day. It was Mrs. Bradley's
secretary.

"A Mr. Joshua Devizes has called," said the telephone in refined accents. "I did not say where you
were, but promised to let him know whether you could
see him, and, if so, when."

"Tell him I'll see him to-morrow at four," said
Mrs. Bradley. She returned to her barn-like bedroom
to find young Tom in possession.

"What is it, child ? " she enquired. Tom grinned.

"Will thee tell I something if I ask thee ? "

"Yes, Tom, if I can."

"Well, who be fellow watches in at thy window,
like, of nights ? Because tidden one of our chaps as
I knows on."

"I don't know, Tom, who it is. I haven't seen
anybody. At what time, do you mean, does he
come ? "

"Oh, middling in the night, like."

Unable to interpret this reply, Mrs. Bradley decided
to return to it later. She then enquired :

" And what sort of person is he, would you say ? "

" Oh, middling, like," said Tom.

Mrs. Bradley kept careful watch from seven o'clock until twelve that night, and was prepared to swear that nobody, middling or otherwise, had been near her window between those hours. At twelve she went to bed.

She broke the news next morning that she would be catching the ten-thirty-nine to London. She even, to the distress of all concerned (herself included, for she had liked the inn) paid her bill, in case she should not be able to return.

" Oh, us have so enjoyed thee," Tom's mother almost tearfully protested. " Such a change, thee is, and give us so much to laugh over in the evenings."

Uncertain as to the significance of this ingenuous and apparently well-meant remark, Mrs. Bradley grinned in an amicable manner, and packed her suitcase hastily but well. She caught the train with just three minutes to spare, but this was sufficient for the porter, who said, as he hurried forward to take her bag :

" What, off again already ? Soon got tired of we, thee have."

Mrs. Bradley pleaded an urgent call from relatives in London, and promised to return if that were possible.

She had every intention of returning, but she thought that it might be as well, when she had disposed of Mr. Joshua's business, to go north and interview Gillian's Mr. Geoffrey. She felt that to miss Mr. Joshua would be tragedy beyond belief. After all, the whole magnificent fabrication, according to Mr. Geoffrey, had been his.

"He *says*," said her secretary, as soon as Mrs. Bradley arrived, "that his *uncle* is being *murdered !* "

"He may be right," said Mrs. Bradley, taking off the veil in which she usually travelled. "Except that I don't believe for a moment that the man he means is his uncle. Tell Henri I'd like some sherry, and then an omelette, and then he can send up what he likes. What did *you* have for lunch ? "

"Curried chicken, Mrs. Bradley."

"Don't tell me you went *out* to lunch, dear child ? "

"Well, when Henri heard you were coming in to lunch, he couldn't be bothered with me, so I went to the Corner House."

"Which you really enjoyed much better than you do Henri's lunches. Don't tell me. I know. What it is to be twenty-two," said Mrs. Bradley. "And what did you have to drink, child ? "

"A Horse's Neck," said the child, with an air of defiance.

"And I bet you had ice-cream," said her employer. She sighed and grinned, and produced an envelope. "And now you can take that charming young man of yours to a *matinée*," she said. "And don't get back until dinner-time."

"He can't—I don't know that he can . . ." began the secretary, who had not known that Mrs. Bradley knew of the young man.

"What ! Not from the Board of Trade ? " said Mrs. Bradley, horrified. "Go to the telephone, child, and act like a dying grandmother."

E

"Oh, he doesn't need *that*," said the girl, with a cheerful smile. She considered her employer eccentric, but no one but Mrs. Bradley herself was aware of this. "He *could* get leave, but he's *rather* conscientious."

Mrs. Bradley moaned faintly, and then cackled. "Anyway," said the girl, obtaining the last word, "you needn't bother about Henri and omelettes and things. He knows *exactly* what he's giving you for lunch. He's been in a trance ever since your telegram came."

Having, in her own view, cleared the decks for action (for any notes which the interview with Mr. Joshua might require could be made more exactly in her own peculiar shorthand than by the efficient but unimaginative child whom she had just sent out for the afternoon), Mrs. Bradley thoroughly enjoyed her lunch.

When it was finished she sent for her cook, congratulated him upon the meal, and then observed :

"Henri, I have heard many times from Célestine of your prowess with weapons, have I not ? "

"As madame pleases," he replied, with extreme wariness.

"I am expecting a visitor at four this afternoon. I want you to stand by with a heavy rolling-pin or something, and, if I order you to attack this man, you are to do so without hesitation."

"He dies," said Henri obligingly.

"Well, no, perhaps that would be going a little too far. Stop just short of that."

"In my youth," said Henri, "I am crossed in love by a girl who has the largest *dot* in our village. She runs away, isn't it, with an English lance-corporal, and her father does not give her a *sou*. It goes all to her younger sister, who will not look at me, and her father is so much afraid of other English lance-corporals that he marries her off quick to Jean Delabroue, and I am prevented by the tears of my mother, that only, from joining the Legion in North Africa."

Mrs. Bradley supposed that this speech had some bearing upon her request for an armed guard, but its obscurity remained unchallenged, for Henri, in a military manner, removed the dishes, brought the coffee, and, giving vent to the exclamation, "En haut, les franc-tireurs!" closed the door and left Mrs. Bradley alone. She occupied herself, when she had had her coffee, in writing up her notes of the case—if case it could be called—as far as it had gone.

There was no doubt whatever, she felt, that, for some reason, her presence in the neighbourhood of old Mr. Lancaster's house was desired by some person or persons. Moreover, Gillian's Mr. Geoffrey must be a party to the plot, if plot it was, or else the most extraordinary coincidence had occurred. Mrs. Bradley disliked coincidences and distrusted the circumstances which led to them. Her view was roughly that of Mr. Shaw's Bishop of Beauvais upon miracles—that coincidences were part of her profession ; that they may seem very wonderful to people who experience them and very simple to people who bring them off. She herself had caused the most extraordinary coincidences to happen. It was part of the "shock" treatment she used for some of her patients.

The facts that Mr. Geoffrey had told his sad story to the one person in Newcastle who happened to be in direct communication with Mrs. Bradley, and that Mrs. Bradley, in her turn, happened to be both a psychologist and a private investigator of crime, made a coincidence which did not particularly please or excite her, although she found it interesting.

Then there was the clumsy device to bring the fact of the strychnine poisoning to her notice. This was an extremely odd feature of the case, and, so far, she could not fit it in. It might mean that the house-keeper, loyal, and fond of her master, was giving a hint (which she dared not give in words) that the old man's death by poison was already planned by those who knew his idiosyncrasies, but this seemed unlikely.

On the other hand, it could be argued that the housekeeper herself might be in the plot, since she had allowed Mrs. Bradley to see for herself that the old man's complaints were groundless. But that being so, why had she put the strychnine in the cocoa ?

There was one bright spot in all this puzzling affair : it was that the doctor would be a good friend, she thought. She had made enquiries, along the proper channels, and was assured that he was a young, not very clever man who had recently bought his first practice and had not yet completed the first year of his professional career.

Other strange features were the gamekeeper who was, obviously, nothing of the sort, and the house itself, which, either deliberately, or (as she was inclined to believe) by accident, had not been quite correctly described by Mr. Geoffrey. There was the assertion about the hill, whereas there were no hills in the vicinity of old Mr. Lancaster's house, and, an equally noticeable error—there was no rushing stream to tumble through the garden. The house, in fact, had been quiet ; as quiet, thought Mrs. Bradley involuntarily, as the outside of a mental hospital.

Taking the hill and the stream both into consideration, Mrs. Bradley came to the interesting and (as she admitted, at once, to herself) possibly erroneous conclusion that there must be another large house connected with the mystery ; a house from which the drive to the station was uphill, and a house which had a rushing stream through the garden. On the other hand, the two houses must have a good many features in common, since roughly the same description would suffice for both.

She sighed, and began to sketch out the ground-plan and front elevation of the house she had in mind. She took out Gilliam's letter and re-read it, sifting it for any further clue to the identity of this mysterious residence whose site the interested parties (whoever they were, and that in itself had not yet been made at all clear) were so anxious to keep secret. But she had scarcely read the first five closely written sheets when the maid announced Joshua Devizes.

Mrs. Bradley's godly, righteous and sober life, as she would sometimes point out to her sister-in-law and other fermenting relatives, was hedged with but few temptations, and to these she rarely succumbed, for she was in agreement with the dictum of Gerald Gould—"for God's sake, if you sin, take pleasure in it." Some Puritanical streak in an otherwise untainted ancestry caused her to look upon sin as the last resort of the feeble-minded, however. She could perceive no pleasure in it at all.

Nevertheless, when she first met the pale and sandy-haired Mr. Joshua Devizes she was tempted to sum up his character, and this from his personal appearance. She yielded to the temptation, grimaced hideously, and wrote in her notes the following prejudiced observation :

Enter Three Murderers.

She then bestowed on him a grin of welcome which made him blench, and pushed open the door of her consulting-room.

"Come in," she said invitingly. Mr. Devizes, looking nervous, seated himself, dropped his umbrella with a clatter, apologised, dropped his gloves, licked his lips, and observed :

"I want you to find out who is murdering my uncle."

"But I am not interested," said Mrs. Bradley winningly, "in finding out who is murdering your uncle. Kindly cross your legs."

"It is no good your hitting me under the knee-cap and all that stuff," said Mr. Joshua, recovering his nerve and speaking petulantly. "You solve these cases, don't you ? Well, just you listen to this. And then I want to know how I'm to call in Scotland Yard. These local bobbies are nuts."

"If," said Mrs. Bradley, taking up her notebook again, "you are proposing to tell me the story of the wicked housekeeper, the sinister gamekeeper, the victimised old gentleman, the rival nephews, the penniless niece and the Irish groom, pray spare yourself the trouble. I have already heard the tale. I find it interesting, credible, and second-hand."

"Second-hand?"

"Well, yes, I am afraid so. Did you come to ask my professional advice?"

"No. Your professional assistance. But, perhaps, under the circumstances . . ." said Mr. Joshua. "I suppose you mean my cousin Geoffrey has already——"

"Only by proxy," said Mrs. Bradley firmly. "Haven't you heard of the East Bierley murder of 1910?"

"The East . . . I beg your pardon?"

"It doesn't matter in the least. May I ask, Mr. Devizes, where Miss Phyllis is staying?"

"Who the deuce is Miss Phyllis?" His high thin voice became peevish. "Who *is* Miss Phyllis? Has Geoffrey been spinning some yarn?"

"How should I know? I am asking for information. Your cousin's story partly involves a Miss Phyllis, in whom I am interested. If there is no Miss Phyllis, my curiosity is out of place and shall be controlled. But *if* there is no Miss Phyllis——"

"I suppose he means Madeleine," said Mr. Joshua sourly. "And if he does mean Madeleine, why on earth shouldn't he say so?"

"I don't know. He did admit that he had altered some of the names."

"We've got to be careful," Mr. Joshua admitted.
"It's terribly worrying. You see, there are the three
of us—Geoffrey, Madeleine and myself—and none of
us know how we stand. I believe he likes Madeleine
best. She makes a companion for him, and he can
have her at his beck and call, and old men with money
like that.

"Geoffrey isn't so popular. In fact, the old man
kicked him out. All the same, he liked Geoffrey's
mother better than he liked my mother. They were
sisters—the old man's daughters. With Madeleine it
was her father, the old man's only son. He cut him
off with nothing but an order on his tailor and hatter
for two suits and three hats, and I've got an idea that
he's sorry, because the chap was killed in the war.
Now I think he'd like to make it up to Madeleine.

"But this business of trying to poison him—I tell
you, we're all at sea. None of us would do that. It
must be the servants. I can't suspect Mrs. ——"

"Norris?" said Mrs. Bradley helpfully.

"Is that what Geoffrey called her? Her name's
really—that isn't really her name. Still, it'll do; it'll
do. Well, now, how about it, do you think?"

"How about what?" Mrs. Bradley coldly
enquired.

"You'll undertake the case, I suppose, at a
premium?"

"What case are we talking about?"

"Oh, I see. You won't take it? Well, why not?
If you undertake it I will, of course, let you have the
names, and full authority to act as you think best.
We've got to find out who's doping the poor old boy."

" That is a task for the police.   It has nothing to do
with me."

" But the police are not any help, not any help at
all ! " wailed Mr. Joshua.   " They do nothing but tell
us that the poor old man has had these suspicions for
years.   They say it's old stuff, and they've been had
like this before, and that the best thing we can do is
have him certified."

" It isn't that at all ? He's being murdered ? "

" Come now.   Name your own figure.   Money's no
object."

" So Mr. Geoffrey says," said Mrs. Bradley.

" Well, if you act for Geoffrey, you're acting for me."

" That is not what I was given to understand," said
Mrs. Bradley, abandoning her attitude of slightly
scornful calm, and lobbing a spanner adroitly into the
works.

The resulting dislocation was immediately and
convincingly apparent.

" What !   The double-crossing tick ! " shouted Mr.
Joshua, leaping up and down in his arm-chair. " Don't
tell me what he offered you !   I'll double it !   The
dirty, treacly little toad !   But I'll get even with him,
don't you worry about that !   Now, will you take on
the case for me, or won't you ? "

" I will not.   And I ought to add that neither have
I accepted Mr. Geoffrey's offer," said Mrs. Bradley
rising.   " I don't like your story, Mr. Devizes.   I don't
see why the police cannot be convinced that your uncle
is being poisoned.   If he is," she added.

" You'll know better, one of these days, you obstinate
old woman ! " shouted Mr. Joshua.   " Why did I come

to a woman, anyway ! Geoffrey's a fool ! No wonder
I can't get satisfaction ! "

Furiously he took himself off. Mrs. Bradley sighed,
then went to the window and watched him get into a
taxi.

" Curiouser and curiouser," she observed.

Gillian walked to the window and waved to the
handsome Mr. Geoffrey, and watched him get into his
car. She noted, with some satisfaction, that the car
shot off along the North Road. She then took out an
Ordnance Survey map of the Border, which had street
plans of the chief towns, and turned to the plan of
Newcastle.

The North Road led to Morpeth, Alnwick, Coldstream and Berwick.

" So what ? " said Gillian, in unconscious imitation
of, among others, Mrs. Bradley's great-nephew, an
engaging child named Denis. With the problem
unsolved, she went to bed, and, as her habit now was,
slept lightly but sufficiently, and no longer cried about
her lost love before she went to sleep.

Next day she took a packed lunch out with her and
went to visit Hexham. This first bit of the journey
she made by car, intending to see the Fridstol sanctuary chair, the monks' night-staircase, the Saxon crypt
(although she was not sure whether it was possible to
visit this and to see the Roman stones from which it
had been built), and the beautiful north transept.
After that she proposed to walk to Fourstones, and

thence along the Roman road to Hotbank and, by the footpath past Broomlee Lough, on to the high road by Tepper Moor and so to Chesters and Humshaugh. Here the car, driven by one of the garage hands and having cut across by way of Wall from Hexham, would pick her up again and take her back to Newcastle.

It was not a long walk for anybody as energetically fond of walking as Gillian was, but, although she had planned the excursion with considerable care, and had even asked Geoffrey to let her have her walk by herself, she did not really enjoy it. Her mind was preoccupied. She saw, but with only half an eye, the gateways, streets and barracks, the law-courts, baths and bridge, the villages and temples, of the Romans. She made no speculations about the wide deep Vallum. She took little heed of the snake-like writhings of the Wall. She mused on a second telegram she had received from Mrs. Bradley. "Do not trust Geoffrey," Mrs. Bradley instructed her. "With you on Wednesday." This was Wednesday.

By Broomlee Lough she paused, not for the view, but for the sake of one moving figure which she recognised immediately. It startled as well as pleased her, and she was glad that she had received the warning telegram, for it was Mrs. Bradley in the distance. Her grandmother's friend was walking, at a good rate and swinging a stout ashplant as she walked, towards the river.

Gillian longed to yodel, but doubted whether she could. A mere shout, she surmised, would not sufficiently carry over the moor. She essayed it, however, but the hurrying little figure in front gave no sign that the shout had been heard. Gillian began to run, but soon gave up, partly because the nature of the country was not conducive to running, but also because she did not think she would be likely to overtake Mrs. Bradley, who was moving at a quite remarkable speed.

She continued her own walk, therefore, but with a lighter heart.

" Fun," she thought, " about Geoffrey. Something phony in that story he told me at the castle. Wonder how Aunt Adela tumbled to it, though ? . . .

" She *must* have been interested," she thought, " all the same for that, to come straight up here like this."

The fact that several days had elapsed since Mrs. Bradley had received the letter did not weigh with Gillian. She had been enjoying herself, and the passing of time had seemed swift and relatively unimportant.

Mrs. Bradley had heard the shout, and knew who it was who had shouted, for she had happened to see Gillian before Gillian spotted her. She did not want to meet her at that moment. She was making for Chollerton, where she intended to meet George with the car. The car would take her back to Newcastle and the hotel at which Gillian was staying, and at which she herself had booked a room. Exactly what she was going to say to the girl she had not decided. It would depend upon whether Gillian could add anything to the information contained in the letter. She had known Mr. Geoffrey for several days now, and might have found out more about him.

Between Chollerton and Low Brunton her car passed that of Mr. Geoffrey, who was doing some casual cruising before going on to pick up Gillian, whom he had followed over the moor. He had not, on the previous day, gone further north than Morpeth. He smiled slightly, and raised a hand to his cap in ironic salute when Mrs. Bradley had gone by. They, of course, did not recognise one another.

"That young man wants the road to himself, George," was her comment. But she had no idea, at the time, that her words were prophetic.

Gillian reached her hotel to find Mrs. Bradley in possession of the lounge, the current number of *The Psychologist*, a cup of tea and the hotel cat.

"I knew it was!" she said. "But you wouldn't look at me. Aunt Adela, guess what!"

"Mr. Geoffrey Devizes has proposed to you!"

"Oh, somebody told you!"

"No, child. It was to be expected, and I expected it. Would it shatter love's young dream if I asked you to refuse him, at least temporarily?"

"No. You see, I haven't given him an answer. Do you think he really yearns for Phyllis, whoever she is?"

"I don't know, child, and her name may be Madeleine, it appears. And I don't think I care about this story told you by Mr. Geoffrey."

"You don't believe it?"

"I believe it and more," said Mrs. Bradley exasperatingly. "Gillian, are you seeing a good deal, then, of this young man?"

From her mother, Gillian would have resented this question. From Mrs. Bradley's beaky little mouth it took a different and unexceptionable tone.

" We go out every day and every evening," the girl replied. " Except last night, when he motored north towards Alnwick."

" You've given up the thought of your holiday in Galloway ? "

" Well, no, not altogether. But Geoffrey says it isn't the best time of year, and that he wants to show it me at its best."

" Is it his part of the country ? "

" No. The family live on the Sperrey Marshes, he says—wherever that may be. It means nothing to me. Do you know where they are, Aunt Adela ? "

" I have visited them. I have also visited the house in which, by his own account, his Uncle Lancaster lives."

" The house in the story ? "

" The house in the story. But not the right house, child, I am inclined to think. Now I want you to help me. Set your brains to work. I am looking for a house like that house, but with a rushing stream and near a hill. This house may be anywhere in England, Scotland or Wales. It may even be in Ireland, for all I know."

" But that isn't much to go on, is it, Aunt Adela ? You could never find such a house."

" ' What say you, Bottom ? ' " quoted Mrs. Bradley under her breath. She paused, raised her eyebrows at Gillian, grinned, and then continued : " ' Some man or other must present Wall : and let him have some plaster, or some loam, or some rough-cast about him. . . ' "

Gillian giggled.

" You mean that we are to provide a house as a bait ? " she suggested. " But whom are we baiting the hook for ? For Geoffrey ? Am I to be a sort of decoy duck, or something ? "

" For your Mr. Geoffrey first. I want to learn how much that young man knows. He must be in the plot. . . ."

" What plot ? "

" That is exactly what I have to find out, child. What plot ? Not the plot detailed to you with such delightful, racy and inaccurate detail by Mr. Geoffrey. That seems absolutely certain. Besides, a Dark Gentleman may be involved. What do you think of that ? "

Gillian stared at her hard, unable to make out how much of this was said in jest.

" So *that's* why you think Geoffrey must be mixed up in something. Was the story just an invention, then ? " she asked.

" By no means, child. Every bit of it was the truth, if police-court witnesses can be trusted to tell the truth. And there was more than truth in it, too."

" I'm afraid I don't understand."

" Let us go to my room—I have engaged a room here—and I will explain what I can. Your Mr. Geoffrey is not staying here, I imagine ? "

" He *was*, but he said that if there was a chance of our being engaged later on, it would be better for him to leave. I thought it showed strength of character."

" I am sure it did," said Mrs. Bradley. " I don't suppose for one moment that Mr. Geoffrey wants you to know what he does with himself all the time."

They went up in the lift, although Mrs. Bradley's room was on the first floor of the hotel.

" I am afraid of stairs," she said, grinning.

" Oh—Freud ! I thought that was old stuff now," said Gillian.

" Not Freud," said Mrs. Bradley.

" Fortunately," she added, when they were seated in arm-chairs by the window which was a wide and handsome bay, " I have a patient in Newcastle—an ex-patient, I should say—who has often suggested that I should visit her. I shall call at her house—it is out on the Otterburn Road—as soon as I have finished with Mr. Geoffrey."

" Tell me about your discoveries, Aunt Adela, please. And tell me why Geoffrey is suspected. I can't believe it of him—he seems so very truthful and sensible, and, really, I rather like him, I ought to tell you."

" Someone has been plumming him up, if he is truthful," Mrs. Bradley pointed out, " and if he were sensible, this would not have been possible by the crude methods which, so far, in this case, are being employed. Take your choice, child. He may be either truthful or sensible, but, even at this extremely early stage of the investigation, it is very difficult to see how he can be both."

" Truthful, then," said Gillian.

" Right," Mrs. Bradley answered. " We will begin

with the assumption that he is truthful, and see how far that leads us. When are you meeting him next?"

"This evening, I'm afraid."

"Do not say that. Nothing could be better. When he is at his best, ask him to take you to visit this dying uncle of his. I want you to notice and remember the words of his reply. Can you do that?"

"Yes, of course."

"And you will?"

"Yes, I will. I'm sure he has told the truth, so far as he knows it."

"In that case, his sudden appearance among them should startle the conspirators into a fit," said Mrs. Bradley. Gillian stared at her, but the brilliant black eyes gave nothing more away, and the beaky little mouth was pursed frighteningly. Mrs. Bradley looked like a bird of prey. She stared at Gillian for a minute, and when she spoke her words conveyed nothing to the girl.

> "There were three ravens sat on a tree,
>   They were as black as they might be.
>   The one of them said to his make,
>   'Where shall we our breakfast take?'"

Gillian laid a hand on the yellow-sleeved, thin, old arm.

"You think there's dirty work going on, Aunt Adela, don't you? But so does Geoffrey, you know. That's why he wanted someone to take up the case and investigate his uncle's illnesses. He'll be ever so

F

pleased to know you are going to do it. I know he will."

"I know he will, too," said Mrs. Bradley.

Mrs. Bradley dined alone, for Gillian was first dining with Geoffrey and then was going with him to the local music-hall. She left the hotel at half-past six. The "second house" was at nine, and this was the performance for which their seats had been booked.

It occurred to Mrs. Bradley that an evening spent at the Hippodrome would be preferable, in some respects, to one spent alone in the hotel, and so, at seven-thirty-five precisely, ten minutes before she had her dinner, she called up the music-hall and asked for a seat. She had to give her name and the name of the hotel, and secured a good seat in the front row of the dress circle. Gillian and Geoffrey, she knew, had booked two stalls. At half-past eight she drove off in a taxi, and was in her seat, studying the programme, at twelve minutes to nine.

She had looked carefully at all the people in the stalls the moment she took her place, but Gillian and Geoffrey had not then arrived. They came in at about four minutes to nine, however, just as the orchestra had begun to take their places, and Mrs. Bradley watched them settle into their seats in the fourth row.

She took no further notice of them after that, for almost immediately the lights were lowered, the orchestra struck up, the fire-curtain, a depressing view of Windsor Castle by moonlight, was raised, the curtains behind it parted and, as soon as the orchestra had finished, the first act was on.

Mrs. Bradley, in common with most philosophical human beings, held that, although to obtain the maximum of entertainment from any music-hall performance one had to be in the right mood and, she rather thought, in company with friends whose temperaments were equally attuned to the rarified atmosphere of Variety, it was always possible, granted that one was experiencing neither pain, sorrow nor serious worry at the time, thoroughly to enjoy any vaudeville programme, good, bad or indifferent.

This philosophy she was effectually realising, when, at the end of the third item, there was a noticeable scuffling down below on the floor of the house. This disturbance was followed by some audible North-country protests, and then the house lights went up, the curtains came together, and the manager stepped out through a flashing central aperture and asked, in the tones of a man trying to make his voice heard above the roar of Niagara, whether there was a doctor in the house.

Mrs. Bradley had begun to get out of her seat—with some difficulty due to the small space at her disposal between the front edge of the balcony and the bodies of the people in her row—when she was addressed by an agitated, breathless, white-faced Gillian. The girl seemed unable to express herself clearly at first. She was suffering from shock, there was no doubt.

"Aunt Adela! Do come. They say it's Geoffrey. He's been stabbed! I'm afraid it's—I'm afraid it's serious."

"So he's truthful but not sensible," said Mrs. Bradley. Nevertheless, she could not believe that this was so. She herself considered him neither. Gillian's observation that he might be a bit of a heel (made suddenly and ingenuously at the tea-table) she herself amended to the thought that, so far as Mr. Joshua was concerned, he might possibly prove to be Achilles' heel.

There was no doubt but that Mr. Joshua had made the appointment at her London house merely to size her up. It would be his bad luck, were any villainy toward, that Gillian (Mr. Geoffrey's innocent witness to the incredible story he had told her) should have brought into the case not only an expert in morbid psychology but an amateur of crime.

CHAPTER IV

" ' O ye take my riches to Bee Ho'm,
    And deal them presentlie
    To the young that canna, the auld that maunna,
    And the blind that does not see.' "

MRS. BRADLEY AND GILLIAN HAD REACHED THE GROUND
floor and were walking, after a murmured word to one
of the programme girls, along the left aisle of the stalls,
before the performance was resumed.

From the front of the house a short passage led to
the stage and also to a door through which they
passed. They were met by a man with a beard.

"We brought him in by the stage door," he explained in a whisper. "He's in the acrobats' dressing-
room, they not having come in yet, owing to being
the last item on the bill."

They continued to follow this informant and soon
reached a dingy but brilliantly lighted dressing-room
in which was a small group of people. One of these,
who was in evening dress, turned out to be the manager.
At least three of the others, two men and a woman,
were doctors, Mrs. Bradley surmised. A fat little Jew,
still another doctor, it seemed, was on his knees by
the body. Mrs. Bradley heard Gillian make a little
choking sound, and suggested that she should sit at
the further side of the room and not worry.

At the sound of her voice the manager turned round.
He spoke with a slight American accent.

" I guess we've gotten assistance, thank you, Doctor,"
he said.

" Yes, but I think I may know the young man," said
Mrs. Bradley. She walked round the body via its
feet, and watched the little Jew. He lifted his black
eyes to hers, squatted back on his heels so that his
plump thighs seemed ready to burst from his trousers,
and said, with a slight but pleasant lisp :

" I'm sorry, Doctor. I hope he was no relation ? "

" No relation," replied Mrs. Bradley. She, too,
knelt down beside the body, but opposite the other
doctor. " Dear, dear ! Very bad, very bad."

" Not a lot of blood. It was a very clean, quick
work, this," said the little Jew.

" Dead ? " said the manager. " Heck ! We'll
have to call up the police."

" Yes, do," said Mrs. Bradley. " Tell them, when
they come, that his name is Geoffrey Devizes, and
that his uncle lives . . ."

There was a shriek from Gillian. The door slammed.
The Jewish doctor felt the top of his head, and smiled.
Mrs. Bradley went over to the opposite wall, and,
taking a piece of coloured chalk from her pocket,
made a ring round the spot where the bullet had
pitted the plaster.

" It was one of those other doctors ! The woman
doctor ! " cried Gillian.

Gillian went to her room that night in a state of
mind to which she had long been a stranger. She

could have fancied that the shadowy man seen by the housekeeper, stood, a darker shade, against her shadowy curtains ; that beneath her window walked a ghostly groom in conversation with a cut-throat gamekeeper. But when, nerving herself to get out of bed, she walked over to the dressing-table, the shadow was only the shadow of two heavy, narrow curtains against a background of broader, thinner ones ; the two men walking below were only a couple of drunks turned out of a public-house at closing-time. She made a face at her own vague shadow in the mirror, and went to bed again.

She dreamt of green bottles and of purple ones ; of a rose window in a church she had known in her childhood ; of the Five Sisters of York Minster ; of a window at home which had a coat of arms in it.

Mrs. Bradley, who had had no dreams, rose very early next morning and went out for a walk before breakfast. She was thinking again about the house in the marshes. There were two people (according to Mr. Joshua's story) whom she had not seen when she visited there. One was the Irish groom and the other the penniless niece. She was inclined to think, with the farmer who would not believe in the giraffe, that there weren't no such animals. But it did not do to be too sure, particularly as, to her, the house already had the heavy compelling horror, yet utter incredibility, of a nightmare. As an equally fascinating side of the investigation, she went over in her mind the events of the previous evening. Who, she wondered, and where, was the woman who had fired the shot across the dead youth's body ?

She wondered, also, for whom the shot had been intended. It seemed that it must have been aimed either at herself or at the little Jewish doctor. At that moment she had been speaking, she remembered. She had mentioned Mr. Geoffrey's name and she had been going on to mention the house in the marshes. Was it that someone was sensitive enough not to wish Mr. Geoffrey's name or his (alleged) uncle's address broadcast? On the other hand, the shot might not have had any connection with her remarks at all.

There were two other puzzles which she could not solve. One was the effect of the young man's death on Gillian. The girl had had a shock, it was true ; but it was not the shock of personal terror or loss. The young man might have been a stranger, from the way that the girl had behaved and spoken, after the first panic was over.

Then there remained the nagging little question of how it was that Gillian had known exactly where to come and find her at the music-hall on the previous evening. She could come to no conclusion about this, and decided that she would ask the girl about it as soon as she returned to the hotel.

She got back from her walk before nine, and found Gillian still in bed.

"Get up, lazybones ! " said Mrs. Bradley. "And come along down to your breakfast."

"Oh, Aunt Adela ! Isn't it beastly ! I've got to go and identify the body, and I'm sure I can't," said Gillian, looking fresh and pretty. "And I've had such beastly dreams ! "

"There is a good deal I'm still in the dark about,"

said Mrs. Bradley, sitting in Gillian's arm-chair. " Do
you feel able to enlighten me ? "

" Why, of course, Aunt Adela. But you ought to
go back to London. I'm sure you were shot at last
night. What a mercy the woman couldn't aim
straight ! I saw the gun. A beastly little black thing.
She had it in her coat pocket and whipped it out, and
fired, and was off like a shot herself."

" *He* had it in *his* coat-pocket," amended Mrs.
Bradley. " I think, child, that our inefficient friend is
the poor Mr. Joshua of the story. And that's another
interesting point. He and Mr. Geoffrey were supposed
to be cousins, weren't they ? Did you gather whether
they got on well together ? "

" Well, Geoffrey didn't sound malicious about
Joshua when he told the story ; and it did seem as
though Joshua must have consulted him about the
way things were happening to their uncle ; and, the
queerest thing of all, there was no suggestion that
the uncle was a bit—well—how shall I put it ?—you
know, batsy or anything."

" I noticed that particularly," said Mrs. Bradley.
" In fact, in the story, he was a hale and hearty old
gentleman who was accustomed to travelling every
day to his business to keep an eye on it ; he was
capable of kicking his groom in what can only be
called a full-blooded, eighteenth-century manner, and
he gave parties for his relations if he liked them, and
turned them out of doors if he did not—behaviour, in
every case, which, partly by reason of its sheer un-
Christianity, would be accepted as sane and normal by
the majority of people everywhere."

" You sound like the conclusion to the Children's Hour," said Gillian flippantly. Then she added soberly : " What do you make of it all, Aunt Adela ? "

" What do you, child ? "

" Nothing. I think I'd like to go back to London, and I think I'd like to forget all about the beastly story. I wish I'd never met Geoffrey and I certainly wish I'd never got mixed up in his affairs. I shall never get over having mixed *you* up in them, that's another thing. I'm really terribly sorry it's all being such a nuisance."

Mrs. Bradley cackled.

" There's one more thing I wish you'd explain to me," she said. " I know, from what the police were told last night, and from what the manager said, that Mr. Geoffrey was not in his seat in the auditorium when he was stabbed. On the other hand, it was not the interval in the performance, so why had he left you, and where had he said he was going ? "

" He said he hadn't any cigarettes and could not sit through a performance without smoking. He apologised, but said it really was just like hell to him if he couldn't smoke when he wanted to, so that, if I would excuse him. . . . So, of course, I did, and off he went. That was almost as soon as the lights went down. He was gone an awfully long time, but I didn't think anything of it, although I did think perhaps he could have got some in the bar. Well, just before the manager came on to the stage and asked if there was a doctor in the house, the man who had been sitting in the seat next to Geoffrey leaned over to me and said he'd just had a message that my ' young man ' had met with an accident, and had given my name, and I was to go up to the dress circle front row, and fetch the old lady who was sitting there, because she was a doctor and would know exactly what to do."

" So that's how you knew where to find me ? "

" Yes. Of course, I didn't know it was you at first, and then, when the lights all came on, I saw you as soon as I began to walk down the gangway. But I can't think how Geoffrey could have known you would be in the house."

" No, but we can easily find that out," said Mrs. Bradley. After breakfast she went to the advance booking office of the music-hall, and came directly to the point.

" I am very anxious to have a description of the man who asked for the number of my seat in the house at last night's second performance. My name is Bradley," she said. " I booked my seat by telephone last evening."

" We do take the name and address of telephone bookings," said the clerk. " Bradley ? From the *Dillinger* ? "

" Yes."

" Dress Circle A 21 ? "

" Yes."

" Young fellow came in about eight and asked for it specially. I had to tell him it had gone. He said he wanted it for his aunt, name of Bradley. I said that was the lady's name who had booked it. He said that was all right, then, and went off whistling."

" A tall dark young man, of course ? "

" That's right," replied the clerk, who appeared to

have strayed north from Shoreditch. Mrs. Bradley added another leading question.

" Accompanied by a small, reddish-haired man, somewhat older ? "

" That's right."

" And the conversation did not seem to you at all strange ? "

" Who, me ? "

" Yes. Do people often come and make these rather odd requests at the box-office ? "

" We get all sorts. A man wanted to book three seats for self and two chimps the other day. In fact, he *did* book them. Then the management threw out the chimps."

" Indeed ? "

" Not 'arf. Then the man went, too, and claimed his money back."

" He got it ? "

" No. Nobody getting thrown out of a music 'all gets their money back. One of the Queensberry rules, that is. You'd have no check on anybody's behaviour, you see, and behaviour's everythink in a music 'all, especially in the first 'ouse, which is what it was."

" I see. Thank you very much," said Mrs. Bradley. She took her leave, frowning thoughtfully.

" Well ? " said Gillian, when she got back to the hotel.

" Geoffrey and Joshua were together yesterday evening, after Geoffrey took you out to dinner. At what time did he leave you ? "

" He didn't leave me."

" Don't be tiresome, child."

"But he didn't, Aunt Adela. Not until after the beginning of the performance, and you mean earlier than that, I suppose."

"I do mean earlier than that. I mean at about eight o'clock."

"We were eating quail at eight o'clock."

"A repulsive gesture," said Mrs. Bradley absently. "Why quail?"

Gillian might have retorted, upon classic authority, 'Why not,' but, instead, she said :

"Why, what's the hitch at eight o'clock?"

"At about that time, child, or a little after, Mr. Geoffrey and Mr. Joshua were together in the advance booking office at the music hall, demanding to be allowed to book the seat I had just acquired for myself. The booking office recognised my description of Geoffrey. That's all."

"But it couldn't have been Geoffrey, Aunt Adela," said Gillian firmly. "I am ready to declare—upon oath, if necessary," she added histrionically—"that Geoffrey was with me from the time we left the hotel until just after nine o'clock, inclusive."

"He didn't leave the dining-table at all?"

"No, of course he didn't."

"Perhaps, then, you did, child?"

"Of course I didn't. One doesn't, unless one is going to be sick or something. It's bad manners to leave the dining-table in the middle of a meal. I should have thought you would have known that."

"Be quiet, child. This is serious ; serious, and extraordinarily interesting. By the way, you say the

police have informed you that you will be called upon
to identify the body ? "

" Oh, yes. But, Aunt Adela ! I *can't !* You've
got to get me out of it. I can't go *near* the beastly
body ! I couldn't stand it."

Mrs. Bradley, looking at her, decided that this was
very probably true ; and yet the tempting theory of
impersonation which, against her better judgment, was
rapidly forming in her mind, required unbiassed
testimony.

" If they make me, of course," the girl continued,
" I suppose I'll have to do it. Will they let you come
in with me ? "

" Yes, I think so, child."

" Oh, well, I don't mind so much, then. But I'm
sure the dead man isn't Geoffrey, you know, any more
than your box-office impersonator. Ask me, there's
more in this than meets the eye."

Mrs. Bradley thought so, too.

The mortuary was, like all mortuaries, cold and
unattractive. Gillian shuddered as soon as the door
was opened for them, and, without knowing that she
was doing so, kept a tight, childish clutch of Mrs.
Bradley's yellow claw.

The police inspector was, in the Northern manner,
kindly. He led the way past a sheeted suicide to the
resting-place of the stabbed man, and drew back the
covering from the face.

" Now, lassie," he said encouragingly. Gillian shut

her eyes tight, gave, unconsciously, a very faint moan, opened her eyes, looked, looked again, and then, gazing candidly at the inspector, said, clearing her throat, and avoiding Mrs. Bradley's compelling and basilisk eye :

" But this—this isn't Geoffrey."

" You don't identify the body, then, lassie ? "

" No. I've never seen this man before."

" You're certain sure of that ? "

" Yes, quite, quite sure. This—this isn't the gentle-man I thought it might be. It's something like him—in fact, it's very much like him, but Geoffrey was longer-faced and had more chin, and, anyway, he wasn't dressed like this. He had a heather mixture suit on, not dark blue. And—was there anything funny about this man's hands ? Because Geoffrey had lost a finger. Anyway, I'm absolutely positive I don't know this man at all. I have never seen him before."

" But the really odd thing, you know," she con-tinued to Mrs. Bradley, as they made their way back to the hotel, " is what has happened to Geoffrey. You don't think *he* could have killed this man, Aunt Adela ? "

" Are your bags packed, child ? " asked Mrs. Bradley.

" I've only got a suitcase. I can pack it in half a jiff."

" As soon as we get in, child, I want you to run up and pack it."

"But I don't want to go home *now*! I want to know what has happened. Of course I didn't go and bother round the body last night while the doctors were busy, and then they took it away as soon as the police had done their stuff, and it *looked* like Geoffrey, and everybody *said* it was Geoffrey, and—I was scared and upset, I suppose—I took it for granted, until I thought it over, and realised that the clothes were wrong, you know."

"It looked like Geoffrey from the side of the room where you were sitting?"

"Exactly like him, and I didn't think at first about the suit. But if it isn't Geoffrey—and it *must* be some relation—who is it? And if Geoffrey isn't killed, where is he? Anyway, it was jolly rude to bung ho like that without a word, and all on the excuse of cigarettes, especially as I had some in my bag which he's always accepted before."

"'Now, husband, thou hast nicked the matter,'" quoted Mrs. Bradley solemnly. "'To have him impeach'd and hang'd at the next Sessions is the only thing that will ever make me forgive her.' What did you mean about the hands?"

"Only one hand, Aunt Adela. Geoffrey's lost the index finger on his left hand. A monkey bit it off when he was two."

"I don't see, ma'am," said the inspector, a little ponderously, "how the young lady came not to recognise last night that it was the wrong lad, all the same."

" Oh, but I do, Inspector," Mrs. Bradley responded. " And I take it that she will no longer be required to attend the inquest ? "

" Well, it doesna appear that she kens any more than the rest of the public, ma'am. All the same, maybe she should have waited a bit before making off the way she has. But doubtless ye were both in a swirl."

" Well, she's better out of it," Mrs. Bradley said pacifically. " And I don't see how you could have called her. What about the young man who has disappeared ? "

" Not a bleat about him, ma'am, from anywhere. We were speiring about him, naturally, as you'll understand, seeing that the dead man was so readily taken for him at first by the young lady, but he seems to have disappeared from the city, and I've no authority, I need not remind you, to look for him. We can't prove that he had anything at all to do with the other lad's death. They've not been seen together, so far as we can hear tell. No. No. But I'll need to get this poor lad identified before we can proceed, and then, ten to one, it'll be suicide, the knife left in the wound and all, you ken."

" Yes. Fingerprints ? "

" Not one. The hilt of the knife—it was a sharp, wee thing, the kind they call in the Highlands a sgian-dubh—they'll wear it in the stocking—had been wiped, I would say, and then had been handled with gloves."

" And the dead man was wearing gloves ? "

" Aye. He had one gloved hand—the right hand—

G

and the position of the knife in the wound would accord pretty well with the suicide theory if the man was right-handed, and most people are, thank the Lord. A perfectly new glove it was—we've had it identified—bought yesterday here in the city. The description would fit the young fellow himself pretty well——"

"Or the missing Geoffrey Devizes," interpolated Mrs. Bradley. The inspector glanced at her sharply, then smiled, and observed that she had anticipated his next remark. Mrs. Bradley grinned in response, and said that she could not see why a suicide should trouble whether he left his fingerprints on the knife or not.

The inspector wagged his head, remarked that all suicides were fey, and, in the Scots manner, embarked upon religious controversy.

Mrs. Bradley feared that they were in for a theological discussion of some magnitude, but she could not bear to abandon it in its interesting preliminary stages, and so she observed, after that the inspector had laid it down that St. Peter was a right-handed man :

"You draw that deduction, no doubt, from the incident of the left ear of the High Priest's servant. I agree. A right-handed man would tend to cut off the left ear of a person standing opposite to him. But, Inspector, you surely were born on the further side of the Border."

"Aye," the inspector admitted. "I'm from Kelso. There's a town for you," he continued enthusiastically, abandoning theology in favour of local patriotism. "Have you seen Kelso ? "

Mrs. Bradley admitted that she had, and they discoursed lyrically and almost in chorus upon the

beauties of the town ; its bridge over the Tweed ; its
Abbey ruins ; its associations with Sir Walter Scott ;
the tale of his ancestors who had been buried in the
Abbey aisle.

"It is a small point," said Mrs. Bradley (for,
although a theological discussion, even with a Scots-
man, can sometimes be warded off by those with their
wits about them, it is a different matter altogether to
cut short a man who is praising his native town),
" but, I think, an interesting one, which of the great
abbeys is referred to in the old ballad of *The Queen's
Marie*. You remember ? :

> " The King is to the Abbey gone,
>   To pull the Abbey tree,
>   To scale the babe frae Mary's heart ;
>   But the thing it wadna be."

The inspector admitted that he was not conversant
with the ballad, but suggested that the Abbey, no
doubt, would be Melrose."

" Not Kelso ? "

Not Kelso, the inspector thought ; nor Dryburgh.
Melrose would be the place. It had been called Holy
Melrose from time immemorial.

Mrs. Bradley then mentioned Glastonbury, and back
they soon came to Kelso, and from there parted firm
friends.

The identity of the dead man remained a mystery,
and the inquest ended in a verdict of suicide while the
balance of his mind was affected. The police, however,
continued their search for clues to the reason of the

death, and waited for relatives or friends to turn up and give a name to the dead man.

It was just over a week before anybody came forward, and then it was not a relation or a friend, but a landlady. She had little that was good to relate concerning the young man. He had left, she said, owing her money, and it seemed as though he must have sneaked back under cover of night and rifled the house, particularly his own bedroom. She gave details of pillage and damage. She herself had been "from home the night," she said.

" What gave her the idea that the dead man might have been her lodger ? " Mrs. Bradley wanted to know.

" Well, she thought she recognised the police description, which was broadcast, you remember, and then, when, two nights afterwards, her house was turned upside down, she seems to have had some odd notion that the young man was a criminal, and had brought his old associates to the house to help him burgle it. Now, however, she believes they killed him and were helping themselves to what they thought was his property. She has some idea, too, that he's been a schoolmaster at some time, but since he came to her he seems to have been out of employment. Often he would be away a couple of nights, but she doesna ken where he went."

" Where does the woman live ? "

" In Edinburgh."

" Will you give me her address ? "

" You're interested in her, then ? "

" Yes, of course. After all, you must remember, the

young man for whom this dead youth was mistaken has not been traced yet."

"We've no authority to trace him, unless he's concerned with the death. That much I told you."

"Yes, I know. But doesn't it seem odd to you, Inspector, that a young man dies and another one disappears, and they are sufficiently alike in appearance to be mistaken, from a short distance, for one another?"

"It's just coincidence, so far as we know at present," the inspector soothingly answered. "And you'll mind that the young lady was suffering from shock, when she wished to impress on us how much alike they were."

"I wish I had a description of the man who sat in the next seat but one to her at the music-hall, and first interested her in the matter. He is responsible, and, I should say, deliberately so, for her having made the mistake."

"Did she no confide to you the description?"

"Well, she was, naturally, vague. And it doesn't do to be vague about such things if the description is going to be helpful."

"Dod, no," said the inspector. "But, ma'am we are doing all we can. We'll need to know a deal more before we can make another move."

"I entirely agree," said Mrs. Bradley. "Oh, and the woman doctor who is supposed to have fired that shot across the body——?"

"That business we have in hand. You'll need to hear more of that later. There is an explanation due to you there, I agree—or to Doctor Abrams. Have you any enemies, ma'am?"

" Not homicidal ones, at any rate.   Had Doctor
Abrams enemies ? "

" Not that he kens ; but all Hebrews have enemies
nowadays."

With this retort upon our civilisation, he took his
leave, and Mrs. Bradley went back to the hotel and
packed a bag.

" We're leaving for Edinburgh at once, George,"
she said to her chauffeur.

" Very good, madam," said George.

CHAPTER V

" ' The only boon, my father dear,
  That I do crave of thee,
  Is, gin I die in southern lands,
  In Scotland to bury me.' "

THE ROAD, WHICH RAN BY WAY OF OTTERBURN, JEDBURGH
and Galashiels, passed Melrose, and they parked the
car and went across to the Abbey. Almost no trace
of the Norman buildings remain, but the fourteenth-
century eastern end of the nave and some parts of the
choir and transepts give glory to, and are glorified by,
the beautiful, fine red sandstone of which the medieval
church was made.

The presbytery, with its fine window, the magnificent
decorated window of the south transept, and the
delicate, traceried pillars were so beautiful that they
spent more time at the Abbey than they had anticipated, for George, to Mrs. Bradley's secret enjoyment,
had recently become a keen student of ecclesiastical
architecture as a result of a series of University
Extension lectures he had attended during the
winter.

Glancing at her watch, she perceived that she was
unlikely to reach Edinburgh until the late afternoon.
This did not matter, she decided, and they continued
the exploration of the ruins.

There was a fine view through the high and empty

windows. Wooded hill-sides, yellowish-green in the
sunshine, with blue-massed shadows where the trees
grew thick and deep, rose against a delicate sky.
Birds flew past ; there were flowers on the ground
where the feet of the monks had trodden. The heart
of Robert Bruce was buried at Melrose, George, who
had been seeking information, returned and told her.
Mrs. Bradley countered this educational attack by
giving him a short lecture on the turbulent house of
Douglas.

There was one other visitor to the ruins that afternoon
—a Scotswoman, gentle in manner, and with the
deceptive appearance of frailty which is apt to startle
and confuse the peoples of lesser nations when they
discover how tough, resilient and unconquerably
enduring is the stuff and the spirit of this race. In
answer to a question from Mrs. Bradley, on George's
behalf, this lady entered into conversation about the
place, and pointed out, among other things, the spot
where the fabulous wizard sleeps under the aisle of the
south transept. She talked also of the families who
were buried there, and described the arms and crests
of these families.

" Unicorns ? " said Mrs. Bradley. " Very interesting
indeed. And have you heard of the old belief, I
wonder, that the horns of these creatures are antidote
to poison ? "

The Scotswoman said that she had heard of this
belief, and twenty minutes (during which the two ladies
seated themselves, and George strolled off to smoke a
cigarette and, Mrs. Bradley suspected, make notes upon
what he had learned) passed very pleasantly in a

discussion of witches and warlocks, the water-kelpie, Hern the Hunter, raising the wind (in the magic, not the financial, sense), and other old wives' tales.

Mrs. Bradley, like most English people who know and love the royal city, had her favourite hotel in Edinburgh, and to this George drove immediately. A Scots tea, of enormous proportions, fortified her against her quest of the young man's lodgings, but before she could depart in search of them—in fact, whilst she was still enflanked by scones and apple jelly— a young, female, and, to Mrs. Bradley, who had expected some such manifestation, dreaded voice, exclaimed :

" I thought you'd arrive about now. Are you staying here again, Aunt Adela ? "

" But you're in London, Gillian," said Mrs. Bradley distastefully. " I saw you off on the train."

" Yes, darling, I did start for London. But if you think I'm going to stick about London with mother while you're getting yourself shot at across dead bodies, you've got another think coming. And don't argue, because I'm going to stick around. Besides, I need some excitement, and I must know what happened to Geoffrey."

One thing was certain, Mrs. Bradley concluded, looking up at the girl. The broken heart, however occasioned, was now a thing of the past. If there were a spiritual scrap heap for broken hearts, Gillian had cast hers on it. She looked alert, healthy and energetic, or, as others have expressed it, and as she herself proceeded to do as soon as Mrs. Bradley commented upon her changed appearance, bloody, bold and resolute.

"In fact, what I really feel like," she announced, "is Up, Guards, and at 'em."

Mrs. Bradley was reminded, in this chivalrous gesture of the girl's return, of Sir Giles de Argentine, who, having escorted Edward II from the field of Bannockburn, turned about with the immortal rebuke : "It is not my custom to fly."

Gillian seated herself, spread a scone until it dripped apple jelly, wolfed it with mannerless hunger, and then looked wide-eyed at Mrs. Bradley, whose experience of the psychology of persons aged twenty caused her to know better than to send the girl away again. She said, therefore, formally :

"And what does your mother have to say ? "

"Mother dithered a bit, when she had heard all, and wished Lesley was with us to keep me from being bored at home, but grandmother said I ought to be ashamed of myself to leave one of her generation to face the pop-guns while I came back to London to laze, dance and tipple."

Mrs. Bradley, whose contemporary, the grandmother, had been a militant suffragist leader for old, unhappy, far-off things and battles long ago, cackled harshly, and bestowed upon the ally the last cup out of the pot and the two scones still left on the dish. Gillian, who admitted to having had her tea, cleared the plate. Mrs. Bradley grinned approval.

"And now," she said, "we have to interview an Edinburgh landlady."

"She won't mind. They're used to the students, I expect," replied Gillian philosophically. The landlady did, in fact, prove perfectly easy to interview, particularly when Mrs. Bradley claimed to be the young man's maternal aunt, able and willing to pay his debts and for the damage done to the house.

"Ye puir body," said the landlady, at this. "He was a braw laddie."

Although both elderly ladies were convinced that this was untrue, it formed a sympathetic bond, and Mrs. Bradley was able to inspect, as narrowly as she wished, the bedroom of her deceased nephew on her sister's side, and to take stock of such of his effects as had been left untouched by a cyclone, it appeared.

"There'll be ane thing mair," the guardian and custodian of the tall, narrow house said suddenly, when Mrs. Bradley's close and detailed inspection was completed and the young man's bills had been paid. "There'll be a wee picture he was giving into my charge. It's just a map."

She led Mrs. Bradley to the dark-walled bend of the stairs.

"Ye wouldn't just notice it," she continued, "and, in my opinion, it's a thing of very small value, but it belonged to him, and maybe ye'd care to take it away for a memento. It's about all that got left, puir laddie, by the time those daft loons had finished wrecking his room. I dinna ken what way he set store by it."

"I'd very much like to have it," Mrs. Bradley responded. The landlady reached up a long arm as

tough as a Border reiver's, and snatched the picture
from the wall.

"It's no old," she observed, as she gave it a hasty
wipe over with her apron. "It's nothing but a bit
picture pulled out of a book."

"Good heavens!" said Gillian, amused. "It's out
of the Book Seven *Piers Plowman*. We used to have
them at school."

"It's written on, over to the back," said the woman.
"A bit verse, maybe, from Sir Walter Scott, I'm
thinking."

The 'verse' was a line or two from *The Lay of the
Last Minstrel* :

> "Shone every pillar foliage-bound,
>   And glimmered all the dead men's mail."

"Will there be anything more for ye?" the woman
enquired ; and upon being informed that there was
nothing more unless she could tell Mrs. Bradley the
names and addresses of any friends the young man had
had in Edinburgh, she showed them out very civilly.
She had no more information to give.

"He lived here four months, and nobody ever came
near him. He would spend the most of his time just
speiring about old books and family papers, and the
like, in the second-hand booksellers, but got nothing,
that I ken, for his pains."

"And his letters?"

"Och, aye, his letters, to be sure! I mind, now you
say it, that some of his letters came addressed to
Graeme, but Carlisle was the name he wrote in my
book, and Carlisle he always signed himself on cheques,

when he could get me to take his cheques, which wasn't after the first two months of paying me, for the second cheque was a wrong one."

"Where did he bank? Perhaps I ought to see the manager. He may have had an overdraft. I want to see, poor fellow, that his effects are finally settled before I leave for London."

"Is it where did he bank? I dinna recollect the name of the bank, but I can point oot the way. I went there myself to speir about the cheque, ye ken. Look. If ye'll take the first turning by the kirk, and then bear round to your left, ye'll be bound to see it."

They walked in that direction immediately her front door closed behind them.

"What do you make of her?" asked Gillian.

"Honest, and a hard woman," Mrs. Bradley briskly replied.

"Are you really going to the bank?"

"No, child. I'm going to make a note of its name and address, though. We may perhaps need it later on."

As they came round by another road, and back on to Princes Street, she added:

"Don't mention the *Piers Plowman* map to anyone, child. Don't forget."

"I wasn't going to. By the way, Aunt Adela, have you noticed one very curious thing about this business?"

"I've noticed several, child. That is why, in spite of the fact that this business is anybody's business but mine, I propose to ferret out the very last fact about it, if it proves to be the last thing I do."

" Attaboy ! " observed her niece-by-courtesy, with marked approval. " But what I was going to point out—although evidently you don't need to hear it—is how odd all the names are in this affair. Lancaster, that's the old uncle—Devizes—that's Geoffrey——"

" And Joshua," interpolated Mrs. Bradley.

" Yes, and now this new one—Carlisle—they are all the names of towns. It seems queer to me. Do you think they can all be false ? "

" There seems reason to believe that the last one was false, child, anyhow."

" You think his real name was Graeme ? Aunt Adela, why did you come to Edinburgh ? Just to interview the landlady ? "

" A rich wedding to see," said Mrs. Bradley absently. " I beg your pardon, child. I should have said ' Shades of Baroness Orczy '—although not yet, I trust, bless her heart ! "

" Oh, I get it—' demned elusive Pimpernel '—in this case the reason for Geoffrey's disappearance and this boy—Graeme-Carlisle or Carlisle-Graeme—stabbing himself at almost the same time. I'm positive Geoffrey did it. How, otherwise, could it all have happened so oddly ? "

Mrs. Bradley made no reply to this, and they walked on until they came to a gunsmith's.

" We are," Mrs. Bradley observed in a firm, low voice, " two weak, defenceless women. We will therefore arm ourselves. Can you, by any chance, manage a revolver, child ? "

" Good heavens, yes, I should hope so," Gillian replied. They stopped at the gunsmith's, and, after glancing rapidly at the window—or, rather, into it to obtain the reflection of two men who had been following them—Mrs. Bradley led the way into the shop.

They spent a pleasant forty minutes—instructive ones for Gillian—in choosing the weapons, and by the time they left the shop the two men were gone. All the same, Mrs. Bradley hailed a taxi, bundled Gillian in, and off they drove to the hotel. One of the men, she thought, was not unlike the gamekeeper from the house in the marshes. The other she did not know.

Dinner was excellent, and as soon as it was over they went upstairs to the double room for which Mrs. Bradley had exchanged as soon as she knew that the girl was going to stay, and, each seated in an arm-chair away from the window, they discussed the case as far as it had gone.

Mrs. Bradley wondered whether to mention the fact that she believed they had been followed. Gillian was practising whipping her revolver in and out. She looked absorbed, happy and young. Mrs. Bradley decided to risk it.

"Oh, them!" said the girl. "Yes, I saw them. I shall complain to the police if I see them hanging about again. They positively dogged our footsteps all the way from those lodgings. Silly apes! What did you do with the map?"

"I have it here," said Mrs. Bradley, taking it out and spreading it upon a small table by her bedside. Gillian came and looked over it.

"Taken, I imagine, from the plan of Edinburgh published by de Witt in 1690," Mrs. Bradley remarked. "I see that it has been torn or cut down the middle, and then—oh, no it hasn't. There's thickness through. Something has been folded over, or joined."

"I can explain that, I think," the girl remarked. "I remember that, in the book, the plan was in two halves, on two opposite pages. It used to irritate me a bit, because it left a wide white margin of page between the two halves of the map, so that you got——" she traced it delicately—"this letter K, which marks the High Street, separated from the rest of the High Street looking towards the Castle by an inch-wide strip of white paper. It made the plan seem not real. Of course, it was better to have the plan on a larger scale, I suppose——"

She picked at the thickened paper as though to prise it up. Mrs. Bradley gently but firmly removed her hand, and said :

"At any rate, somebody so far shared your objection to the way the plan was set out on opposite pages as to go to the trouble of folding the second sheet over and sticking it along that white margin to which you refer, and—you know, I think I'd like to see——"

She did not finish the sentence, but, taking out a penknife with a very long thin blade, she began, with the most extreme delicacy and care, to separate the pages again.

The sticking had not been done by an expert, and her precise handling of the knife began to have its effect. She worked very slowly indeed ; so slowly, that Gillian suggested that wet warmth applied to the gum would take effect more quickly.

"Like you steam open an envelope," she suggested. Mrs. Bradley, however, preferred, as surgeons must, the knife, with its nicety of judgment. Her patience and skill were rewarded. Page one hunded and three fell back from one hundred and two, and, except for one obstinate sliver of paper which had elected to be sliced from the parent thickness rather than yield, the plan was in two perfect parts, as the bookbinder and the printer, between them, had ordained that it should be.

" Why, there's something written," said Gillian. " There's the word Acrostic—beastly things !—and then some Latin. Oh, it looks like the beginning of a psalm."

" Of the fifty-first psalm," amended Mrs. Bradley. " And that is interesting, too. It is the Criminals' Psalm. It used to be read or repeated by criminals before their execution. Scott has a stanza about it :

" And safer by none may thy errand be done,
    Than, noble dame, by me ;
Letter nor line know I never a one,
Were't my neck-verse at Hairibee."

" Hairibee ? " said Gillian.

" The place of execution, child, at Carlisle. Wait a minute. There's more here, written small, and in ink not ten years old. Look. Here."

Gillian followed the yellow finger, and read aloud, like a child :

" You will find me in title but not in deed of gift."

She looked up and said :
" You're not a Borderer, Aunt Adela ? "

H

"There is good Scots blood in me," Mrs. Bradley replied. "But not a lot of it," she added, with a cautiousness which appeared to give the amendment the lie. Gillian giggled, met a reproachful grimace, and subsided, elbows on the table, to brood again over the map.

"Why should anybody take the trouble to write the first two words of a Psalm, and then stick it down inside two pages like that? And that's something legal, isn't it—title, and deed of gift?"

"Time will show, child. I wish I could be certain that we have now obtained possession of the only object for which the murderers were searching when they wrecked Mr. Graeme-Carlisle's rooms."

"The murderers? You mean—Geoffrey——?"

"And Mr. Joshua. That precious pair, I fancy—and, mind, it is nothing but fancy, for I can't prove a word of what I'm saying—tracked down the man they afterwards murdered, made an appointment to meet him in Newcastle, and afterwards searched his rooms, but unsuccessfully."

"How do you work that out? You can't *know* that they were after this plan."

"No. But one thing about it struck me as being a trifle odd. Why was it handed to the landlady?"

"He hadn't room for it on his walls."

"And yet a man wouldn't trouble to frame a thing of this kind unless it had some particular interest for him. I should rather like to find out how long he had had it, and whether there were any conditions made at the time that he handed it over into the landlady's care."

" He probably bought it framed and mounted, and then didn't want it any longer."

" Nevertheless, I am interested in our *Miserere mei*, inscribed on the margin of a modern book. I am interested in the sticking together of the two pieces of the plan. I am interested in Mrs. Landlady——"

" MacWhirter."

" MacWhirter, who minds her lodger's business as well as her own, and who, in spite of a shrewd, and even suspicious temperament, accepted our bona-fides on sight and without investigation."

" Oh, I don't know. You look awfully like most people's aunts and godmothers. I'd swallow you myself, without a blink, if I were a landlady, particularly if you were going to pay up old debts and so on. I mean, that puts the O.K. on any sort of snooping, I should say."

" I see. You may be right, but I'm thinking of paying another call on Mrs. MacWhirter—possibly to-morrow. And now—this plan. When we have scrutinised it a little more closely—for I perceive on it certain tiny arrows formed with Indian ink, and not, I venture to suppose, by the authors and printers of the book—we will post it to my friend the inspector at Newcastle."

" Why ? "

" It will probably be among the exhibits passed round to the jury at the trial, child."

" You're pretty sure it was murder, Aunt Adela, aren't you ? "

" I am of the considered opinion that the murdered man was left-handed, child, that's all. The development of the forearm muscles, the size of the left hand compared with the right, point to the facts that the dead man had been a manual worker and a left-handed manual worker. The point did not escape the police doctor nor the inspector, but they are content to abide their time."

" But I thought he was a schoolmaster."

" He had retired from that profession. We knew that from his landlady. Now, then, hand me my magnifying glass, and let us see what we can find."

The plan* was so clearly set out, and so fully annotated, that it was easy enough to follow the course of the arrows. They were very tiny, and, without the aid of the magnifying glass, which was a powerful one, they might easily have been mistaken for insignificant marks on the paper. The magnifying glass, however, showed them up for what they were—the track or trail leading from the West Port, just south of the Castle, along the Grass-market, along a dog-leg street below the Castle Hill, round by the Weigh House, and so along the High Street to the Tolbooth.

Here the arrow had a ring round it. The next arrow pointed eastwards, past St. Giles', and the trail continued by way of the Market Cross and out at the Netherbolb, or Netherbow Port (the former spelling was given on the plan), out into Canongate. Here was sketched (only to be seen through the magnifying glass because it was so small and faintly drawn) a gallows on a raised platform. One thing more, which Mrs.

---

* *Piers Plowman Histories*, Junior Book Seven ; by E. H. Spalding, M.A., and Phyllis Wragg. George Philip & Son. 1914.

Bradley noted and Gillian did not, was that the Tron
Kirk, built, according to the annotation of the plan,
in the ten years between 1637 and 1647, had been
crossed out, having been shaded over very carefully
and finely. The letter I which indicated its position
on the plan had been crossed through.

"Well, well," said Mrs. Bradley, "we have learned
what the plan has to tell us, so now to post it to
Newcastle."

"Why not to London, Aunt Adela?   It doesn't
tell anything about the murder, does it?"

"Be very careful, child, how you talk about murder.
Suicide was the verdict, remember. We have not
altered it yet."

" I mean suicide "

"And I think perhaps you are right about London.
I will post the thing to my bankers. They will keep it
safe. As you say, it has no significance, at present,
with regard to its late owner's death."

"Shall I slip down to the posting-box with it,
Aunt Adela?   There's one in the vestibule."

"Very well, child, but I shall come with you. You
will need, I imagine, armed escort."

She wrapped her revolver round with a small silk
handkerchief so that only the little black muzzle was
showing, and, after glancing both ways along the
passage, she and Gillian walked to the head of the
stairs. The posting-box was just inside the entrance
hall. They reached it without encountering anybody
on the stairs except a sandy-haired waiter who was
carrying an empty tray. Against him Mrs. Bradley
clumsily and unpardonably cannoned, to send the

tray spinning off towards the door of a room marked
eight and the man himself almost head-first down
the stairs.

Waiting until she had seen Gillian shoot the hotel-
embossed envelope into the box, where it became,
presumably, indistinguishable from several dozen
others, except for its superscription, which would
convey little to anybody who saw it since it was
directed to the bank manager's private address, Mrs.
Bradley helped the man up, apologised earnestly to
him, re-equipped him with his tray, tipped him, and
followed Gillian upstairs.

Throughout all these manœuvres, the waiter,
apparently dazed, had made no remark. He stood
gazing at the money in his hand, and his lips moved,
but not, Mrs. Bradley suspected, in thanks, or in words
which any Scottish dialect might excuse.

" That waiter is cursing both of us, I think," said
Gillian, when they had re-entered the bedroom. " He
took a nasty toss."

" Yes, I meant he should," said Mrs. Bradley
calmly, " and I have been to the cinema far too many
times now, I regret to say, not to know how to trip
up people on the stairs."

" Why, what on earth——"

" Our friend Mr. Joshua. Unfortunately he knows
I've pierced the disguise. I had to let him see my
revolver. Lock the door, child. Are you nervous ? "

" Good heavens, no ! My generation isn't nervous.
We just get beastly bored. This, I think, is grand.
This sleuthing about, I mean, and barging people
downstairs. Let me do the next one, Aunt Adela."

"Your part," said Mrs. Bradley, "is to keep both eyes wide open for Mr. Geoffrey."

"What shall I do if I see him?"

"Perhaps you'd better yell for the police, child."

"Oh, rot. Of course I shouldn't. I should pounce on him and ask him what he meant by leaving me flat, and going off for good like that in Newcastle."

"He'll plead loss of memory, child, and will probably ask you who you are."

"If he did, and if I knew him the slightest bit better, I'd sock him, and tell him that's who."

"Dear, dear! Do *you* go to the cinema, too, then, child?"

"You wait until you see me slinging pie," replied Gillian tersely. "Attaboy!" she added, with unnecessary dramatic effect. "But——"

"One thing at a time, child. From the plan we have learnt that a line of research in connection with Mary Hamilton awaits our examination."

"Mary Hamilton? Never heard of her. Mary Tudor, yes; Mary Queen of Scots, yes; various Bible Maries, yes; Mary, Mary quite contrary, yes; Mary Beaton—in a play by John Drinkwater, yes; various authors called Mary Something or other, yes. Mary Hamilton, no."

Mrs. Bradley grinned, and quoted solemnly:

"Yestreen the Queen had four Maries,
    The night she'll hae but three;
There was Mary Beaton, and Mary Seaton,
And Mary Carmichael, and me."

" Mary Hamilton ? "

" Mary Hamilton ; executed outside the Netherbow Port, not far from Holyrood Palace. Now, we really need a copy of the ballad, although I think I could recite it from memory."

" Recite away, then. This is most gripping. I wouldn't give up your society, Aunt Adela, for any man on the face of the earth."

" Sour grapes," said Mrs. Bradley, prodding to find out whether the wound was healed, and not in very much doubt about the result of this crude test.

Gillian laughed, and picked up the house telephone.

" Aren't you really going to recite it ? " she enquired.

" I beg your pardon ? " said the telephone.

" Send the porter out for a copy of a book of Border ballads containing——" She put a hand over the receiver. " What's it called, Aunt Adela ? "

" *The Queen's Marie*, child."

—" *The Queen's Marie*, please. And could he be as quick as he possibly can ? I want to read it before I visit Holyrood Palace or the Castle."

" You are speaking ? "

" From Number Six."

" It's no part of the porter's duties, but will the *Oxford Book of Ballads* be what you're seeking ? "

" Is it, Aunt Adela ? The *Oxford Book* ? "

" Yes, of course, child, that will do, at any rate, for a beginning."

" Yes, the *Oxford Book*."

"In just eleven minutes, if the library copy will not content you. I'll just see whether it's in. A peety to spend eight and sixpence for just one ballad."

"No wonder the Scots are the greatest people on earth," said Gillian, awed.

CHAPTER VI

" ' Get up, get up, Marie Hamilton ;
    Get up and follow me ;
    For I am going to Edinburgh town,
    A rich wedding for to see.' "

" NOW," SAID MRS. BRADLEY, " WILL YOU HAVE THE
book or the map ? And I'd better warn you at once
that, if we've got hold of the wrong collection of these
ballads, our efforts at the moment are doomed."

" I'd better read the ballad first, I think," said
Gillian, going to the door to answer it.

The book, brought by the porter with a piece of
paper to mark the place, was the copy from the hotel
library. Gillian put the book down when she had
finished reading, and said :

" I can't see that it gets us anywhere. Do you really
think it will ? "

" Yes, child. Now, then."

" I'll have the plan, please."

They exchanged, and Gillian sat, chin on hand,
staring down at seventeenth-century Edinburgh. Mrs.
Bradley handed over the magnifying-glass, and then
began to read.*

---

* It is not necessary for the reader to be conversant with any of the
ballads mentioned in this book in order to follow the story. Apposite
quotations are given by the author, who, nevertheless, heartily recom-
mends the Oxford Book to any who do not know it.

" Do you think they started out from Holyrood Palace ? " asked Gillian.

" No, child ; from Stirling Castle. Holyrood would be too near, I think. You see, it says :

> ' And every town that they came to,
> They took Marie for the Queen.'

" And, again :

> ' Why weep ye sae, ye burgess wives,
> Why look ye sae on me ?
> O I am going to Edinburgh town,
> A rich wedding to see.' "

" Oh, yes, of course. Besides, Mary Queen of Scots was often at Stirling before the death of Lord Darnley, wasn't she ? And look at the arrows on the plan ! They come from the West Port. If the procession had started out from Holyrood, it would have come in by the Netherbolb Port, wouldn't it ? "

" We have no proof yet that the arrows have any connection with the route taken by the two Maries, child."

" No, but we're working on that hypothesis. Don't queer the pitch, Aunt Adela."

Mrs. Bradley subsided meekly.

" Go on reading," said Gillian, " from the bit about the Tolbooth."

> * " ' When she gaed up the tolbooth stairs,
> The corks from her heels did flee ;

---

* Many of the quotations have been very slightly Anglicised in deference to the modern English prejudice against any form of dialect.

And long or e'er she came down again,
She was condemn'd to die.

' When she came to the Netherbow port——' "

" Ah, that's it ! " cried Gillian. " That's where
the spelling is altered on the map. The printed
spelling on the map is Netherbolb. In the ballad it's
Netherbow. Is that what you partly based your idea
on ? "

" My idea, child ? "

" Yes . . . about Mary Hamilton. But of course it
was. It must have been. Go on, please."

" ' She laugh'd loud laughters three ;
But when she came to the gallows foot
The tears blinded her e'e.' "

" That's it. And then comes all that bit about
rewards and things, and not letting her father and
mother know what has happened to her. I don't
really see that it helps much, Aunt Adela. We've got
nothing really to go on."

" We've as much to go on as the precious Mr.
Joshua has," said Mrs. Bradley sturdily. " And
probably a great deal more. Let us be up and doing."

" Doing what ? "

" Going on pilgrimage, child."

George stared up at Stirling Castle, his cap tilted
over his eyes. He fully approved of the expedition. It

was his creed that if you had a car it was a sin not to use it. They had come by way of Linlithgow, Falkirk and Bannockburn, and although he had been bidden to drive at an average speed of thirty miles an hour, and although there had been several, to his mind unnecessary, stops, George was content.

The day was calm, clear and warm. The castle, an untidy, impressive, strongly-walled building, isolated by reason of its height above the surrounding country, rose, in a dignity rendered somewhat ugly by successive, individual-minded builders, proudly upon its sheer rock. Below the buildings and their walls were deep dark woods on one side, a scaur with bushes and trees upon another.

George got a view of the darker woods, and, beyond the lower slope of the scaur, of two lines of low-crowned hills. He lit a cigarette and smoked placidly, oblivious of everything except that the day was fine, the car was running in its usual faultless manner, and that some miles still remained to be covered, as they were due back in Edinburgh that night.

Meanwhile Gillian and Mrs. Bradley strolled and talked. At last, having viewed the castle from every possible angle, they fixed upon a return route from their maps and by half-past two were again getting into the car.

" Back by the same route as far as Falkirk, George," said Mrs. Bradley, " and then we had better take the road by way of Kilsyth, Kirkintilloch and Coat-bridge, to Hamilton. We shall stay in Hamilton for a bit—possibly for tea."

" Very good, madam," said George.

"I don't see how we are going to get on the track like this," said Gillian, hopelessly. "We've learned nothing whatever from this morning's drive, or from seeing Stirling Castle."

"No news is good news," said Mrs. Bradley. "But it is not going to remain no news much longer," she added suddenly. She picked up the speaking tube. "George," she said, "go north towards Callander instead of the route I gave you."

"Very good, madam," said George.

"Why, what's happened, Aunt Adela?" Gillian demanded, looking out of the window.

"Mr. Joshua and Mr. Geoffrey, on motor-cycles," Mrs. Bradley replied. "They probably know the country better than George does, too." She picked up the speaking tube again. "Can you manage to lose a couple of motor-cycles, George?"

"A red Charleroy and a green-picked-out-dark-blue Wurton, madam?"

"Those are the colours, yes."

"Very good, madam. I'll step on it. I'd seen them coming up."

He stepped on it with some success, and, at the end of a lively little run, pulled adroitly across a small bridge, swung left into a lane, came out of it in front of a wider bridge across a wider stream, crossed the water, pulled up, got out, and, coming round to Mrs. Bradley, observed :

"I fancy we've left them behind, madam. Do you still require to go to Callander?"

"We're headed south now, I take it? Is this the River Forth?"

" Yes, madam. Just above Buchlyvie. I once drove a couple of American gentlemen round here. We can be *en route* for Hamilton safely now, if you say the word."

" I'd say the word at once, if I were certain we had lost those motor-cycles, George."

" We lost them the second time we went through Aberfoyle, madam. It was a manœuvre they were not expecting. You remember we waited at the cross roads ? We then returned via Aberfoyle, and so to Buchlyvie, madam."

" Very good, George. Hamilton, then ; and if you know of any short cuts you had better use them."

" But what can we do in Hamilton when we get there ? " Gillian had asked at Stirling.

" Start again, child. It is possible, and we should not overlook this fact, that the name Hamilton refers to the town, and not to the person. At any rate, the appearance of our young friends and would-be employers is a very good sign that we are being a nuisance in some way, or else that they still imagine that they can obtain our help."

" And which do you think it is, really ? "

" Time will show, child." She closed her black eyes, and lay back against the corner of the car, but whether she wished to sleep or to meditate Gillian did not know. She remained silent, however, and the car, having crossed the Clyde, slid, like a great marauding cat, thought Gillian, into Hamilton.

" I don't really like manufacturing towns," she said.

" Neither do I," said Mrs. Bradley. " Let us drive straight through it, and go back to Edinburgh."

"Which way, madam?" enquired George, when this decision was communicated to him.

"Any way you like," said Mrs. Bradley, "and you can go as fast as you please," she added kindly. "I can think better," she said to Gillian, as the car crossed the Clyde into Motherwell, "when I am travelling."

"I don't see that there's much to think about," said Gillian rather crossly. Mrs. Bradley opened her black eyes wide and looked at her in acute distress and with sympathy.

"My poor, poor child! You haven't had your tea!" she said. "I suppose that *was* Mr. Geoffrey?"

Gillian went to bed at midnight—her usual time—but Mrs. Bradley, seated at a small table with a shaded lamp to keep light from the sleeper's eyes, worked and computed for another hour or two, and then slept, on sentry-duty, in her chair. At seven the maid knocked, and brought in the early tea.

"Good heavens!" said Gillian, when the girl, having bade them good morning in her pleasant Scottish voice, had gone out. "You haven't been up all night!"

"I have enjoyed myself thoroughly," said Mrs. Bradley; and, indeed, she looked fresh and alert. "I believe, child, that I have gone some way towards solving part of our problem."

At this moment the telephone rang. Gillian picked it up.

"Here, it's for you," she said. It was the inspector

at Newcastle. He requested Mrs. Bradley's presence.
There was a clue. He could not say more over the
telephone. Mrs. Bradley promised to drive back to
Newcastle straight away.

"Oh, damn!" said Gillian. "Must you go? I
thought you thought you were getting somewhere
with this Marie Hamilton stuff."

"I am," said Mrs. Bradley. "And even a day may
make a difference, but I've said I will go to Newcastle,
and I must go. Look here, I'll leave you my notes,
and you can see what you make of them. I shall be
back this evening, I hope. I'll try to get back in time
for dinner. Don't go about alone. I doubt whether
we've shaken off our Mr. Joshua. You've got your
revolver. Don't use it, of course, unless it's really
necessary."

"I wonder whether Mr. Joshua is still holding down
his job as waiter here?" Gillian enquired.

"I discovered, by tactful enquiry, that he never had
a job here as waiter, child. He had put on his evening
clothes and flung a face-towel over his arm. They are
on the look out for him now as a possible thief. Now,
child, do be reasonable whilst I'm away."

"Rather. I wouldn't queer the pitch for words,"
said Gillian, whose metaphors were trite and limited
in number. She saw Mrs. Bradley off from the steps
of the hotel, and then went upstairs again to their
room. The notebook Mrs. Bradley had left in her care
was gone from the table. A man was climbing out of
the window.

Gillian had had the education considered suitable,
in the early twentieth century, for young gentlewomen,

I

so she leapt for the window, and, despairing of catching
the man and taking back the notebook which she felt
quite certain he had stolen, she gave him a hearty,
weighty, forceful, two-fisted shove. With a shriek and
a curse, he shot off the sill as though an elephant had
charged him from behind.

Gillian tore for the self-operating lift, and burst from
it across an astonished reception hall and out into the
garden. The man had been surrounded. The porter,
a couple of page-boys, two gardeners, a man who had
been delivering stores to the hotel kitchen, a policeman,
two maids, three or four residents (one an octogenarian
who had made up his mind that the whole thing was
a cinema stunt, and, in this belief, had enjoyed it
enormously) were formed two or three deep round the
dazed and abrased young man, and were asking him
whether he was hurt.

Gillian joined the group, and shouted :

" Geoffrey, you silly ass, you've got my notebook !
He was snooping round my room," she added naively.

At this the policeman drew out *his* notebook, and
began to ask for particular information.

" Oh, I don't want to charge him," said Gillian,
" but I do want the notebook back. Give it up, will
you ? " she demanded. " And what a sight you look ! "

The young man did indeed look more like one who
has been pushed from a first-floor window than Gillian
would have believed possible. He seemed dazed, too,
and Gillian, deciding that possession was going to be
all ten points of the law so far as she was concerned,
put her hand into his blazer pocket and picked out the
book.

The policeman told her she could not do that. Gillian pointed out that she had already done it. She also challenged the young man to prove that the book was his. The young man created a diversion at this point by shamming loss of consciousness. In the subsequent excitement Gillian quietly walked up the steps of the hotel, went to her room and locked the door. There she picked up the house telephone and informed the receptionist that if she was wanted by the policeman she would be in her room (of which she gave the number).

She then took out her revolver, laid it on the table, drew the curtains, switched on the light, and sat down to read Mrs. Bradley's notes. They were as follows (and the further she read the more deeply she frowned in perplexity) :

" *Cypher* may read ten,
Then (but we must deduce here the best, or a combination of some or all), twelve or thirty-three or ninety-two or one hundred and fourteen or one hundred and fifteen or one hundred and forty.
Then ninety-three followed by one hundred and four. (I see here no alternatives, owing to the spelling.)
Then again one of, or a combination of, or from, twenty-five, thirty-seven, thirty-eight, sixty-five and seventy-seven.

" This completes the first. If the old spelling is not to be used, we could substitute for our fourth line, and should not need a fifth.

" After this we get (if I am on the right track) something from one or more of thirty-five, thirty-six, seventy-nine, one hundred and thirty-nine, one hundred and forty-three and one hundred and fifty-two.

Then we can have another look at our second line,
And at our third line,
And even at our fifth line, which may save both time and trouble.
Then we get a good deal to do, for we should look carefully and judicially at fifty, fifty-one, fifty-four, fifty-six, sixty-six, seventy-three, seventy-eight, eighty-six and one hundred and fifty-one.
Then perhaps a teaser. Let us, in addition to one and two, which are obvious, select, from a host of applicants, thirty-nine. You will be able to see why.
Then fifty-three.
Then one hundred and twenty-nine.

" If you can get all this done during the day we can argue about it after dinner."

Gillian's first reaction to this singular document was to moan and give up the struggle. From the time when long division of money had been, to her mind, impossible, it seemed, of comprehension, she had detested any puzzle of which integers formed the chief, or, indeed, any important part.

Impatiently she flicked over the next page of the notebook to see whether Mrs. Bradley had made any further notes. She had. The next page was headed :

" Let us by all means try for a biggar and
    better house south of where culter flourishes."

It then went on :

" Young Hunting kens all the fords of Clyde,
    He'll ride them one by one ;
    And though the night was ne'er so mirk,
    Young Hunting will be home."

Gillian sighed and shook her head. She turned over
the next page, and there found :

" Some would say thirty, or perhaps one hundred
and twenty-nine."

Gillian stared at this, and then impatiently flicked
back the pages again, but still no chord of memory,
imagination or, as she herself expressed it, " ordinary
gump," was stirred by anything she read. She tried
the fourth page :

" Now there," Mrs. Bradley had written, " is what
I call the Murderer's Vade-Mecum or Murder, not as
a Fine Art, but as a Botched Job."

" Good Lord ! " said Gillian aloud. " She said
that yesterday. Apropos of what ? Oh, Lord, what
was it ? The Murderer's—— Got it in one ! A-ha !
Now, then ! Where's that cypher ? "

Full of confidence, she turned to the bedside table
on which the *Oxford Book of Ballads* had been lying. It
was no longer there.

" Oh, *damn* ! " said Gillian, dismayed. Her mind
leapt to conclusions. " That brute must have had it
when he snaffled the notebook. Then he must have
dropped it, because it certainly wasn't on him. It's

too big to go into a pocket. I wonder whether, by any chance——"

She descended. At the entrance to the lift a page was waiting. The book was under his arm.

" Miss Macrae was thinking ye'll be speiring after your book," he observed as he handed it over. " It was on the gentleman that fell frae your window the now, and as it was marked with the name of the hotel, the pollis gave it into our charge. . . . Thank ye kindly. No, they didna take him up. He said he was frae the University of Cambridge, and it was a' a joke."

Gillian leapt upstairs again, only to fall sprawling as a foot, which shot out from a man who was leaning over the banisters gazing into the well of the hall, caught her completely unawares. The book flew out of her hands, but a girl accustomed to ' wild, rough games ' was also accustomed to recovering quickly and neatly from falls. Picking herself up, she went for the man's legs as he dashed to pick up the book. She had never brought off a rugby tackle in her life, but fortunately the man was small and light. He was, in fact, Mr. Joshua. He came down, hitting his head a sharp crack against a door which immediately opened. Gillian stood by for a second, breathing heavily and feeling slightly dazed, the book clasped to her breast. Mr. Joshua, wiping his face, apologised to the man who had opened the door. He had slipped, he said. The man, an elderly Canadian, seemed disposed for conversation. They should not put polished linoleum in hotel corridors, he said. He drew the protesting Mr. Joshua firmly inside his room, talking, with nasal hospitality, on the subject of ' a straight rye.'

Gillian, grinning, went back to her room and locked the door.

Mrs. Bradley's fourth-page clue had given Gillian's brain the fillip it needed. It referred to the last ballad they had read, which was called *Young Hunting*.

There were, as Mrs. Bradley had pointed out, a great many alternatives and/or possible combinations, in the working out of the acrostic. These, however, would be subject to trial. Obvious errors would tend to eliminate themselves upon inspection, she imagined. The results could then be tested, and the correctness of the final result would be, she hoped, self-evident. Stimulated by her successful physical countering of Mr. Joshua's villainy, she settled down with zest to elucidate the puzzle.

The numbers, it was clear from Mrs. Bradley's third page, referred to the numbers of the ballads in the Oxford Book.

"And that means," thought Gillian, "that the person who made the cypher may still be alive, or, at any rate, must have died fairly recently, because the Oxford Book was not published until 1920. That might account for this ' house to house ' business which otherwise seems such a mystery. Well, anyhow, let's get on."

Young Hunting, which was the ballad obtained by reference to Mrs. Bradley's last page, was numbered thirty, and the number of the page on which it commenced was one hundred and twenty-nine. Once this had been established, the rest was easy going.

By inference, the ballad numbering, and not the page numbering, was the first clue, since there was no number higher than one hundred and fifty-two in the cypher, and this would restrict the number of ballads used to thirty-six, if the page numbering had been employed. There was no particular reason against this, however, she reasoned, if the acrostic could be worked out from those few ballads, but very soon she realised that it could not, for the cypher was, in its first stages, very simple.

The title *The Queen's Marie*, on which, in view of the plan of Edinburgh they had found, and the obvious references on it to Marie Hamilton's execution, she set to work, mindful also of their apparently abortive pilgrimage to Stirling, did not work out at all from Mrs. Bradley's figures, but as soon as she tried the name *Marie Hamilton* she knew she was on the track.

The titles of the ballads, as worked out by Mrs. Bradley, ran thus :

M ay Colvin
A lison Gross
R are Willie Drowned in Yarrow
I Saw Three Ships
E arl Mar's Daughter

H ynd Horn
A lison Gross
M ay Colvin
I Saw Three Ships
L ittle Musgrave and Lady Barnard
T homas the Rhymer
O ld Robin of Portingale
N orthumberland Betrayed by Douglas.

Alternatives were :*

For letter *A*

    A Lyke-Wake Dirge

    Annan Water

    Adam Bell, Clym of the Clough and William of
        Cloudesley

    A Little Geste of Robin Hood and His Meiny

    Archie of Cawfield

For letter *E*

    Erlinton

    Earl Brand

    Edward, Edward

    Edom o' Gordon

For letter *H*

    Hynd Etin

    Hugh of Lincoln

    Hobbie Noble

    Hughie the Graeme

    Helen of Kirconnell

For letter *L*

    Lord Ingram and Childe Vyet

    Lord Thomas and Fair Annet

    Leesome Brand

    Lord Randal

    Lady Maisry

    Lamkin

    Lady Elspat

    Lord Maxwell's Last Good night

For letter *T*

    Tam Lin

    The Douglas Tragedy

---

* This list can be omitted by bored or lazy readers. It has academic
interest only.

This last ballad had been selected from some dozens, all beginning with the word *The*, but, as Mrs. Bradley had pointed out, there was reason for the selection, in that the name *Douglas* constituted, in itself, some sort of possible pointer, owing to the context formed by the location (as Americans might say) of the mystery.

Gillian sat back, and tapped on the table with her pencil. "First catch your fish and then cook it" pretty well expressed her state of mind. She put down the pencil and commenced to read the chosen ballads carefully. Where she hit upon a stanza which seemed to have some bearing upon wealth or treasure (the obvious motive for murder, in her opinion) or upon lines which seemed to give a hint of the situation of the so-far undiscovered house, she noted it.

It became a fascinating game, and she was surprised when she heard the gong for luncheon. She wondered where best to hide the book of ballads and Mrs. Bradley's notes, and hit upon the plan of leaving them, as though by accident, in the ground-floor ladies' lavatory. She was a confirmed cinema-addict, and had often seen this device used upon the screen to foil the machinations of men. It was not, perhaps, the perfect repository, in some senses, but she thought that its advantages, in the present instance, outweighed any nice objections. So she unlocked her door, felt for her little gun, and shot into the lift, which fortunately opened to let out a resident who had been down to the dining-room already, but had returned to get her spectacles because the fish was not filleted that day.

The lift descended ; Gillian shot out, and darted for the sanctuary she had decided upon for the documents. She put them down on a glass shelf above one of the washing basins, entered one of the compartments, came out, and said to the attendant-maid :

" I say, can I leave them ? I don't really want to be bothered with them at lunch. There's so little room at my table."

With an easy mind she washed, powdered her nose, and added, as she reached the swing door :

" Please don't give them to anyone else ; all sorts of sharks in this hotel are wanting to read that book, and I'm not ready yet to return it to the library."

The Scottish maid smiled, put a small pile of clean towels on top of the book and the note-book, and then said (for, like most Scottish maids, she was the soul of democratic friendliness) :

" I'll see ye get them."

Gillian enjoyed her lunch. When it was over she watched her chance, retrieved her property, returned safely to her room, locked the door again, and then re-read Mrs. Bradley's notes. She remembered that there was a page she had not tested ; a page whose odd spelling intrigued her. She took up the house-telephone. She knew that she was being a nuisance, but she did not much want to walk about the hotel, in view of her promise to Mrs. Bradley.

" I'm so sorry to bother you again about books," she said, " but is there an atlas in the library ? "

The page who had given her the book of ballads

after it had been taken from Mr. Geoffrey, brought her the atlas.

Biggar was marked ; so was *Culter*.

" So what ? " thought Gillian, longing for George and the car. At that moment the telephone rang.

CHAPTER VII

"The lady ran up to her tower-head,
   So fast as she could hie,
   To see if by her fair speeches
   She could with him agree."

HAVING ENTIRELY MISSED—ALBEIT BY A MINUTE OR
two only—Mr. Geoffrey's unceremonious descent from
the window-sill, George and Mrs. Bradley drove
sedately out of Edinburgh along the road to Peebles.
From Peebles they followed the Tweed, cut off a loop
of it between Melrose and Dryburgh, continued along
it to Kelso, and then, by a long road avoiding the hill,
came to Wooler. From here it was south and a little
by east for Morpeth, and then almost due south to
Newcastle.

"An enjoyable run, George," said his employer.
"We shall go back after dinner, unless the police
detain me."

"Very good, madam," said George.

"And this time," said Mrs. Bradley, "we have
not been followed, have we?"

"Not to my knowledge, madam, no."

"Ah. I trust your knowledge, George. Besides,
I expect our friends are busy trying to steal her books
and things from Miss Gillian."

George, whose sense of chivalry had been outraged
at leaving Gillian alone in Edinburgh, did not reply

to this statement of opinion.   Mrs. Bradley cackled,
and then added :

"Miss Gillian will give as good as she gets, George,
never fear."

George parked the car at a garage almost next door
to the police station before which he had stopped.
Mrs. Bradley went in and asked for the inspector.

"It's like this, ma'am," said the inspector, after
he had asked whether Mrs. Bradley had lunched.
"We've got another line on that young suicide lad."

"The lad who was murdered, you mean ?" said
Mrs. Bradley.   She pulled off her gloves, avoiding the
inspector's surprised and reproachful eye.

"And how did you get on to that ?" the Inspector
enquired.   Mrs. Bradley cackled, and observed that
sometimes the right hand did not know what the left
hand accomplished.

"Tell me all, child," she added.

"Well, I'll admit he was murdered.   But, first, to
who he is.   His previous employer wrote to us ; said
he understood the lad hadna been identified, but that
from the description he believed he might be able to
place him for us.   Sure enough, too, he did.

"A dominie *he* was—the employer.   Runs a wee
school for delicate and backward laddies.   Hochen !"
said the inspector, with an unreproducible snort of
blended irony, irritation and amusement.

"Where, child ?"

"At a place in Lincolnshire.   I dinna believe it

matters, but I have the address, and I'll give it you.
Well, this man gave our lad the sack. He came in
drunk from his half-day out once or twice, and he
tawsed one of the wee laddies, which, it seems, was
against the rules of the school, and he was untidy in
his clothes and didna wash himself overmuch, and a
two-three things a schoolmaster-body should frown
on."

"So the headmaster frowned on them for him, and
turned him out?"

"That's about it. Well, the lad had expectations
from his grandfather, and on his birthday—that was
about a week before the old dominie—not *that* old,
you ken, but older by twenty years than the laddie—
showed him the gate—he was in a great state of excitement showing off to the others a letter he had had from
his grandpa, promising him all he could find at the
time of the old man's death.

"'And I ken where it is, all of it,' he says. 'Every
piece. *Find* it?' he says. 'It *takes* no finding,' he
says, 'for I ken where every bit is.' Now, what can
you make of all that?"

"Quite a lot," said Mrs. Bradley drily. "What
happened when he lost his job?"

"I dinna ken. That's as much as the dominie could
say. But he identified a two-three things we were able
to show him, and he described the lad, and there's not
much doubt they're the same. Graeme his name was,
and that's gospel, because the dominie had seen his
birth certificate."

"And the headmaster was above suspicion?"

The inspector chuckled.

"We sorted him. Aye, he was above suspicion, the wee scantling."

"Where did the grandfather live?"

"Eh, that has us beat. I speired at the dominie about that, but he couldna tell me any more."

"Well, that's something anyway. I knew that no one but a schoolmaster or schoolmistress could have got on to a *Piers Plowman* history book plus a copy of the *Oxford Book of Ballads*. But what do you make of the fact that the dead man had been indulging (let us say) in a good deal of manual labour before he died?"

"What are you talking about now?"

"Nothing much, child. What about the murder?"

"Aye," said the inspector, with great good humour. "What about the murder! Well, I'll tell ye. Ye'll call to mind yon wee knife he was stabbed with? And no fingerprints on it, and the corpse in gloves? Well, one glove, anyway. Well, now, here's something to make you laugh." He paused, so that she could savour to the full the point of the story. Mrs. Bradley attempted to look eager, attentive and impressed, and apparently succeeded, for, after a short pause, the inspector continued, with relish:

"Dod, aye! You'll mind that the wee knife was up to the hilt in the wound?"

"Yes."

"And that there was blood?"

"Yes."

"There wasna a drop of blood on the glove at all."

"That isn't proof positive of murder," said Mrs. Bradley, "and——" she hesitated delicately, "I *had* noticed it."

"It isna proof positive; it's what you might call, if you'd a mind, though, truth presumptive," said the inspector. "But, to clinch it, what do you think we found?"

Mrs. Bradley could not bear to ruin the dramatic effect of this question, and so she did not make the obvious reply.

"Anither pair of gloves!" said the inspector, almost dancing with pleasure. "Aye, ma'am! Anither pair of gloves, in his pocket! Wash-leather yellow, gey old, and one of the fingers bitten through on each, where he pulled them off with his teeth. And not a mark on the ones he had on! Not a single mark! Will you add that up, ma'am, and see what you make it come to?"

"Yes, it might be," said Mrs. Bradley, speaking doubtfully. "Anyway, what about it?"

"Well, we traced Graemes here and Graemes there —'tis a good Border name, you ken—but we couldna trace the rich grandpa. All the same, we found a cousin; or, rather, we found a cousin's cousin, a lassie. Her name was Graeme, too. She put us on to the grandpa. He lives in East Anglia, it seems——"

"I like the lassie," said Mrs. Bradley, grinning. "But, the grandfather's house is at a point where a line drawn from Edinburgh—or let us say, Leith—to Port Patrick, or perhaps Stranraer, intersects with a line drawn from Lochgilphead to Peel Fell. Have you a map on a conical projection with two standard parallels? If so, I can show you what I mean."

"I ken well enough what you mean," said the inspector. "I learned my map of Scotland at school!

K

Yon wee point you're making will be on the upper
Clyde, not far from Lanark, I'm thinking. Woman,
you're an old witch! How did you get on to that
now? And what does it mean?"

"I have my methods," said Mrs. Bradley, grinning.
"But you need other bearings before you can find the
treasure. That young man got himself sacked from
his school to avert suspicion, I think. There are
family ramifications, Inspector, I think. He had
worked out his grandfather's rather childish will, and
did not want to wait until the old man died before he
plundered the family hoard."

"You're beyond me," said the inspector.

"So was the arrow beyond Jonathan," Mrs. Bradley
reminded him, "but it was not for *Jonathan's* safety
that that was so."

The inspector looked at her searchingly, but
her brilliant eyes told him nothing. He merely
remarked,

"Ye maun hae been a sonsie lassie."

Mrs. Bradley, grinning her acknowledgment of a
compliment which had not been paid her for nearly
forty years, enquired in a business-like tone:

"And what have you brought me down here for?
You could have telephoned all this."

"Well," said the inspector, glancing cautiously about
him, "I'll first say this, and no more: we've had
a message from somebody else, you ken. We've had
a nod and a wink from Scotland Yard about ye, and
I don't mind telling ye—although it's no an inter-
county match"—he chuckled hoarsely, "there's folks
that were at a public school with your son, and *you*

ken, better than I ken, where that can lead an English body, do you not?"

"I do," said Mrs. Bradley. "Bring out the rest of your information, then, Inspector, and let's see what we've got."

"It's just another death," said the inspector. "Did you warn the police they might expect a murder at Cawby-on-the-Sperrey, down to the south?"

"I did. Do you tell me that old Mr. Lancaster has been poisoned?"

"I do that. By strychnine, without a doubt, and that, I'm told, was your prophesy."

"Yes, it certainly was."

"And, what's more—and it's the strange thing, this!—not a soul nor a body, except the dead man, in the house, from roof to cellar. It was a wee boy found him, a laddie who lived at the inn."

"It would be. I told him to keep his eyes open," Mrs. Bradley murmured. "All, right, Inspector. I suppose the papers haven't got it?"

"My certy, no! Those laddies will climb up glass to get their news, but they've not been let in on this. Mind you, we canna keep them from it for long. Could you get along, right away now?"

"Yes, if I can use your telephone, and if you can find my chauffeur."

She called up Gillian at the hotel in Edinburgh. This was the call which Gillian received after lunch.

"I am sending George for you," said Mrs. Bradley. "If you lose the note-book, and so on, it won't matter now."

"You need not send George," replied Gillian. "I

can send the porter out to hire a car. I've got my
little gun. I shall be with you all the quicker. I've had
a lovely time with your puzzle, Aunt Adela. I believe
I've solved it right. All the rest when I see you."

"Bother your murders!" said Gillian. "I thought
we were going to hunt for buried treasure."

"We are, child; later on. Meanwhile, you are
going home to your mother."

"Oh, no, Aunt Adela! Why?"

"Because, although I've been called in by the police,
I have no official standing, child, and so I can't take
you with me into this house in the marshes, or give
you any of the fun. It isn't a place you'd care for;
there wouldn't be much for you to do——"

"And I'd only be a drag and a nuisance. I see.
O.K., then. But you've got to promise to let me
treasure-hunt afterwards."

"Willingly."

So at York Mrs. Bradley put Gillian into a train,
telephoned her mother to be sure to meet her at the
other end, and, relieved to be rid of a responsibility,
returned to the car.

"So thee be back? I thought us should see thee
again, but never dreamed so soon," said the landlady
of the *Rising Sun* hospitably. "Have thy same bedroom,
will thee? Soon turn that out for thee, I can."

"No, our mam," said Tom, between whom and Mrs. Bradley a conspiratorial wink had passed as soon as their glances had crossed. "Thee give she a room on top of house. That don't require to be on ground floor this time."

"Nervous?" said the landlady anxiously. "Time enough, poor old man, to be left a-laying, and not a soul to stay beside him. Heartless, don't thee think? How come they all to cut and run?"

Mrs. Bradley said that she supposed it was human nature, and that, by all accounts, the old man had been a queer creature.

"Queer? Ah, that was daft," said the woman. It was clear that the secret of the poisoning had been well kept, since she, living so close at hand, did not know of it. Mrs. Bradley felt an increased respect for young Tom.

She got him away from his mother as soon as she could, and went out with him to see the pigs. She could talk pig fairly fluently, and with correct appraisal of points, for her nephew bred pedigree stock and had educated her carefully. There was, too, something appealing, she thought, in the psychology of the pig. She had studied it, not without benefit to some of her wealthier patients.

"Tell me all about it, Tom," she said.

"Well, I went up there every day, like how thee telled I," Tom began, "and met doctor sometimes, and passed time of day, like thee said, and asked sometimes about poor old chap, and one day I got me a job there, like, cleaning trap and grooming horse, rightful chap being took bad, doctor says, and nobody suspicioned I, I don't think so, anyway, and come yesterday morning I went up along there with a two-three eggs, our mam sending sometimes when we was glutted, and the gates all open, and nobody when I rang bell, and nobody round to back, and gamekeeper and groom gone, horse and trap likewise, so, thinking it was come like thee said, I breaks window and gets in, and there be poor old chap on bed, blue-like, and died ugly, thee could see by that's face, and out I come, quickern I go in, and get Billy Blandy, and Billy put on uniform, like, and take up helmet, and that do come along of I up to house, and that do tell Inspector over telephone at house to come quick and bring sergeant with note-book."

"Well, you've done remarkably well, Tom," said Mrs. Bradley, scratching a pig with the corner of a stiff-covered note-book. "What did the doctor say?"

"Nought to I, like. Happen that'll talk to thee, though."

"Happen that will," said Mrs. Bradley grimly. "Have they traced the housekeeper yet?"

"That, again, I can't tell thee. They police do know how to hold their tongue."

"And you know how to hold yours, too," said Mrs. Bradley, with approval.

"Had a rare old time with our mam," said Tom appreciatively. "Come in, I did, in a rare old bat and a sweat, after I found him dead. That wasn't pretty, I can tell thee. Our mam, that demand to know where I been, and what up to, so I tell that to ask Charlie Kepple."

He chuckled.

"Who's Charlie Kepple?" Mrs. Bradley dutifully enquired.

"Oh, that do be our old way of saying mind thy business. That did make our mam so wild. Clouted my head for me, that did, but no astonishment."

"Well," said Mrs. Bradley to the young doctor, "and what have you got to say for yourself?"

"It's the very devil, isn't it?" he said. "I was there the day before, you know. They sent for me because he had one of his fits. There wasn't a trace of strychnine in him, though; of that I'll take my oath. This is the finish of my work here. I'm only staying on for the inquest."

"And the trial," said Mrs. Bradley. "I wish I could see the whole plot, and what it's intended to lead to; but I can't."

"You worked out this bit, anyhow. What are you going to do next?"

"I am going to see the body, child. Are you coming with me? I am in with the police over this."

"I might as well come with you. I've nothing to do except visit a couple of invalids on whom I live."

They drove in his car to the house. The body had been left where it was, and the inquest was to be held in the dining-room. Mrs. Bradley led the way to the bedroom. The police were still busy there, and the inspector rose from his seat at the dressing-table, where he had been going through drawers, to give her a nod and a slight, official smile.

" Pleased to see you, ma'am," he said gravely. " This is a very queer business. Nothing's been stolen from the house. There's plenty of ready money about the place, the safe hasn't been touched, there are a few odd bits and pieces of old-fashioned, rather valuable stuff (belonged to his wife, we suppose) lying about in jewel boxes shoved into drawers—not a thing missing, so far as we can tell. And yet, if nothing's wrong, where be the servants and the housekeeper ? "

" Had he a watch ? " asked Mrs. Bradley.

" Watch ? Oh, yes, he had a watch. Want to see it ? "

" Yes, if it was on a chain."

" It's on a chain, of course, with the usual seals, and coins, and miniature compass, and things that these old fellows like to have."

" Interesting. Where is the watch, Inspector ? "

The inspector put his hand in his pocket and drew out a key. With this he unlocked the top drawer of a cabinet, took out a piece of cotton-wool, unwrapped it, and displayed the watch and chain.

" No need to tell you not to touch it, ma'am."

" Fingerprints on that won't help much," said Mrs. Bradley, grinning.

" None, except the old man's. It's just routine. We've not had a murder here for seventy years, so we're all a bit new to it, like," the inspector said, grinning in his turn.

"Aha!" said Mrs. Bradley. She indicated, with the end of her pencil, one of the coins on the watch-chain. "That's surely unusual in this part of the world, Inspector. Do you know what coin that is?"

"Gold, ma'am, anyway."

"Yes. It's a gold bonnet-piece, of the time of James V of Scotland. It is only the second time I have seen one, except in collections."

"Are they rare, ma'am?"

"Rare in England, anyway. But that isn't the point, Inspector. Thank you. You can lock it up again."

The inspector put away the watch and chain, and Mrs. Bradley went over to look at the body.

"The inquest is in half an hour, ma'am," the inspector told her. "I daresay you'll like to attend."

"Yes, of course, child. But this man isn't everything he seems." She bent over the body, pulled back the eyelids, and then took out her powerful magnifying-glass and inspected the skin of the face. "His skin has been bleached. He ought to be brown," she said.

The inspector caught the eye of the young doctor. "You identified him as your patient, Doctor?" he said.

"I identify him, too," said Mrs. Bradley. "He is certainly the man I saw when I came here to visit the housekeeper. Inspector, you must get on without me here. This is not where I ought to be. Who is making the coffin?" she asked suddenly.

"Sam Wiveller," said the doctor.

"Drive me to him, child."

Leaving the inspector to his researches, which, with a slight shake of the head, he resumed as soon as he had covered the face of the corpse, she went out on to the drive.

Sam Wiveller was a craftsman. He was an old fellow, certainly over seventy, with shrewd eyes, large, powerful hands and a little thin voice which came oddly from such an old oak tree of a man.

"No, I don't want to order my own," said Mrs. Bradley, when the introductions had been made. "I want to see old Mr. Lancaster's."

"Ah, had the order for that these two years and a half come Saturday midday," said old Wiveller. "Screws. It must be screws. No nails for him. Screws with great big yeads you could almost take out with your fingers. 'I don't want they angels to have any trouble,' he says."

"Who said so?"

"Why, the nevvy. It were the nevvy ordered the coffin for uncle."

"Mr. Joshua?"

"Ah, Mr. Joshua Devizes. Didn't know him, I didn't, till he told me his own self who he was."

"Ah?" said Mrs. Bradley. "Where is the coffin? Is it finished?"

"Ah, that be finished all right. Don't do to be behind time in this yer job. Here her do be, and better work I never have done in my life. Thee take a good look at that."

"Lead, oak or elm?" asked Mrs. Bradley absently.

"Oak, that be. I had to get her special. Don't

get no oak about year. Ellum, aye. Oak, no. Had to send special, I did.

" ' Oak's honest wood,' says Mr. Joshua Devizes, the nevvy. Took a real interest, that did, same as you do now."

" Red-haired man ? " asked Mrs. Bradley.

" Foxy-like. That's right. Thin-haired and whitey. Should never have took that for old man's nevvy myself. But, then, it must be three year, near enough, since old chap took to his fits."

" Do many people go mad in these parts, Sam ? And how long is it since people set eyes on the dark Mr. Frere, I wonder ? "

The craftsman looked at her with his bright old eyes and smiled.

" Thee be a good workman thyself, missus, I'll be bound, whatever it be thee might do," he said appreciatively. " What thee be working at now I don't altogether follow, but thee got something back of that head of thine, I'll be bound. We be all a bit touched, these parts, missus. Thee'll be touched thyself, stay long enough. And folks as take queer fancies hereabouts, well, nobody take much notice, holding it be folk's business what they do see and believe."

Mrs. Bradley gazed at him for a minute. It seemed as though some chord of communication hummed between them. The doctor, in his sensitive, nervous state, could feel the vibrations but could not interpret their message. Mrs. Bradley turned and dug him in the ribs.

" We now want the vicar," she said. " Which, from here, is the quickest route to this haunted church

where ghosts tap housekeepers on the back at the end
of Evensong ? ''

" I want to know," said Mrs. Bradley to the inspector,
" something about our Dark Gentleman, Mr. Frere."
The vicar had been unable to give any explanation
of the haunting of his church by an invisible ghost
which tapped people on the back. Mrs. Bradley neither
affected nor felt the slightest surprise at this. It was
part of Mr. Geoffrey's embroidery of his tale, un-
doubtedly. She dismissed it in favour of realities.

" Mr. Frere ? " said the inspector. " Ah, we could
do with a bit more information about him ourselves,
ma'am, I might tell you."

" I see. How long has he been resident here ? "

" Thirty years, more or less, so they tell me."

" Then he can't be the person I'm thinking of,
Inspector."

" That's a real pity, ma'am, because *my* money
was on him as well."

" Do you know him by sight, Inspector ? "

" Did, ma'am, three years ago, I reckon. I haven't
seen him since then. Became a kind of a recluse, after
his son died, they say."

" Oh, he had a son ? "

" Yes. The old doctor attended him. Died in
a fit, so I heard. After that, Mr. Frere he shut himself
up and carried on with his experiments, and nobody's
seen very much of him since then."

" Where was the son buried ? "

" Oh, in the churchyard, like everyone else around here."

" Oh, I see. The Dark Gentleman hadn't a dark religion of some kind, then ? "

" Now you mention it, ma'am, I believe he was a Parsee. But the wife was English."

" Is she dead ? "

" Oh, yes. She died soon after they came to live here."

" Frere is not his real name, I take it ? "

" It's the name he always went by."

" Frere is a French name, Inspector. It's a French Creole name. Your dark gentleman can't be a Parsee. What gave you that idea ? "

" I forget, ma'am. The vicar would know."

" All right. You send one of your young men to him this time, then. He didn't like *me* very much."

" He don't like trouble in the parish. Very quiet they've been, this seventy years."

" Yes. That must have been pleasant. Now, Inspector, I want to know where this idea came from that Mr. Frere was a Parsee, together with any relevant details, apposite observations or colourful hints. I also want to get in touch with anybody who knew Mr. Frere by sight, say, five years ago."

" I'll go down there myself. I guess what you're after, ma'am. Don't these Parsees burn their corpses, like ? "

The inspector, having obtained permission to do this, took down the vicar's replies in writing, to submit them verbatim to Mrs. Bradley. It appeared that

Mr. Frere had asked to have his son's ashes buried in the churchyard. There was no question of anything except cremation. The vicar had never heard that Mr. Frere was a Parsee ; he thought it must be village gossip. He would not dream of allowing a Parsee to be buried in consecrated ground. The body, however, had not been cremated, after all. The vicar did not know the reason for this.

" Very starchy he was about the whole thing," said the inspector. " Said he supposed it was none of his business, and that he supposed I knew what I was doing, but that he couldn't think what was inducing me to connect Mr. Lancaster's death with Mr. Frere."

" So it was a child he buried," said Mrs. Bradley. " And, although the father favoured cremation, the body never was cremated, but was buried in the ordinary way." She looked at the inspector. " The grave will have to be dug up. But that can wait. I can't stay here any longer, Inspector, but I'll give you a hint. Keep your eye on the body—Mr. Lancaster's body, I mean. Have you heard of cataleptic seizures ? "

" Yes——"

" Well, catalepsy can be self-induced. I've seen it with my patients. You mind that corpse doesn't come alive on you."

With this piece of advice she included a hideous cackle.

" Edinburgh, madam ? " said George. He handed her into the car.

" Well, Edinburgh will do to begin with," said his employer, " but I may give you another direction later. And hurry. Don't stop for police traps, gunmen or even the demon king."

" Very good, madam," said George.

CHAPTER VIII

" Upon a morning fair and dear,
　She cried upon her sister dear,
　' O sister, sister, take my hand,
　And we'll see our father's ships to land.' "

GILLIAN SAT IN THE TRAIN AND STARED SOMBRELY OUT of the window. Then, in defiance of good manners and the regulations, she put her feet up on the seat. She had the compartment to herself, for the other occupants had got out at Huntingdon.

She opened the book of ballads and took out a pencil. There seemed little point in it, she thought, since she was ordered out of the hunt, but it might pass the time to work out the bearings of the house of which they were supposed to be in search.

She did not get far in her research work, for the train reached London almost before she had begun. Having been warmly greeted by her mother and one of her sisters, she said she would like to rest, as she was tired. Her mother, who was greatly relieved at seeing her looking so much better than when she had gone off, broken-hearted, to stay with Mrs. Bradley, assented readily to this reasonable suggestion. Gillian touched her sister's hand as she was following her mother out of the room.

" Come with me, Lesley," she said. " I want you to help me unpack. I've got something for you."

Once inside Gillian's room, however, the two young ladies made no attempt to unpack. Lesley, the younger by two years, lay flat on her back on Gillian's bed, rested her hands beneath her head, and said :

" Go on. Tell me all about it."

" You must help me first," said Gillian. " You read better than I do. You read aloud, out of this book, the numbers I tell you, and stop when I say so, and go on again when I say so, and don't ask questions or waste time. There's a lot to get through."

At the end of two hours they had achieved the following result, which Gillian then read aloud :

Treasure	*Locality*
Go fetch me some of your father's gold	North land
And some of your mother's fee	
And she's taken the red and she's left the white	
She showed me a cup of the good red gold	
Well set with jewels so fair to see.	
	O boatman, boatman, put off your boat
	Put off your boat for golden money.
	He has ta'en the ford at that stream tail

L

She sought him east, she
    sought him west,
She sought him braid and
    narrow ;
Sine, in the clifting of a craig,
She found him drown'd in
    Yarrow.

As I sat under a sycamore
    tree
I looked me out upon the sea.

And landed near the Earl
    Mar's castle

If she be sick and like to
    die,
Then why wears she the
    gold on high ?

They rode till they came to
    the water of Doune.

Foul fall the breast first treason
    bred in !
That Liddesdale may safely
    say,
For in it there was both meat
    and drink,
And corn unto our geldings
    gay.

May Margaret sits in her
    bower door
Sewing her silken seam ;
She heard a note in Elmond's
    wood,

And wished she there had been.

For I have a bower in Bucklesfordberry.

If I go a step for Childe Vyet,
For Lord Ingram I'll go three ;
All for the honour that he paid
At Mary Kirk to me.

And he has broken my bonny coffers,
That was well banded with oaken band,
And he has stolen my rich jewels. . . .

Then he writhe the gold ring of his finger
And gave it to that gay ladye ;
Sayes 'That was a legacye left unto mee
In Harley woods where I could be.'

Adieu !   Drumlanrig, false wert aye,
And Closeburn in a band !

Adieu !   Dumfries, my proper place,
But and Carlaverock fair !
Adieu !   my castle of the Thrieve,
With all my buildings there !

Adieu !   Lochmaben's gate so fair,
And Langholm, where birks there be :

Then he took off a gay
   ring,
Whereat hangs signets
   three.
'Hae, take thee that,
   mine own kind thing,
And still have mind of
   me!'

Adieu! Fair Eskdale up and
   down,
Where my poor friends do
   dwell;

And she has kilted her green
   kirtle
A little abune her knee;
And she has braided her
   yellow hair
A little abune her bree;
And she has gaen for Carter-
   haugh
As fast as she can hie.

He put a silk cote on his
   back
'Was thirteen inches folde,
And put a steele cap upon
   his head
'Was gilded with good red
   gold.

Now hold thy tongue,
   thou goodly lady,
Now let all this talking
   a-be;
For all the gold that's in
   Loch Leven,
William would not deliver
   me.

"There's far too much of it," said Lesley, laying aside the book. She yawned with fatigue, for some of the ballads had been long ones. "You've still got to dig out the bits that matter, and how on earth do you think you're going to do that?"

"Where's your Ordnance map of the Border?" demanded Gillian.

"Why, you borrowed it when you made up your mind to have a holiday up there. Don't you remember? I sent it on to you, when you said you were leaving Aunt Adela."

"Goodness, yes! I'll get it."

She burrowed into her suitcase, scattering items of silk underclothing, stockings and toilet accessories much as a terrier scatters earth.

"Here it is. Where's a ruler or a pair of dividers, or something?"

"Here's a postcard and a pair of scissors. Chop off some straight bits. You don't want to measure things, do you?"

"No; only find some intersecting lines."

"O.K., then. Let me chop."

"Mother will be coming in to say good night in a minute. We've been ages over this reading and writing stuff. I'll get ready for bed. You do, too. Then you can sneak in here again when the family has gone to bed, and we'll get on with the job."

This plan was carried out. The two, feeling as though they were once more engaged in the nefarious pastimes of childhood, smuggled themselves away until "visiting rounds" was over, and Lesley could return to her sister's room.

"The bearings are too many and too various," Lesley again objected, when they had been working away for some time—the one with the Ordnance map, the other with the sketch-map which was printed on the inside cover of the *Oxford Book of Ballads*.

"Mustn't forget it's still the hotel copy of the ballads," muttered Gillian. "What did you say?" she added. "Oh, that! Well, look here——" with hazy recollections of fourth-form geometry—"you can always prolong or extend your lines until another line crosses them, can't you?"

"Yes, but even then, you get more than one point of intersection if you use all these places you've written down."

"I bet Aunt Adela's worked it out all right; and if she can, so can we. Bend your brains to it, my girl. I'm going to find out where that treasure is if it takes me all night to do it."

"Much better get a possible selection of places, and then go up there and visit them," Lesley suggested.

"That's not a bad idea, either. Well, come on; let's go on with it."

"Just one point then. What do you do with all these *Adieu* places?"

"All those what?"

"You know—all those bits you've written down under *Locality* that start with *Adieu*. Do you think it means leave them out?"

"Well, why mention them, then?"

"That's just the trouble. You haven't got enough to go on."

"Just now you said there was too much. Do the

best you can. How do you think the sailors get on at sea ? "

" That's all right how the sailors get on at sea. They shoot the moon. Roger told me all about it when he was home. Oh, by the way, your beastly Gerald's married."

" Is he ? Who to ? "

" Oh, nobody we know. She's rich or something. Didn't you see it in the papers ? "

" No. Haven't looked at the papers much these last three weeks."

" Do you mind much ? "

" Mind what ? "

" Gerald."

" Gerald who ? Oh—Gerald ? Good heavens, no. I'm glad. Don't waste time. Get on."

By two o'clock in the morning the maps had been criss-crossed with lines, but a motoring route had not been planned, because they could not agree upon one. The arguments, however, were amicable.

" Mother will have a fit, you know," said Gillian.

" She won't, as long as you don't mention guns, and shoving young men out of bedroom windows. I've got another five weeks to get through before college. I might just as well spend them with you. Mother can't say anything to that."

Gillian thought this, too. A spasm of conscience, which suggested that, as the elder, she ought not to lead a younger sister into danger, she soon contrived to soothe. That sort of thing had been all right when they were little children, she reminded herself. She had then received the blame for every untoward incident which befell the pair of them. Yet Lesley, bigger and bolder, had often been the leader, and would now be invaluable if there were trouble in the North.

She giggled, and suggested that they should make an early start.

" We can't go to-morrow too early," Lesley objected. " Mother will have to be told, and she won't be up before nine."

" All right. We must tell her at breakfast. I've left Cynthia's sports in Newcastle. We can go up by train and fetch it, and tell mother we're going to tour in it from there. It's a good idea in every way, because we can take turns in driving. You go back to bed now. We ought to be able to start after lunch, with luck."

" Aunt Vera's coming," said Lesley.

" Oh, bother ! Still, it can't be helped. She and Mother really prefer to be on their own without us. Funny, sisters being such friends all their lives."

She punched her own sister lightly upon the shoulder.

The light-hearted young, having managed to borrow from their mother enough money for two first-class fares, so that they could " have a bit of peace for some more map-reading," as Lesley put it, made a swift hop to York on a good train, and another to Newcastle.

They were in their double room at the hotel before midnight, and slept soundly.

By eight next morning Gillian had breakfasted, and Lesley, who had gone out earlier, reported that a garage hand would bring round the car by nine. By half-past nine they were cruising northwards towards Berwick, which they had decided upon as their starting-point in their search for the house.

"Wonder where Aunt Adela is now?" Gillian observed, at lunch. She spread out on the table the small map they had made from the Ordnance map and checked their position on it. They had been unable, after much argument in the train, and again as they drove north, to reach any conclusion as to where their objective might be. Yarrow Water and St. Mary's Kirk, both marked on the map at the beginning of the book of ballads, seemed to be a good starting-point, however, they agreed, and so, from Berwick, thither they made their way. They came into Kelso through Swinton, Leitholm and Ednam, went on to Selkirk and thence to St. Mary's Loch, all the way beside Yarrow Water. It was a lovely drive, and they took it slowly through the long and winding valley, as the road turned gloriously among the hills.

"Now what?" said Lesley, stopping the car on a by-road to Cockburn's Castle.

"Sure to be a hotel along the side of the loch," said Gillian. "Let's go there for tea, and ask them about a big house and people called Graeme. That ought to help, I should think."

"There's plenty of time," said Lesley. "Let's have a walk. The car will be all right. I've parked it well

off the road. I could stay here for weeks. It's lovely.
Look how green and smooth the hills are, and all the
reflections in the loch ! "

" All right, then," Gillian answered. " But we've
taken longer than we thought we would since Selkirk.
Still, one couldn't hurry. Isn't it lovely here ! But
we mustn't be too long now. We've got to sleep
somewhere, remember. No night driving for me in
country I don't know at all. A smash would put the
finish on everything."

" It would certainly finish Mother," said Lesley,
grinning. " Better bring the Ordnance map, I
suppose."

" Aunt Adela," said Gillian, as they walked, " had
some stuff in her notes about Biggar and Culter, but
they're further north than we are here. If we can't
find out anything at the hotel, I suppose we'd better go
there and start again, but I'd rather we followed our
own trail. It's more fun."

They sat down and spread out the Ordnance map,
compared it with the smaller map they had made, and
picked out the position of a hotel and an inn, both
beside the loch. They soon identified these, and kept
them in view as they climbed. They had seated
themselves for a rest, and to look at the view of smooth
hill slopes ending in gentle-tongued spurs as they met
the smooth lake water, when Gillian suddenly said :

" Lie flat a minute, Lesley. Now look down there
on the road towards our car. Do you see two motor-
cycles ? "

" What's more, I see two men. Don't tell me
Joshua and Geoffrey have hit our trail ? " said Lesley.

"I don't know whether it's them. It probably isn't. I don't know why two motor-bikes should give me the jumps. I expect lots of people come here, but they do happen to be the right colour——"

"If you can tell at this distance. You probably can't. What do we do? Lie doggo until we spot the owners? They've probably gone on to the hotel."

"No, they haven't," said Gillian. "And they're having a look at our car. Now what on earth do we do?"

"Go back and ask them what they want. At least, I will. You stay here. They don't know me from Adam, and we're not a bit alike. If they mention they know the car, and ask after you, I shall say it's my car, and I'm Cynthia. I suppose you mentioned Cynthia to Geoffrey, and the fact that you'd borrowed her sports?"

"Yes, I'm sure I did. All right, then. I'm in London. I went back by train from York. I bet they know that already. Mr. Joshua must be pretty fly. Where will you take the car from here?"

"To the hotel, I should think. You'll have to go hungry and thirsty for a bit if you don't want to meet them. Do you suppose they're really on our trail?"

"I don't know, I'm sure. They might be on Aunt Adela's track, for all we know, so I don't think we ought to lose sight of them. On the other hand, it's quite likely they're simply prospecting, the same as we are."

"Then that means they don't know where the house is, any more than we do, and, if that's true, a lot of things go wrong, according to what you've told me. Oh, well, we might as well not worry. I'll go down

and do Horatius Keeping the Bridge. You keep an
eye on me, and if I can, and the coast seems clear, I'll
signal you, and then come back and pick you up.
Where does that road I parked the car on go to ? . . .
Yes, look. . . . You can get round to Biggar that way.
It makes a short cut, instead of going to Moffat.
Work round to it, if you can, without being spotted,
and I'll pick you up when I've shed the two men.
Rah ! Rah ! "

And the spirited girl, crawling onwards until she
was sixty yards from her sister, rose to her feet and
began to stroll back towards the car.

She had little difficulty in recognising Mr. Geoffrey
from her sister's description. The two men stood back
from the car as she approached it, but as she got in and
took the driver's seat, Geoffrey came up and saluted.
His motor-cycling helmet suited him. Except for the
fact that his mouth was weak, he might have been a
young airman.

" I say, look here," he said, " you must be Miss
Cynthia—what ? "

" Sorry," said Lesley, " your 'van."

The young man laughed, and put his hand on the
door of the car.

" No, but look here," he said. " My name's
Devizes. Surely Gillian told you about me ? I know
this car. In fact, I've been out for a drive in it."

" Oh—Gillian ? " said Lesley. " No, she didn't
mention you, except once."

" What did she say ? Nothing very complimentary,
I guess."

" It depends upon what kind of compliments you're

used to," said Lesley, who could have kept up this kind
of quarter-staff—it was too crude to be called fencing—
all day long. " I'll tell you what she said, and you can
judge."

She saw, out of the tail of her eye, that the sandy-
haired Mr. Joshua had come nearer.

" She said she was sorry you'd left no address, as she
would have enjoyed telling a man who thought he
could leave her cold in Newcastle, and then wanted to
climb in at her bedroom window in Edinburgh,
exactly where he got off."

She looked severely upon Mr. Geoffrey, and then
pulled the knob of the self-starter.

" Hey, wait a minute ! " Mr. Geoffrey protested.
" You tell her from me——"

But Lesley had let in the clutch, and the car rolled
forwards towards the open moor, and then, reversing,
returned towards the young men. Pulling it round
when she was clear of the secondary road, Lesley, her
brain working busily on the subject of how best to
choke them off, and how to pick up her sister without
their knowing that Gillian was in the vicinity, drove
sedately towards the hotel.

She left the car at the roadside, walked into the
hotel, made up her mind in a second, and approached
a young man whose open-necked shirt, knapsack and
ash-plant proclaimed him to be a hiker. Lesley
accosted him peremptorily.

" Look here, I don't know you, but would you do
me a favour ? "

" Oh—yes ? " replied the young man, on the
slightly rising inflection of the æsthete.

"Come outside with me and get into my car. I've got to drive you a mile or two away from this hotel. Which way do you want to go?"

"Oh—thanks. Across to Tweedsmuir, if I may."

"Come on, then. It's quite all right—I mean, I'm not trying to kidnap you or anything—but there's a man outside who wants a lift, and I don't like the look of him much, so I said I already had a passenger, only, of course, I haven't."

"Oh—quite," said the young man. "Why don't we have tea together first? I mean, that would perfectly put him off. Or not?"

"Well, yes, it would, but you've had yours, I expect."

"One's alimentary canal is at your service," said the young man exquisitely. He led the way back to the lounge.

"We mustn't be long," remarked Lesley. "My sister will wonder where I am. I'm picking her up on the road."

The young man asked no questions, ate a scone, with a detached air, and did not attempt to offer to pay the bill, for which Lesley was particularly grateful. It would have been, she said later to Gillian, too, too awful to make use of him like that, and soak him for tea as well. She had seen Mr. Geoffrey and Mr. Joshua enter the room, and had heard them order tea. She had pointed them out to the young man, who had given one horrified glance in their direction and had exclaimed, faintly but clearly (like the horns of Elfland, thought Lesley, giggling suddenly):

"My God! What offal!"

Lesley saw food brought to their table, and Mr. Joshua fall to, and then she finished her tea, and she and the young man were soon in the car. She saw, to her immense satisfaction, Mr. Geoffrey come to the window which looked on to the road, and knew that he had seen the young man get into the car beside her.

She drove off carefully, turned at the road which runs between the end of St. Mary's Loch and the much smaller Loch of the Lowes, and soon was on the road for Tweedsmuir and (if they decided upon it) Biggar.

They picked up the hungry Gillian, who walked on to the road by Cramalt Tower. The hiker had some chocolate in his pack. Gillian ate it, and they stopped the car whilst she drank a little water out of the stream. This was Meggat Water, beside which the road ran for several miles before it climbed steeply upward at the head of the stream before dropping to Talla Linnfoots and the narrow reservoir.

Tweedsmuir, where they set their cramped passenger down, was only about a mile beyond the reservoir, and here they turned northwards along the Tweed to make for Biggar.

During this part of the drive Lesley was able to explain more fully to Gillian the strategy by which she had outwitted, she hoped, the cousins.

"I can't think there's much harm in Geoffrey, though," she concluded. "He just seemed to me one of those boobs. Joshua, of course, could murder anybody. He's just the type. I'm sure it was he who stabbed that poor boy in Newcastle."

"Yes," said Gillian, "so am I. So is Aunt Adela," she added, "but nothing can be proved."

"There must be proof, though. And somebody must have seen it done, that's another thing."

"Yes, but you might easily see a stabbing and not know that's what you were seeing. I mean, you might just imagine two people had collided, and yet one might have stabbed the other."

The road turned west for Biggar at Broughton, just beyond the railway station. It was towards evening by the time they reached the town, and as Gillian was resolute not to travel after dark they had then to decide upon the next part of their plan. Biggar itself was a very small town, and so there was no disagreement when Gillian suggested that they should go on to Lanark and put up there for the night.

The incidents of the day were not yet over. The railway ran with the road, or very close to it, for the first few miles of the way and just outside Symington there was a level crossing. The gates were closing, and Lesley, who was driving, pulled up. Just as the car slowed, there was a roar from behind, and two motor-cyclists, tearing along as fast as their machines would move, shot by, and narrowly missed the closing gates.

"It was them! Did you see?" cried Gillian. "Where are they off to, at that pace? We ought to get after them and see. I bet they're up to no good. Why, they weren't even following us up. They just rushed by as though they'd got to get somewhere as soon as ever they could."

"I don't know so much," said Lesley. "We don't want to be ambushed on the moor. The country looks pretty lonely after the next main road junction—

look, see what I mean? Just here is where we are—
and there are several side-roads, and at least two
water-splashes, where they could pretty well pounce,
if that's what they mean to do. I vote we don't take
any chances. It isn't dark yet, by a long chalk. Let's
back down here through the village without taking
this crossing at all, and then cross the railway again—
it makes a jolly good landmark—and join this other
main road. We don't have to get to Lanark unless we
want to. We can take it as far as——" Her voice
trailed off as her forefinger travelled southwards down
the map.

" That's the trouble. I think it's a good idea, but
where do we go? " asked Gillian. " Besides, I don't
really think they're going to wait for us. For one thing,
they came at such a rate that I don't believe, really,
they saw us. You see, they wouldn't expect to see *me*,
in any case, and they would expect to see that boy
with *you*. By the way, we never even asked his name."

" I did. It was Smith." She giggled. " Anyway,
I shall never sneer at intellectuals in future. He was
a friend and a brother, and asked no questions at all."

At this point the train went through, the gates
opened, Lesley let in the clutch, Gillian felt for her
gun, and the girls drove onward. But by the time
they reached the turning to Thankerton Station
Gillian's heart had failed her.

" I wish now we'd done what you suggested," she
said.

" Well," said her sister, in the practical tones she
had used over Gillian's broken engagement, " I'll tell
you what we can do. I've been thinking over the

M

map, and what you said about Aunt Adela and her
notes.   Remember Culter ?   Well, look, if we turned
off here——" she indicated Thankerton Station—
" and turned the car back on its tracks "—she per-
formed these manœuvres—" we could go back through
good old Symington——" this time the level-crossing
gates were across the railway line, and the road was
clear and empty—" go on to Coulter Station—God
bless the L.M.S.—switch off *comme ça* "—she twiddled
the wheel, and the car turned off the main road for
just about a mile.   " I've lost the thread of my
remarks," she added, as they came on to a main road
again, " but this is A702 in the book of words,
and here——" she paused for dramatic effect—" is
Culter, specifically mentioned by Aunt Adela in her
notes, and as such—great jumping fireworks ! "

Culter was a very small place.   The two motor-
cycles, one a red Charleroy and the other a green-and-
dark-blue Wurton, lying abandoned by the roadside,
were quite a feature of the village.

" Now how on earth did they get here ? " Lesley
exclaimed.

" And where are those two men ? " demanded
Gillian.   " Lesley, I don't like this a bit ! "

" At any rate, they weren't chasing us," said Lesley.
" That seems fairly obvious.   But let's push on a bit."

She drove onwards, and then, the car bumping
gently on the uneven ground and over the heather, she
left the road and took to a dip in the moor.   Before the
car had quite come to rest, a motor-cyclist tore past
on a red Charleroy.   He was wearing a fur-lined
helmet, and was easily recognisable as Mr. Geoffrey.

He left the highroad and took a narrow, winding track southward by Culter Water.

"Funny," said Lesley, scowling at the map in the fading light. "Wonder where he's off to? That way doesn't seem to lead anywhere much. And what's Mr. Joshua going to do?"

"The sight of Geoffrey now gives me the creeps," confessed her sister. "Do you think he noticed us?"

"I should say he was going too fast. Pull yourself together, old soul. He wasn't a ghost," said Lesley. "Let's get on our way a bit, in case Mr. Joshua's still in the village."

CHAPTER IX

" ' O open the door to me, Marg'ret !
   O open and let me in !
   For my boots are full of Clyde's water
   And the rain runs o'er my chin.' "

IN MRS. BRADLEY'S MIND AS THE CAR FLED NORTHWARDS
—George did not often receive a commission as much
to h s mind as the twin commands to hurry and not
to stop—were several questions. The most pressing
seemed to her to be these :

First—what had been Mr. Joshua's motive in
calling her into the case ?

Second—a somewhat similar query—had Mr.
Geoffrey's first meeting on the moors with Gillian
been accidental, or was it part of a plot ?

Third—was there the body of a child, or the ashes of
a man—the real Mr. Frere—in the coffin which had
been lowered in a marshland grave three years before ?

Fourth—was there again a plan to substitute one
dead body for another ?

Some questions which her mind had formed previously had already been answered. For instance, she
was certain that the " dead " man at the house in the
marshes was not Mr. Lancaster. Mr. Lancaster, she
suspected, had been dead some time—most probably
murdered. Mr. Frere, too. That could be proved
later. She was equally certain that the man who now

called himself Mr. Lancaster was not dead, but in a cataleptic trance.

This latter certainly seemed to give some sort of answer to her third question. Old Mr. Lancaster—Frere (she was fairly sure that the double impersonation was being carried out)—was not going to be buried, although he might be laid in his coffin—the coffin which could so easily be unscrewed. In that coffin would be buried another man, a man, Mrs. Bradley confidently hoped, who, at the moment of her speeding northwards, was still very much alive.

A further small query remained. Did Mr. Joshua and Mr. Geoffrey know where their next victim lived, or were they depending upon her to locate the house ? An answer to this seemed to lie in Mr. Geoffrey's careless confusing of the two houses when he had described the rushing stream and the hill. They must know where the house was ; they must have been to it ; they might even have been inside it.

What they did not know, and what (having failed to obtain possession of the first part of the cypher from the murdered man's rooms in Edinburgh) they must find out before they committed their next murder, was the place where the treasure was hidden.

She herself believed that she had located this spot. What she had not discovered to her satisfaction (in spite of her bold map-reading with the inspector) was the exact situation of the house. Ironically, in the way that things do so often turn out, it was the thing she did *not* know which was of the greater importance, she believed. The Dark Gentleman's cataleptic trance could not last indefinitely. The villains must have all

their arrangements complete. It might be only a
matter of hours before they accounted for their victim.

The car ate the North Road smoothly. George,
in his element, snicked in and out among traffic, saved
a second here, split one there, and by the time Gillian
had reached her mother's house after the journey from
York he was gliding between a brewer's lorry and a
stationary bus on the road to Newcastle.

In the back seat of the car Mrs. Bradley worked out
another variation or two of the directions given in the
ballads. She went further than Gillian, however, in
her handling of the material. Not content with having
worked out the acrostic and used the ballads thus
given her, she also went through the collection again
to discover any other ballads in which the name
" Hamilton " appeared. There was one in particular
which seemed to hold some promise. It began with
the words *Ettrick Forest*, and the stanzas which impressed her were these :

> " Ettrick Forest is a fair forest,
>   In it grows many a seemly tree ;
>   There's hart and hind, and doe and roe,
>   And of all wild beasts great plentie.
>
> There is a castle built with lime and stone ;
>   O gif it stands not pleasantlie !
>   In the forefront of that castle fair,
>   Two unicorns are braw to see."

Later came the " clue " word *Hamilton*, in the stanza
which began :

> " Then spake the Earl hight Hamilton."

Mrs. Bradley sighed. There was really nothing to go on. All the clues from the ballads might be false. There might be no point at all in having solved the acrostic from the titles of the ballads, although she felt, from the whole naïve character of the clues, that nothing else had been intended. The circumstances that also gave her hope were, first, the wrecking of the dead schoolmaster's rooms, and, second, the persistence with which Mr. Joshua and Mr. Geoffrey seemed to have dogged her and Gillian. If she had seen Gillian's spirited treatment of them, one after the other, after she herself had left the hotel in Edinburgh, she would have felt even more satisfied that she was on the trail. This treat, however, had been denied her.

She spread out the map on her knees again, and considered the claims of Ettrick Forest. True, it was in the neighbourhood of water—a motif which appeared the whole way through the ballad clues—but, to her way of thinking, it was not sufficiently far west. A line of a ballad which did not appear at all in the *Mary Hamilton* acrostic kept running through her head, and had done so for several days.

> " The deepest pot of Clyde Water
> They got Young Hunting in ;
> *With a green turf tied across his breast*
> To keep that good lord down."

On the other hand, she reminded herself, stern on the suppression of fancies, if drowning were essential, there was Yarrow Water, there was St. Mary's Loch, there were other streams in the Border country swift to drown a man and deep to hide him, and the same applied to the treasure.

At Berwick she directed George to drive to a hotel. They would stay the night, she said. In the morning they would make for Lanark, explore the upper waters of the Clyde with an eye to Bonnington Woods, where she fancied the treasure was hidden, and from there——

Suddenly her thoughts took a new direction.

" Don't stop after all, George," she said. " I'm sorry. Go out by way of Coldstream and Kelso, then on to Galashiels and Peebles ; so to Biggar and Lanark. Like our delicious Yvonne Arnaud in that excellent farce : I've got an idea."

" Very good, madam," said George.

" You'd better have a rest and get something to eat and drink," his employer added.

" Very good, madam. Could I perhaps bring you something, madam ? "

" Yes, George. Whatever you're having."

" Fish and chips and beer, if I can get it, madam."

" Good. Bring enough for two, get some cigarettes, fill up with petrol in case we get lost on the moors, boot, saddle, to horse and away ! " exclaimed Mrs. Bradley, *crescendo*.

George made his usual response, drove first to a garage for the petrol, and then went off for the food. He returned quite shortly, and displayed the results of his explorations.

" And the salt, madam," he concluded, handing it in a little screw of newspaper.

" George, this is marvellous," Mrs. Bradley asserted.

"Only one thing disappoints me. I wish Miss Gillian were here; and, better still, Miss Gillian plus her younger sister, Miss Lesley. I feel that we approach the crisis of the affair, George. What say you?"

"I have no idea, madam."

"Do you think you can find your way on the moor at night?"

"Yes, I fancy so, madam. I anticipate not much difficulty. It is a very romantic countryside, madam, the Border. I enjoyed it very much when I was driving my two American gentlemen. One of them, it appears, had ancestors living just north of the Border. Very gone on them, he was. Name of Ker, this gentleman. His family crest, he was telling me, was unicorns, a most unusual thing, surely."

"George," said Mrs. Bradley, "this is fate. I now know why the bonnet-piece struck me all of a heap." She ate the last of her fillet of fish, and gobbled up the rest of the potato chips with the infinite relish which almost everybody, of whatever age or type, displays for this particularly democratic food. "The beer, George," she observed.

George, who had discovered, in the recesses of the car's boot, a picnic basket containing glasses, poured beer with Cockney accuracy and affection, and handed her a frothing tumbler.

At Biggar George went wrong. On the west side of the town there were two possible roads. One ran past the next railway station, Coulter, and, after a southerly

loop, north-west to Lanark. The other went south by
Culter village, joined the Clyde at a little place called
Lamington and followed the river along its valley.
This, the way that they were going, narrowed to a
pass near Abington, and then mounted steeply between
Wellgrain Dod and Rake Law, towards the Lowther
Hills. It was on this rapidly-steepening road that
George decided he had missed the way.

" I'm very sorry, madam," he said, engaging his
lowest gear, " but we've come wrong somewhere."

" Interesting," said Mrs. Bradley. " But my fault,
as I'm holding the map. What shall we do, George ? "

" I don't think I'd better try and turn her, madam,
particularly as we don't know where we are, and it's
going on dark. I think we'd better persevere, and ask
at the next place we come to."

" If they're not all in bed and asleep, George."

" I think, anyway, madam, we'd ought perhaps to
shelter for a bit. It's blowing up wet, and if it does
that on these moors the visibility is not everything it
should be."

" True, George. All right, then. Stop at the first
inn we come to, and we'll be on our way as soon as we
can in the morning. I only hope," she added, " that
the murderers will find it as difficult to go on as we do,
if the weather turns really bad."

" The murderers, did you say, madam ? "

" Why, yes, George. I'm saving an old man's life,
I believe and hope."

" Then perhaps we should push ahead, madam."

" Oh, no, George. We must inevitably follow the
fashion, and think of ourselves first. Besides, we should

be of very little use to the old gentleman if we got ourselves bogged on this moor."

Beyond Abington the road had forked. George, hopelessly lost, hesitated at a secondary road which turned off to his left and which seemed to run with the railway.

" Go ahead, George," said Mrs. Bradley, for once in her life as lost as she might have been in the Sahara Desert. The secondary road continued with the railway. Then it picked up a burn, but did not cross it.

They came to a station at last, and George got out and asked the way.

" I'm afraid we're right off our track, madam," he announced. " They say our best plan is to keep to the left all the way. That should take us back, more or less by the way we have come, to Biggar, so they tell me, if I've properly understood what they say."

" Very well, George," said Mrs. Bradley. But to keep left, in the dark and the rain, was not as easy as it sounded. Around them soon stretched the moor, with its hundreds of glens and hills, its bogs, burns, tracks and sheepfolds. The road they were on petered out with dramatic suddenness.

" I see nothing for it, madam, but to wait until morning," said George.

Mrs. Bradley, like an old campaigner, could sleep anywhere, if she liked, no matter what the discomfort, and the car was far from uncomfortable. She insisted that George should come inside with her, gave him one of the cushions and a rug, and the two of them settled down in their respective corners to make the best of the night.

Some large part of it was gone. By dawn Mrs. Bradley, having had four hours of dreamless sleep, woke cramped but rested. Quietly opening the door on her side of the car, she stepped out on to the road.

It was no more than a track, which ceased in the sudden and inexplicable manner of many moorland roads, and beyond it there was nothing but the moor. Heather-covered, misty, alluring, beautiful, it stretched as far as she could see in rolling hills, deep violet-coloured dips and gradually rising uplands.

In the soft soil near the car were the prints of horses' hoofs. As soon as she saw them, Mr. Geoffrey's story, told to Gillian, came back into her mind, and she looked for the marks of wheels. Not far away, she knew, there was the railway, although how far away she did not remember. There were streams in plenty, too, and here were hills.

She remembered the Irish groom. It would be much more likely to find one here than in the marshes among which Geoffrey had pitched his tale.

She walked on, following the hoof-marks and the track of the narrow-wheeled gig. She had not far to go. There stood the house, very much as she had imagined it ; in fact, as she stood at the iron gates and gazed in, it had the familiarity of things seen in a dream.

It was George who translated the mystery.

" Why, madam," he said, as he came up with her, " surely that must be the house Sir Walter lived in ? It would be in these parts, I believe."

" Sir Walter ? " said Mrs. Bradley. " Oh—Sir Walter ! Yes, of course. Not his house, though,

George. The house you are thinking of, and to which this house does bear the most extraordinary resemblance, is that called Ashestiel, near Caddonfoot."

" That's it, madam. I have illustrations of it. I used to know the whole of ' Marmion ' by heart, madam, when I was at school."

" Admirable, George. Keep an eye on the car—in fact, get steam up—in case I am pursued. I am going to gate-crash this house, and that in the literal manner."

The iron gates were not high. Two stone pillars crowned with stone urns, supported ironwork of a plain, strong pattern, offering plenty of foothold. Mrs. Bradley looked about her, perceived nobody but the obedient George, who had turned his back on her and was walking towards the car, placed a thin foot, sensibly shod, upon the bars, and mounted with the swift agility of a monkey, or a small boy bent upon orchard robbery.

A close-cut lawn formed a semi-circle in front of the house. The long frontage was broken (rather than graced) by a pointed-topped porch. A wing at right angles to the main building formed stables and a coach-house. Here all resemblance to the house in the marshes ceased, for to the right was a tumbling stream which, even in the height of the summer, held enough water, on those high moors, to rush shouting through the garden between its silver birches and its foxgloves, and over its clear grey stones.

Mrs. Bradley was so entranced by the stream that she could have drunk from it, she said afterwards. From the stream to the house ran a meandering, pleasantly informal little path, and beyond the stream the moors sloped up to form the shoulder of a great, warm, heather-covered hill. Above the pointed porch was a long window. Above that there was a rose-window. Above that again came a dormer window set in an ogee-arch which terminated in a weather vane. But what caught Mrs. Bradley's fancy was, first, that the rose-window bore a coat of arms, and, second, that the weather vane had a peculiar and individual shape. It was in the shape of a unicorn's head, and the coat of arms in the rose window was a shield on which appeared, on a chevron, three unicorns' heads in the position known in heraldry as being *erased*.

Mrs. Bradley went up to the door and knocked very loudly. A tall, rangy, elderly woman, with the long legs, light, alert, easy stance and steady gaze of the Border, opened wide the door and stared at her unfavourably.

" What would it be ? " she enquired.

" I want to see Mr. Ker," said Mrs. Bradley. Mr. Ker, it appeared, was in his bed, and likely to remain there, since he had eaten something which did not altogether agree with him.

" Has he a nephew named Graeme ? " asked Mrs. Bradley.

" Have you come speiring about him ? " the woman demanded.

" He's dead. I know. I want to tell Mr. Ker some more about it," Mrs. Bradley said calmly.

" Deid ? He's no deid ? " The tidings was evidently a shock, although not an unwelcome one, to the woman. " Do ye tell me he's deid ? "

" I do. Let me in. I have more to say than that."

" Until I ken who ye are, ye'll bide outside," said the woman very decidedly.

" Very well. But I ought to tell you that it may mean life or death to your master, whether you let me in to speak to him, or whether you keep me outside."

The woman looked at her, and seemed to make up her mind.

" Come ben," she said. " I ken ye, who ye are. He keeps a picture of ye on his bedroom wall. Ye're gey auld now, but I'd speir at ye whether ye were na sonsie aince."

Mrs. Bradley entered. Cases of stuffed fish lined the walls. There was a pair of old pistols in another case, and in yet another a piece of some sort of woven material so old that it was difficult to tell what its original colour had been.

" Bide here," said the woman. " I'll no be long."

She took the stairs at a dignified gallop, lifting her long, heavy skirt above elastic-sided boots to do so. Mrs. Bradley, who had not seen a pair of elastic-sided boots in wear for more than thirty years, stared interestedly at those displayed by the housekeeper.

In less than five minutes she descended.

" Ye'll no fash him, mind," she said. " The man's no well."

" I'll be careful. I am a doctor," said Mrs. Bradley. " You might, whilst you are waiting, make me a cup of tea. I've spent the night in my car, having lost my way on the moor."

The housekeeper, at this, looked upon her with a miraculously softened eye.

"A' nicht ! Ye puir body ! Bide ye ! I'll see ye get breakfast."

"No. I must see Mr. Ker at once. Lead the way, please."

The Scots are a sensible people. The housekeeper, having accepted Mrs. Bradley, her errand, her hunger and thirst, her status and qualifications, led the way to her master's bedroom without another word, except to say, as she tapped on the door and then quietly opened it, and looked in upon the occupant :

"I said I didna believe her, but I do, and here she is. And dinna get talking ower lang. Ye're sick, and she's needing her breakfast."

Mrs. Bradley walked in, and sat down at the side of the bed. The owner of the house was a personable old gentleman, high-coloured and energetic at all normal times, but, when she saw him, sadly reduced to speaking at first in a hoarse croak which only his will-power prevented from sinking, through weakness, to a whisper. His face was drawn and pale.

"Well, David," said Mrs. Bradley. "I suppose I ought to have guessed it would be you. I've had you in mind ever since I saw a bonnet-piece like the one you used to wear on your watch-chain. I knew you lived hereabouts, but scarcely thought to stumble upon you so easily. What have you been doing with yourself ? "

"You have the advantage of me," said the old man. "David—aye, that's my name—or was, when anyone called me by it, and that hasn't happened these twenty-five years or more."

"Very well ; David Ker, then. I expect I've

changed more than you have, David, but I do think you ought to keep a record of the women to whom you have proposed."

" The women—Lord ! Lord ! So it's you ! Beatrice Adela—damned if I don't forget your maiden name ! You married Lestrange. Too young ! It never gave you a chance to know your own mind, my lass."

" Oh, yes, it did, my dear David. But never mind about that. Tell me what's the matter with you."

" Oh, nothing. Nothing at all. I ate some caviare yesterday, and I daresay it didn't quite suit me. My nephew Joshua sent it, I daresay. He's been making himself very pleasant a year or more now, though the deil kens I've nothing to leave him."

" Opinions might differ about that," thought Mrs. Bradley. Aloud she said, referring to the caviare :

" I should think not ! You'd better stick to fish from your own loch ! Is any of the caviare left ? "

" Oh, aye. More than half. Elspat and the groom won't touch it, and, although there's no manner of doubt I ate more than I should, there's plenty put by for to-day."

" I want you to ring, or shout, or whatever it is you do, for your housekeeper, and ask her to bring us the rest of the caviare, David."

The old gentleman accordingly lifted up his voice in a howl which would have done justice to Mic-Mac-Methuselah, and the housekeeper came running.

" Elspat," he said. " Beatrice wants the rest of the caviare."

" Then she may want on," retorted the house-keeper. " Naebody here is getting any mair o' the

N

stuff. Michael was awa' to the loch with the wee pot, and them that wants it will need gar dive, I'm thinking."

"Michael?" said Mrs. Bradley, when the house-keeper had gone. "Not, by any chance, your groom, David?"

"Aye. An Irishman. Why?"

"Send for him."

The old man looked at her, but her black eyes expressed nothing but amused satisfaction. "Mr. Geoffrey seems to have proved a most unreliable decoy duck," she observed. "Go on, David. Send for him. I have my own reasons for preferring not to wander about your land alone just at present."

"Elspat!" bellowed her harassed employer. "Get Michael."

"He'll be washing the trap."

"Tell him to stop washing it. He's wanted here immediately."

Michael, a short, squat, broad-faced man, with an expression of blended humour and pugnacity, and some characteristic less attractive than either, stood before his master, and bestowed, upon him and upon Mrs. Bradley equally, a singularly sweet smile, demon-strating suddenly that his eyes were deep blue with black lashes, and that his teeth were stumpy and yellow.

"Ah, Michael," said Mrs. Bradley. "How often does your employer kick you, would you say?"

The groom gave the question serious, almost ambas-sadorial, attention. Then he replied, with sweet richness of voice and intonation:

"Why, then, your honour, ma'am, 'tis a very hard thing to say."

"Why, you villain!" said his employer loudly. The groom paid him no attention, but kept his eyes fixed on Mrs. Bradley, to whom he replied with great calmness:

"And, indeed, now I come to recollect it, ma'am, it was by way of being a small matter, itself, between myself and the master here, and that would have been when Mr. Graham was with us, you remember, your honour, sir—'twas the pleasant morning, so it was!— and he wishful to drive over and see the river where it runs below Bonnington Woods."

"Above, he meant," Mrs. Bradley remarked inaudibly. "And now, Michael," she continued, "if you were going to commit a murder, how would you set about it?"

"Sure, I would belt him over the head," said the groom, with obliging readiness.

Mrs. Bradley was silent for about three minutes after they had let the groom go. The old gentleman said nothing; this, to Mrs. Bradley's great admiration. She herself reopened the conversation.

"I'm sorry about the caviare, David," she said. "Tell me about Mr. Graeme. Is he related to you in any way?"

"Related? Aye, we're related. His name would be Graham, not Graeme, although doubtless it's the same name really, ye ken. But, Beatrice, you wouldn't know him. The lad comes and stays here every now and then. He's the son of my oldest brother."

"Unless I am much mistaken, he will come no

more," said Mrs. Bradley. "Were you fond of the boy, David?"

"Me? No. He was a kind of a daft-like laddie— a dominie—so he said."

"It was true, that bit of it. Did he show any particular interest in your library?"

"Aye, he did, that." He raised his voice again, and it took an indignant tone very pleasing to his hearer, whose simple creed about invalids was that they seldom became very angry because they were much too weak. David Ker, she thought, was on the high-road. "He was a regular ferret of a boy; without permission, too. I gave him the run of the library, but he was not content with that. I found him in my bedroom—in here—one day, rummaging. He went out with a flea in his ear, but, for all that, I've an idea he found what he'd come for."

"Oh?"

"Aye. My copy of Sir Walter Scott's poems."

"Annotated?"

"Aye. And an old map I had."

"Not, by any chance, a copy of De Witt's *Edinburgh*?"

"Lassie, you're fey!"

"No, I'm not. But two and two make four, which is a very remarkable fact, as Mr. Chesterton pointed out and not at all, as he has said, the kind of thing to be trumpeted from a hill-top before ten thousand people," said Mrs. Bradley, remarkably.

"The devil," said David Ker, with a deep chuckle, "can cite Scripture for his purpose—especially," he added, "if a fairly free translation be allowed."

" I know. But, listen, David. Did you ever have the Scott returned to you ? "

" I did not. I was grieved about that."

" Then they'll be here any minute, and we must act. How many of your people can you trust to put up a fight ? "

" What sort of a fight ? "

" What sort of a fight ! And you a Borderer ! " She produced her little gun and waved it at him. " This kind of a fight, or with boots and fists, or any other kind of fight. What on earth does it matter ? There has been an attempt to poison you already, and your nephew has certainly been murdered. Wake up, David ! How many people have you got ? "

" Michael—although I believe he'll fight only for Ireland—Elspat (as good as any man, and more obstinate and courageous than most)——"

" Your gamekeeper, housemaid, kitchen-maid, knife and boot boy, gardener—any more ? "

" Any more ? You're daft, woman ! Elspat and Michael are all the servants I have, and Michael I wouldn't depend on, without there was politics concerned."

" Well, you'd better tell him there are. Summon Elspat again. I want her to take me round the house. Have you a dog or two, preferably very savage ? "

" I have not. I dinna keep dogs. The nearest dogs would be the shepherds' dogs, and they'll not be lending us those ! "

" Well, for an intended victim, you're the most unprepared and helpless person I ever met in my life. Will the horse bite ? "

" 'Tis a mare."

" Oh, lie down and go to sleep ! And to-morrow, when I've doctored you a bit, you're going to tell me a lot about buried treasure, so kindly prepare a speech upon the subject. Have you heard of people being murdered for their money, may I ask ? "

" I have no money," said her host. " And what's all this about murder ? "

Succinctly, sparing the detail, but giving all the main facts, Mrs. Bradley told him.

CHAPTER X

"John Steward had a little brown sword
That hung low down by his knee ;
He has cut the head off Childe Maurice
And the body put on a tree."

ELSPAT HAD CUT FOR MRS. BRADLEY THREE KINDS OF bread and butter and put out marmalade and also apple jelly after the porridge and bacon and eggs. Mrs. Bradley spoke about the poisoned caviare.

" So canny a stomach *he's* got, the Loard be thankit, it flang oot the poison as though it were warstling wi' it," was her observation. " And I helpit it as I might with salt and water, washed down by very hot whiskey."

Mrs. Bradley grinned, and then begged her to go out to the patient George, order him to drive the car behind the stables, and see that he got some breakfast. Then she herself went back to David Ker.

" Time is short," she said. " Do you feel well enough to answer a few more questions ? "

He chuckled.

" Any number, lassie. Out with them."

" Tell me about the map young Graham was interested in."

" Oh, it was nothing. It was a copy of De Witt's map, as you guessed, only it happened to be marked with a few wee arrows."

199

" Did you draw a gallows on the map ? "

" Not I, but there was one drawn when I had the map from my father."

" And did the arrows show the route taken by Mary Hamilton to her death ? "

" But how do you come to ken all about it, and all off so pat ? Have you seen my copy of the map ? "

" Not your copy. I haven't seen that. But I have seen a copy made from yours before the book was returned. Did you underline anything in the copy of Scott's poems ? "

" No, not that I remember."

" Are you given to marking your books ?—making marginal comments, and so on ? "

" I might just jot down a thought or two, if I had them. Annotated—that was your word."

" You didn't make any notes about buried treasure, did you ? "

" I dinna ken anything about buried treasure. What are you talking about ? And where would it be buried ? "

" Let me ask you this : do you know a man called Devizes ? "

" No ; only a town."

" Do you know a short, thin, pale, sandy-haired, foxy-looking man of between thirty and thirty-five ? "

" No. I know short men, but they're not thin and pale. I know sandy-haired, foxy-looking men, but they're not short. And I don't know anybody who would be as young as thirty-five, unless it would be— ah, now, but bide a wee ! It sounds like my nephew, Joshua Ker."

" Interesting," said Mrs. Bradley. " Do you think you're strong enough to listen to a very long story ? "

" Aye. Take the easier chair. We lunch at one, but Elspat, no doubt, could put it off."

" I'd like her to hear the tale. She may know some things that you do not."

Elspat, summoned, as seemed usual, by a bellow from her employer, agreed that the lunch could be " arranged." Agog, as her ancestors, generations ago, had been for a long and intimate story, she sat bolt upright upon a hard chair, folded her hands and nodded to Mrs. Bradley to begin.

" Aha," she remarked quietly, when the whole of the tale had been told. " That'll be the Cap of Maintenance."

" The what ? " asked both her hearers.

" 'Tis naething but an auld wife's tale," she explained, in her calm and slightly sing-song voice, " but have ye no heard tell that in times gone the king would have a cap of State made of crimson velvet and lined wi' ermine to be carried before him at his coronation ? There's an auld story says that a cap was made by the orders of Henry, Lord Darnley, him that married on Mary, Queen o' Scots. 'Twas but a toom thing, for she never would ca' the man king, and the story gaes that he filled the Cap of Maintenance wi' bonnet-pieces and jewels, and gied it to one of the Queen's ladies to remember him by, though, by all that ye hear, she micht hae had other reasons ! "

" Mary Hamilton, would that have been ? " Mrs. Bradley enquired, at this point. The housekeeper shook her head.

"There's nae names named, and there's them that think it was a servant lassie in the Castle, and not a Queen's lady at a'. But for a' that, the Hamiltons dree their weird. Aboot it a' I couldna say. But the Cap of Maintenance fu' o' gowd and jewels—that's the tale as I ken it, and as it was told to me by my grand-minnie. Mind, there's them that say it was houkit up and spent on Prince Charlie's wars—and very likely that'll be true, I'm thinking."

"But suppose it were not true," Mrs. Bradley persisted, "where would be the most likely place to find this treasure, do you think?"

The housekeeper almost smiled.

"I dinna ken. If I kenned, so would others, and the treasure wouldna stay very long where it was laid."

"Not even if it had been buried in the bed of a river?" said Mrs. Bradley. "I have a theory about the hiding-place of this fortune, David," she added, "and I'd like to put it to the test. If we took your groom out with us this morning, now, could he guide us? Does he know the country well, about here?"

"I dinna ken, but Elspat will go and speir at him."

The housekeeper went out, returned with a cup of broth for her master and a glass of sherry for Mrs. Bradley, and announced that Michael "kenned a' the roads for thirty miles the other side Glesca and so round."

"George," said Mrs. Bradley, standing, five minutes later, with one foot on the step of the car, "we have to be back here by two-thirty at the latest. Lunch has been put back on my account."

"Very good, madam," said George. In daylight it was less difficult to find the road by the map. They soon gained Abington, and ran north, beside the young River Clyde through Roberton, backed by Roberton Law, past the higher Dungavel Hill and so, in a long bend, rounded the Tinto Hills with their twenty-five hundred foot peak, and at last reached Bonnington.

Through Bonnington Woods the narrow, cascading Clyde enters a ravine. Standing on a flat and mossy rock and watching, first, the sun falling on the branches of a thin larch inclined towards the water, and then the reflections of whitish stones, rock walls, bright branches and the glinting sun itself in the deep, and, after the falls, calm greenness of the river, Mrs. Bradley looked long and silently and with a critical and appreciative eye, upon her chosen hiding-place for the treasure.

Giving the two men time to finish their cigarettes, she went back to the car and suggested that they should drive home.

She decided to check her notes, observations and measurements again, and then to go over the clues from the ballads once more, but she had no reason now to believe that there was anything wrong with her deductions.

Lunch left her sleepier than she could have wished, but, having taken David Ker's temperature and left him drowsy (although the improvement in his colour and pulse were considerable) she went out into the garden with a folding stool which Elspat, who had taken a great fancy to her, had discovered under the stairs, carrying books, notes and map.

As a fresh beginning she decided to include among her " pointers " those ballads whose titles began with Y. She did this because she thought it likely that in modern times a person making an acrostic might have chosen to employ the usual English spelling of Mary, instead of the *Marie* of the poem. This gave her, in addition to the other ballads which Gillian had selected, *Young Hunting*, *Young Bekie*, *Young Beichan*, *Young Andrew*, *Young John*, *Young Waters* and *Young Benjie*.

These claimants upon her consideration gave her the following hint upon the nature of the treasure and the location of its hiding-place :

> " In the deepest pot of Clyde Water
> It's there they flang him in—
> *And put a turf on his breast-bone*
> To hold Young Hunting down."

Young Hunting, from which, already, a haunting stanza had remained in her mind and conditioned her reading of some of the other clues, still seemed to give her the most promising material ; nevertheless, there were four lines in an otherwise non-suggestive ballad which made her frown and ponder. Somewhere they reached back into her memory, and only just failed to connect with some piece of knowledge there. Mrs. Bradley's mind was well-trained, and she knew that at some unsuspected moment the necessary connection would be made. Unfortunately she had no time to

spare for her mental reactions to take their normal
course. She therefore went into the house, found
Elspat in the kitchen reading a weekly journal of an
unexpectedly frivolous kind, and confronted her with
the verse which she had copied out in the hope that
this exercise would assist her memory.

"Now, Mrs. Fenwick," she said, "why does that
verse give me the impression that it's rather like something else I've either read or seen or been told?"

The housekeeper found the spectacles she usually
put on when she read the Bible, and studied Mrs.
Bradley's small handwriting. Mrs. Bradley had
written legibly, for once, and, intoning the lines in the
pious snuffling voice which she kept for her devotional
reading, Elspat gravely murmured :

> "His footmen they did rin before,
> His horsemen rade behind ;
> Ane mantel of the burning gowd
> Did keip him frae the wind."

"Well?" said Mrs. Bradley.

"Did ye ever hear tell o' King James the Sixth of
Scotland, that became your ain King James the
First of England?" asked the housekeeper, taking off
her spectacles. "'Tis said—with what amount of
truth of course I canna tell ye—that—Ah, now !
Bide a wee ! I have the book !"

She went upstairs and returned with a copy of
Mr. H. V. Morton's *In Search of Scotland*. Seating
herself, and wiping her fingers carefully on her apron,
she took up her spectacles again, looked at them and
then firmly put them aside. "'Tis a rare pity he didna

see mair while he was aboot it," she observed, referring
to the author, " but the man meant well, nae doubt
aboot it. Oh, aye, he meant verra well. He's lain
the nicht in Jedburgh, and that's whaur I was born."

The book certainly seemed a favourite with her,
Mrs. Bradley decided, observing its worn appearance
and the ease and speed with which the housekeeper
found the page. " Will ye take leeve note of this,
now," she commanded. Her large, blunt forefinger
found the line, and she began to read aloud :

" ' Is there a story that an infant's body was discovered in these walls some years ago wrapped in
cloth of gold ? '

" ' Aye, that is so ! The body was put back and is
in the walls now.'

". . .' after a fire in Queen Mary's apartments a small
oak coffin was discovered behind the wainscoting in
a recess measuring about two feet six inches by one
foot. This coffin contained the bones of an infant
wrapped in a richly-embroidered silk covering. Two
initials were marked on this shroud and one of them
was clearly the letter J. Was this the body of Mary's
infant and the rightful heir to the throne ? If so,
who was James VI ? ' "

She looked up triumphantly, and repeated the
question.

" Aye," she said, nodding her head with great
satisfaction, as though, if she had cared to do so, she
could have supplied an answer. " Wha was James the
Sixth ? And wha's in the wa' at Edinburgh Castle ? "

" I had always taken for granted that he was the
son of Mary, Queen of Scots until I read that there

were grounds for believing that that baby died at birth," said Mrs. Bradley. "Ah, well, it makes no difference, I'm afraid, to my search. But it's interesting, all the same. Thank you, Mrs. Fenwick."

"Hae ye seen the War Memorial?" Elspat demanded before Mrs. Bradley left the kitchen. Mrs. Bradley was able to say that she had, and the subject lasted them for the next twenty minutes or so. Then Mrs. Bradley said, in a careless tone :

"Are you any good with a gun, Mrs. Fenwick, may I ask?"

"Oh, aye, ye're expecting thae lither lads tae murder Mr. Ker, are ye not? I wadna believe anybody would dae it. What you want is the puir auld body at the Peel Tower to the north-east of us, I'm thinking."

Mrs. Bradley felt a sudden shock.

"*What* did you say?" she enquired. Elspat looked closely at her.

"I didna tell ye before, for I wanted ye should make sure Mr. Ker had got over the poison," she announced. "But I thocht, a' the time, it was *auld* Mr. Ker ye were speiring for. Come, and I'll show ye."

She led Mrs. Bradley upstairs to look out of a top-floor window. Beyond them for miles stretched the moor, now dropped to a patch of grazing ground for cattle, now humped, now hilly, but mostly patched with heather, blue in the distance, brown, purple, wine-coloured, honey-coloured—an amazing and beautiful countryside.

"See now," said Elspat, pointing. "There, beyond tur burn, bigged on the wee knowe."

Then Mrs. Bradley saw it. Its brown-grey stone and lichened walls accorded so perfectly with the colouring of the moor itself that at first her eye had missed it altogether. It was perhaps a mile away, but certainly not more, and as she traced its gloomy walls and the darker slits of its windows, she was reminded of the border tower which Gillian had visited in company with Mr. Geoffrey, although this castle was larger, and seemed in good repair.

" It is naething but an auld toom keep, ye ken," said Elspat, " but the auld man is the last of his line, and he lives there all alone. Mr. David, wha's his nephew, gied him the place tae live in. There's naebody gaes near syne Maggie died, that used tae cook and clean."

" And the unicorn ! Is there a unicorn on the tower ? " asked Mrs. Bradley, feeling slightly light-headed.

" Oh, the same, the same. Ker is his name, just the same—although how many of them's entitled tae flaunt the badge I dinna ken," said the housekeeper darkly.

" So he is uncle to Mr. Ker here," Mrs. Bradley exclaimed. " What would his name be, now ? "

" Old Joshua, son of Joshua. Young Joshua is his grandson. They've had little tae dae wi' each other, these twa branches, syne Mr. David's great-grandfather married on the woman that Jamie Ker had in's ee."

" Why on earth didn't you mention him, David ? " Mrs. Bradley wrathfully demanded, when she had repeated the conversation to her host next day.

" Because I'd forgotten all about him," old Mr. Ker replied with considerable triumph. " Besides, I never connect him with young Joshua, that's lived in London all these years since he was seventeen."

The tower beyond the burn was actually at about four hundred feet above sea level, but only about a tenth of that distance above the level of the surrounding moor. In appearance it resembled, Mrs. Bradley thought, Neidpath Castle rather than Branxholm, for it had the same kind of situation on a sloped steep bank above the clear waters of the burn, and a similar rocky, inviting little path leading up to and beyond it. The burn, however, was narrow, a trickle of moorland water, whereas past Neidpath ran the boulder-strewn, swirling Tweed not more than a mile from Peebles.

In place of the woods opposite Neidpath, and Branxholm's deep grassy bank and delicate birches and its shield of ancient, blue woods, this tower had, without the high, stark, cliff-broken grandeur of Smailholm, something of that tower's romantic remoteness ; its sense of defying time. It had, too, its loneliness, its barren wildness, its treeless, unprotected, defiant guardianship of moor and burn and sky.

The first prospect of the keep showed a low doorway filled with a nail-studded door, a small rectangular window twenty feet up, and above that a double window with a stone baluster separating the two halves. Above this again, and almost at the top of the tower was another and a smaller opening. Its most remarkable feature, however, was what appeared to be a round-headed watergate, although, as it was well

o

above the waters of the burn, it may have been the entrance to a cellar.

" This is as far as you'll take the car," said David. George, who had come independently to this conclusion, pulled up, and came round to open the door. Mrs. Bradley got out. David Ker remained where he was, and Mrs. Bradley walked alone up the steep, rocky path to the keep.

Her first summons, a determined knocking upon a large iron ring fixed in stone, went unanswered, so she took out the police whistle she usually carried, and blew upon it three shrill blasts. For about five minutes after this she waited, and was about to knock again when the door of the keep came open. It yawned before her like a cavern, but, as she took a step forward with the object of addressing herself to whoever had let it fall back, she saw that nobody was there.

The passage behind the door was in total darkness ; not the thick, rich, black, mysterious darkness of a curtained sanctuary, but the brownish void of an unwindowed room. She switched on the pocket torch she always carried with her.

The passage was not tenanted ; neither had ghostly agency opened the door. It was clear that it had been pulled to and that someone had forgotten or neglected or been unable to fasten it.

On the inside there were massive iron bolts, and, for additional security, there was a great iron bar which could be dropped into slots across the doorway.

Mrs. Bradley returned to the car. George had been following her towards the gloomy-looking keep, of which, with Cockney shrewdness and an odd streak of

Cockney inconsequence, he heartily disapproved. He
stumbled on the steep, uneven path and fell forward
on to his hands. The wind, which was now blowing
strongly over the moor, took off his chauffeur's cap and
spun it freakishly sideways on to a patch of heather.

Mrs. Bradley, assured that George was not hurt,
came up to the car to David.

" I think it's a case of home, sweet home," she said.
" I can't get an answer and the occupant has gone out,
leaving the door unlatched."

" Can't get an answer be damned ! Old Joshua
never goes out," responded her erstwhile suitor. " And
it's a pity if I can't get my guests admitted on to my
own premises, anyway. The keep belongs to me."

George had returned to the car, and was standing
beside it, awaiting orders. Suddenly there was the
mild and muffled explosion of a motor-cycle engine
some distance away on the moor. Mrs. Bradley,
followed by George, leapt up the steep path to com-
mand the view, but, although they could see the cyclist,
they could not recognise, at that distance, either the
man or the machine.

" Shall I pursue him, madam ? " George enquired.
" It will not be good for the car, but I think I could
overtake him, if you wished."

" No, no, George. Let him go. I know who he is
well enough, and no doubt you do, too. We have
other business here. With Mr. Ker as our protector,
we are going to storm the castle."

She led the way in to what had been at one time
the guardroom, but which appeared to have been used
by the tenant as a combined kitchen and scullery. It

was lighted by two almost burnt-out candles. Two or three greasy plates, and two glasses still smelling of whiskey, were scattered untidily on a side table and near them was an enamel bowl with a dark ring of grease about half-way up the side.

In a tin dish on the floor, half under the table, were some bones and some vegetable peelings, and a jug of milk, three-quarters empty, and with a yellow, hard crust of soured cream to show where high-water mark had been, stood on the table beside a cocoa-stained cup.

There was an archway, uncurtained and without a door, which led from this deplorable anteroom to the living-room of the castle. Here there was a little natural lighting, for the floor of the room above had disappeared. The joists could still be seen. The lowest window which Mrs. Bradley had seen as the car approached the tower was able to light, although dimly, this lower room.

The most important pieces of furniture here were a table and a large, dark, heavy sideboard, but the most striking feature of the room were its occupants ; both of them horribly dead. They had been seated at the table and their game of chess was still on the chess-board before them. Except that one of the white pawns had rolled over, and a red knight lay messily in a coagulated pool of a darker red than itself, the game did not seem to have been disturbed. Mrs. Bradley, gazing with sharp black eyes at the board, could deduce the course of the play. A knotty point had been reached. It was easy to imagine the rapt concentration of the players. These, however, lay, the one with his split skull down upon the table, the other back in his chair, his head cleft almost to the chin. The dark stone walls and the darker wood of the table discreetly minimised the horrors, among which Mrs. Bradley detected blood, spattered brains and splintered bone.

There was a choked gurgle from David Ker. Mrs. Bradley, turning, signed to George, who was white and whose throat was working, to take the sick man outside. She herself switched on her torch again, and with its added light made a swift examination of the scene.

The weapons with which the double murder had been so expeditiously committed had been left for her, or anybody else, to see. They were battle-axes, one with a thirty-inch handle and a blade the size of an executioner's axe, the other a shorter, lighter weapon such as a man might have swung single-handed from a seat on horseback in a battle.

Plainer evidence of planned and deliberate murder there could hardly be, thought Mrs. Bradley, noting the weapons and the positions of the two bodies. From behind the bent back of the very elderly man whom she supposed to be old Joshua Ker, the long-handled axe had come down with devilish inevitability and force across the narrow table and on to the young man's head. It was he who had fallen forward. The old man was the one lying back in his chair, having looked up, amazed, to see who had smitten the first blow.

Mrs. Bradley approached the younger man with her torch. His face was hidden and she did not propose to touch him until the police arrived. She surmised, however, that she was looking upon the last of Mr. Geoffrey.

She made no further investigation. The facts were facts for the police. David was seated, white-faced and breathing heavily, in the car. George had squatted down upon the step and (old soldier though he was) was wiping his face. Mrs. Bradley grimaced at both of them, wiped David's brow, patted him behind the ears with eau-de-Cologne from the first-aid outfit which she always carried in the car, and told George to smoke a cigarette.

" Don't plaster me with scent," objected David. " A drop of whiskey is what I'd give ten years for. Poor old Uncle Joshua ! What fiend from hell's been here and done such a thing ? Geoffrey, too. Could he have killed old Joshua, and then himself, in a fit of madness, would you think ? "

" They've both been murdered," Mrs. Bradley replied. " A man can shoot or stab another, and then turn his weapon on himself, but I don't believe it's possible to split one's own skull with a battle-axe. I have no whiskey, David, but here's the brandy, my dear. Give George a tot when you've finished. He looks white about the gills. I don't suppose it will upset his driving," she added.

As soon as they reached David's house Mrs. Bradley rang up the police. It was then about a quarter to five, and tea was on the table. David Ker gave the table one glance, and then retched, much to the distress of his housekeeper. She and Mrs. Bradley got him to bed, the tea was " wetted " for the second time, and just as they had finished a call came through from

Lanark. It was turned eight o'clock by the time the police arrived. They announced that they would go immediately to the scene of the murders, and kindly promised not to disturb the household again that night, but indicated that they would be over very early in the morning.

"Nonsense," said David, when this news was communicated to him. "I know Braid. He's a very nice fellow. Tell him that of course we shall put him and his people up for the night."

"He has only one man with him," Mrs. Bradley replied.

"Good sakes! Then tell Elspat to get the beds ready at once. And warn him to look for fingerprints on those two battle-axes."

"I don't think he will need to be warned about that," said Mrs. Bradley. "And now, David," she added, when the two policemen had gone off on their grim and messy errand, "you and I must have a word about your family connections. There appear to be wheels within wheels, a process which invariably excites me."

She settled herself bolt upright in a comfortable chair at his bedside, took out her notebook and pencil, looked at him with the benign interest of a boa-constrictor contemplating its next meal, and asked:

"How many brothers did you have?"

"None. I was an only child."

"Tell me about your family, David, please."

"I have no family. My father died eight years ago. My mother died when I was a wee laddie. That's all."

"I see. How much property have you? This

house, the tower you leased to your Uncle Joshua—
what else ? "

" Why, nothing. There's some tale that my grandfather owned a stretch of the moor with a bit house on
it, over towards Lanark."

" On the Clyde ? "

" Well, not precisely on the Clyde, although a wee
burn runs through it."

" I see. And could there be treasure buried on this
land ? "

" Not that I ever heard tell."

" I see. Now, David, please tell me all about your
grandfather, and all about his children and their
descendants."

" For why ? It isna interesting, lassie."

" It will interest me. Do, David, tell me, please."

" My grandfather was just an old fellow who had
four sons, of whom my father was the third, and poor
old Uncle Joshua the fourth. Losh ! That's an ill
business, in the old tower."

" It is. But I know who's responsible. Come along.
What about the other two sons, and everybody's
descendants ? "

" You're still thinking on buried treasure. But,
lassie, there is no buried treasure ; not so much as a
guinea."

" Never mind that. Go on."

" Aye. Well, the eldest son—my father's eldest
brother, ye ken—was called Graham. He died in
1927. His only son, Graham again, had been killed in
France in 1916. He left a son, too, but we quarrelled,
Graham and I, back in '98 that would have been.

Still, I had the boy here sometimes, for his sake. He wasna much of a laddie."

" Don't you know what happened to the boy ? "

" Not since he was here last, a good many months ago, that was. The dominie laddie, you ken."

" So he had plenty of chance to copy your map-markings. Well, I told you what happened to him, David. To the best of my belief, he was murdered outside a music-hall in Newcastle less than a month ago."

" Murdered ? Aye. Poor laddie."

" Didn't you read about it in the papers ? "

" I dinna recollect. So that would have been young Graham. Eh, me. Well, we were always folk to die by violence. It's a tradition in the family."

" Yes, but that isn't all. Was your second uncle named Geoffrey, by any chance ? "

" He was. And he died two years syne."

" Leaving a son ? "

" No. Thomas was killed in 1915. There was naething but that poor lad—twenty-six would he be now ?—aye, about that—lying killed in the tower with old Joshua."

Mrs. Bradley nodded.

" I thought it must be. He told a young friend of mine that his name was Geoffrey, although he certainly did not give the name of Ker."

" I haven't seen the lad since he was a bairn. I wouldna have recognised him, except he was so like Graham, whom I knew pretty well, you ken, for his father's sake."

" One minute, David. Cannot you tell me more

about this piece of land which belonged to your great-uncle?"

"I canna. Nobody kenned when he bought it, or even, for certain, that he did. There was nothing about it in his will, for my father had a copy which was always kept inside our Family Bible, and may be there yet for all I know. I use a smaller Bible."

"Do look, David, please. I should like to see your great-uncle Graham's will."

David called for Elspat and demanded the Family Bible. This she brought. It was a vast and weighty tome, and it rocked the bedside table as she lowered it on to the edge.

"It would be here," said David, leaning up and turning the first few pages over. He soon found the copy of the will. It was sandwiched between a page for the births and a page for the marriages of the family. He took it out, and handed it to Mrs. Bradley.

For about half an hour there was silence, except for slight crackling of paper, as she remained absorbed in Great-Uncle Graham's testamentary depositions.

"I see that, upon the deaths of the Graham Kers, and the cessation of their male heirs, the property passes to the Geoffrey Kers. From them, if there are no male heirs, it comes to your branch of the family, and then passes, in like manner, to that of the Joshua and James Kers," she said.

"Aye, that's it. Small chance that I would ever have got much, for Graham's boy would very likely have married, and had boys of his own, and, if he had not, there would still have been young Geoffrey and his sons to come before me."

" Yes, it certainly *ought* not to have come to you,"
Mrs. Bradley agreed, with a curious emphasis which
did not pass unremarked by David Ker. " What is
this poem at the end of the will ? " she went on.

" Oh, that ! The old fellow, they say, was a rare
one for quoting the Border ballads. I should think he
put it in as a kind of decoration," David answered.

" Yes, but it isn't a quotation from an old ballad.
It's original, and very bad, at that," said Mrs.
Bradley.

" Original ? But Great-Uncle couldn't write poetry,"
his relative announced with scornful confidence.

" Evidently not. But, listen, David, and tell me
what this conveys to you."

" I've read it before, you ken."

" No, you haven't ; not what I should call reading
it," Mrs. Bradley said firmly. She read it aloud.

> " Go draw to me a chevron vert
>   'Twixt uni-horns erased,
>   In silver these, then mullets black,
>   And so my name be praised.

> " And seek by Clyde, in Clyde, his dale,
>   By Bonnington so free,
>   Nor dead bell wight, nor Border light—
>   But good Saint Rosalie."

" Now," she said, looking up at him, " if you are
not too tired, let us construe this mysterious piece of
verse. First : on a chevron *vert* between three
unicorns' heads *erased*, *argent*, three mullets *sable*.
What is the answer to that ? "

"Why, the family arms," replied David Ker promptly. "We worked out that bit long ago."

"'And so my name be praised,'" quoted Mrs. Bradley solemnly. "Let us continue. We can take for granted that when he says Clyde he means Clyde, and by Bonnington he means Bonnington. I've been there once already, guided by the painstaking and careful research of another of your talented relatives. That leaves us with 'the dead bell wight.' What is the dead bell, David?"

"Oh, it's a Scottish superstition that before the death of a friend you'll be hearing a sort of a tinkling in your ears, that's all."

"I see. Well, we are to ignore this superstition, it appears. That brings us to 'Border light,' which again, we are asked to ignore. What is a Border light?"

"Nothing but a tar-barrel on a pole. In old days they would fire them, you ken, to spread news of war throughout the Border country. 'Border beacon' is the name, by right."

"See, also, how, in England, they spread the news of the coming of the Armada," said Mrs. Bradley. "Now, David, we come to the point. What do you know of good Saint Rosalie?"

But here David Ker shook his head.

"Dear me," said Mrs. Bradley. "Have you not read your Walter Scott?"

"I have that. But the reference escapes me."

"It appears to have escaped the other members of your family, too. Saint Rosalie's body was buried in a cleft of the rocks."

"But I dinna see what that's got to do with my great-uncle's will," said David Ker.

"Very well, child. But don't be obstinate. At this moment it seems to me that you are the heir to all the family property by the deaths—the deaths by violence—of your nephews Graham and Geoffrey."

"But, Beatrice, what's afoot? What does it mean, those murders?"

"Have patience, David, for a bit. Did old Uncle Joshua have sons?"

"Aye, one son he had, a weakly, sickly boy called James. I mind hitting him on the neb when we were youngsters."

"Did he go to the war?"

"No. They wouldna take him; he was always sickly, ye ken. Losh! I can see him now, with his thin, sandy hair and his spiteful white face! He died last year. I went to the funeral, but I only did it for duty's sake, for deil knows I never liked him."

"Did he marry?"

"Aye, he married. She was a lass he got into trouble, a richt bad lot, and more to blame than he was, I would say."

"Did the child live?"

"Aye; with his mother."

"Was he born after the marriage?"

"Aye; three months after. He was as miserable as his father and as wicked as his mother."

"Yes, he is wicked," Mrs. Bradley agreed. "He has murdered three people already, including his own paternal grandfather, and, if we are not very careful, my dear David, I'm afraid he may set upon you. He has made one attempt already—the poisoned caviare."

"And when will be come?" asked David.

"At any time now, I should think. And I don't believe he will come alone. We should take the point of view that we are in a state of siege here. Let me tell you the rest of the story."

"I see," said David Ker, when she had finished. "So the cataleptic Dark Gentleman is to have a share of the spoils for his part in the trick, and the coffin gotten ready for him is really for me." He gave a deep chuckle. "Well, we'll lead them dancing." He looked thoughtful for a minute, and then he chuckled again. "I am in hope they made the coffin wide enough," he said. "I like to turn over, nights."

CHAPTER XI

" ' There came a cat to my cage, master,
I thought 'twould have worried me,
And I was calling to May Colvin
To take the cat from me.' "

THERE WAS NO DOUBT THAT TO GILLIAN THE SIGHT OF Geoffrey had been a shock, although not a severe one. Almost immediately she had pulled herself together, conferred swiftly with Lesley, and driven on farther from the village.

" Now what ? " she asked, as she brought the car to a standstill on the moorland road.

" Obvious, I should say," her sister responded. " You stay here ready to start the car at five seconds' notice or less, and I'll go and see whether I can spot that Mr. Joshua in the village. I suppose it's got a pub. I've got his appearance clear, with any distinguishing characteristics, as the police would say."

" But, Lesley, you can't go alone. I'm coming with you."

" My good ass, don't muck the whole show. These men know you too well for us to take any silly risks. Me they don't really know at all. It's a pity if I can't take a slant at a young man without your assistance. Toodle-pip ! Shan't be long. Don't go to sleep before I get back."

Far from requiring this facetious piece of advice,

Gillian felt nervous and ill-at-ease. She had conceived a horror of Mr. Joshua, brilliantly though she had tackled him at the hotel. She hoped that her sister would not be more than ten minutes gone. She chewed her lower lip and kept glancing at her watch. The sun, which for some time had been giving indications that this was to be its policy, set in a glorious haze which at any other time would have delighted her with its colour. At the end of a quarter of an hour Lesley had not returned.

Gillian was in an agony of indecision and alarm. She longed to leave the car and go in search of her sister, but, at the same time, she realised that on no account must she lose such advantage as the shelter of the car might give her. It would never do to let Mr. Joshua know of her presence in this little village, where, so far as he was concerned, there was no reason for her to be unless she were dogging his movements.

At last she heard lightly running footsteps. Cautiously she backed the car to give her sister a shorter distance to run.

"I've seen Mr. Joshua, I think," said Lesley, tumbling in. "Drive on a bit. I don't think I've been twigged, but you never know. I've messed up his beastly bike."

"We're off the main road," said Gillian. "Hadn't I better . . . ?"

"No. Carry on, and make it slippy," Lesley said urgently.

So Gillian drove on across the moor along a wild rough road which showed signs that at any moment it would peter out altogether. This it did, and Gillian, stopping the car at a point where the dusk of the evening indicated nothing but a slight bareness among the heather, enquired what they were to do next.

"Park for the night," said her sister. "Just take the vehicle out of the fairway, lovie, and we'll try a spot of shut-eye. I've had enough for one day."

They switched on the car lights and lay back, pulling the car rugs up to their armpits, and wondering how much colder the night was likely to grow.

At about midnight Lesley awoke from a very uneasy and rather uncomfortable doze, and said that she thought she could hear someone running.

"What's more, I bet it's our precious Mr. Joshua," she said. "What shall we say if he asks us to give him a lift? Look here, he'd better not spot us. And you lie low, in case."

She switched off the lights of the car.

The runner came nearer, and trotted up to the car. They heard him stumble and curse as he left the path for the heather. He slowed down into a walk, and then flashed a torch. It shone on the gleaming paintwork of the car, and he stopped, with a cry of relief.

"I say," he said, coming up, "do you mind if I ask you for a lift? I'm desperately anxious to get on to Moffat before morning and I've had a breakdown in Culter." It was, of course, Mr. Joshua.

"We're here for the night," said Lesley. "We ran off the highroad further back, and came to a dead-end here. I'm not going any further until daylight."

P

" Oh, no, look here——" began the pedestrian.

" I'm sorry," said Lesley with finality. " And please don't wake my friend. He's apt to be violent when roused." She indicated Gillian hidden in rugs.

" Look here," said Mr. Joshua again, " you've got to take me on. It's a matter of life and death."

" All right. Climb into the dickey, then. But please don't disturb my friend. We've had a very hard day's driving. I'll back on to the road, and then turn."

" No, no. Across the moor is the quickest. I can guide you," Mr. Joshua insisted.

" Well, I don't know . . . I suppose it's all right," said Lesley. She gave an added tug to the rug which was covering her sister. " Get in, then. I'm sorry I can't have you in here, but there isn't room if Geoffrey's to get any rest."

" Geoffrey's to get any rest ? " said Mr. Joshua. His tone was filled with horror. He sounded like a man who had seen a ghost. They knew why, later on.

" Yes, my friend Geoffrey Smith."

" Ah. Yes, well, keep to the course of the burn. We shall come to it in a minute. There's plenty of room to run a car beside it. How fast do you think you can go ?."

" Twenty-five, when I get the hang of the bumps," said Lesley.

It was a most eerie journey. Once they were started upon their way, Gillian pulled down the rug an inch or two, so that she could breathe, and Lesley, her eyes strained forward to the fantastic shadow which lay always ahead of the car and beyond the orbit of its lamps, was racking her brain to remember the map, and to try to make out for what reason Mr. Joshua had chosen this way to get to Moffat.

Just as the day was dawning Mr. Joshua asked her to stop. She obeyed, and he got out. Black against the tender colour of the faint and greyish sky stood one of the Border watch-towers, an ancient keep with narrow windows, one balustered, another almost in the roof, and an arched doorway black as the night.

" ' Childe Roland to the dark tower came '," muttered Lesley.

The light was just sufficient to give some impression of what a truly nightmare journey it had been. Great boulders, lying like dragons' heads cloaked in the heather, were strewn about the moor. Among them the harebells, faint-blue, fragile-stemmed, incongruously, delicately flourished. Lesley looked at the burn, and then at her passenger.

" If we'd crashed, I'd have sued you for damage," she observed, with a grin. In response to it Mr. Joshua showed his little white fangs. In the early, revealing light, his face was wolfish and terrifying. Lesley, fortunately, had almost no imagination. She looked him over with a girl's crude curiosity.

" We didn't crash," said Mr. Joshua, with something more than ordinary satisfaction in his tones. " Now, girlie, you're going to drive straight on, and the sooner you get a move on, the better for everyone concerned."

" Is that so ? " drawled Lesley. She looked enquiringly at the revolver which Mr. Joshua had produced. " Gangster, huh ? " she observed.

" Get going," said Mr. Joshua. Lesley shrugged (as

heroines, she had noticed, usually did on the films at moments of crisis like this one), and let in the clutch.

Mr. Joshua walked down to the burnside, and stooped to bathe his face and wash his hands.

" What next ? " said Gillian, appearing from under the rug.

" Goodness knows. Did you see him pull his gun ? "

" I've got a gun," said Gillian. She produced it.

" Good egg. Give here. I'll go and stalk him," said Lesley.

" Put both your hands on the wheel. You'll ditch us," her sister said shortly. " I suppose we must get *somewhere* if we only go on long enough. How much petrol have we got ? "

" Heaps. As soon as we get beyond that little bend there, I vote we have a look at the map. I—hullo ! Look ! A house ! It looks rather decent, too. Let's go and ask them whereabouts we are."

There was no bridge across the burn, but they found a place shallow and clear of boulders, and put the car across with little trouble. The house was some distance away, but they arrived before its iron gates within twenty minutes of leaving Mr. Joshua and the castle, and both got out of the car to look at this monument of man in a place which nature seemed to have reserved for herself.

" I say ! " said Gillian. She expelled her breath slowly as she gazed at the house which had been copied from Sir Walter Scott's residence of Ashestiel. " Do you know, Lesley, I believe this must be the very house that Aunt Adela's been in search of ? "

As though in echo of her own name, Mrs. Bradley

suddenly appeared at the side of the house, and walked towards the gateway.

Her surprise and that of the two girls was mutual and exhilarating. Explanations were forthcoming, and the girls had parked the car beside Mrs. Bradley's, in the stables, long before the story of their pilgrimage was ended. Mrs. Bradley took them into the house, and Elspat made them up beds. It was still a little before sunrise.

"And now," said David Ker, as soon as breakfast was over, "I think you'd better tell me all about it."

"That's Aunt Adela's job," said Lesley, polishing off her porridge, and seizing (again this was literally true) a plate of eggs and rashers from Elspat Fenwick. "But I expect she's put you wise to most of it."

"We've no time for fairy tales now," Mrs. Bradley observed. "We have to put the house in a state of siege, unless I am much mistaken. Mr. Joshua and his friends must have arranged a meeting-place, and may be here at any time."

"But why? What could they do here?" Lesley enquired.

"Murder me, it seems," said David Ker. "But still I want to ken why."

"I'll tell you; and at the same time I'll apologise to Gillian for having given her a good deal of unnecessary work," said Mrs. Bradley. "Actually the only clue we needed was the one we found in Edinburgh—the seventeenth-century plan. That conveyed the words Marie Hamilton. Now the buried treasure, as I very soon guessed, is not gold and jewels, at least, not in the sense that we thought. By the way, David," she said, breaking off and turning on him, " where is the gold bonnet-piece you used to wear on your watch-chain ? "

" Aye, it's sad about that," he confessed. " I must have lost it, although I can't think how or why."

" Lost it ? Ah, well, you'll likely get it back when all this business is over, and our wicked Mr. Joshua brought to book."

" Why, where would my bonnet-piece be ? "

" On the watch-chain of a cataleptic gentleman named (for purposes of convenience) Frere."

" What is the treasure, then, Aunt Adela ? " Gillian asked. " And why, when I decided that the ballads gave one set of clues, did you go and fix on others ? "

" I didn't, child. We interpreted differently what we read, that is all. Take the name Hamilton. What do you know about it ? "

" Well, it's Mary Hamilton's surname, and it's a town and——"

" That will do, I think. Whereabouts is this town ? "

" Oh, well, somewhere in the Lowlands—I could find it on a map."

" Yes. And now I'd like Elspat to read you an extract from Mr. H. B. Morton's *In Search of Scotland*. What do you make of this ? Go on, Elspat, please. You know the passage I mean—the one we discussed this morning."

" *A few miles from Glasgow are the chimneys of Hamilton.*

. . . Over the Clyde, winding here in almost a country mood, the sullen stacks of Motherwell's steel furnaces lift black fingers to the sky. In the middle of this is the saddest house in Scotland. It is the ancient home of her premier dukes, the ancestral seat of the princely family of Hamilton," read Elspat, in a drone.

"Now," said Mrs. Bradley, "it seems to me that the treasure which is indicated all the way through this rather extraordinary story which we have been tracing out, is *either coal or iron*—both, perhaps. So when I worked out my topographical clues from the ballads I went always considerably further west than most of the references seemed to indicate. To give you one example of what I mean : you won't remember Gillian, the ballad called *Young Hunting* ? In that it seemed possible, and, considering our object, quite likely, that we were intended to take as our main clue the stanza :

"' Young Hunting kens all the fords of Clyde,
    He'll ride them, one by one ;
    And though the night was ne'er so mirk,
    Young Hunting will be home.'

"Well, having taken that as a starting-point, I then looked for any further indication of *direction*. I was not always lucky, but these I did get : in the very same ballad, too :

"' Leave off, leave off, your day diving,
    And dive upon the night ;
    And where that sackless knight lies slain
    The candles will burn bright.'

" Note the play upon ' sackless ! ' Rather neat ! In another stanza we obtain :

> ' The deepest pot of Clyde Water
>   They got Young Hunting in,
>   With a green turf tied across his breast
>   To keep that good lord down.'

" Of course," Mrs. Bradley went on, " none of this was conclusive, either to young Graham or to me, when first he and then I began to work out the clues. But there is, all through, the striking indication that the wealth in question was, as I said just now, coal or iron, or both."

" But you spoke of *direction*. I don't see much direction, except the Clyde," said Lesley.

" Of course, a good deal of it was guesswork," Mrs. Bradley admitted. " You see, although it did not come in as part of the acrostic, I could not avoid the implication of the *title* of the ballad *Young Hunting*, especially as I was looking for a reference to the Clyde. At first I was on the look out for one particular spot, but it soon became obvious that, if *coal* was in question, a whole stretch of country was the correct answer to my riddle. David is still the only one of us, however, who knows the exact position and extent of that stretch of country, I imagine."

" I do not, though," said David Ker, " but I mind me, now you say it, of some tale of lost title deeds ; and I mind me of something further. I told you I had little to do with my kin ; that I didn't like them. But here's two bits of news may stand you in stead. You remember, maybe, speiring at my groom did I kick him? Do you ken when that would have happened?"

"Yes, of course," Mrs. Bradley replied. "It happened when you received a short visit from your nephew Geoffrey Ker, although his visit was a surreptitious one, and you never knew anything about it. I wonder who first discovered, by the way, that there was coal under that part of the family inheritance, David?"

"That must have been old Joshua. He was for ever poking about. It would never surprise me if the whole scheme of the murders originated with my Uncle Joshua. Aye, there's black blood in our family, and old Joshua had his share of it, I'm thinking."

"Aiblins!" said Mrs. Bradley, in the belief, apparently, that this peculiarly Scottish word was either an expletive or conveyed some impression of regret. David Ker looked slightly bewildered, Gillian and Lesley giggled, and Elspat, who had begun to clear away breakfast, clicked her tongue and observed, in sibylline tones:

"Dule and wae is me!" And added, "Ye'se gae busk and boun, I'm thinking."

"You believe, then," said Gillian, "that *old* Mr. Joshua, not *young* Mr. Joshua, first made the murder plot: but why?"

"He was the youngest of the family," David Ker explained. "Graham was the heir; next came Geoffrey; after him I should have the property, and after me old Joshua, my uncle, the only one of his generation left alive. Failing him, of course, it would come to young Joshua, his grandson."

"So Geoffrey did not realise that you and old Joshua were to be murdered?" Lesley enquired.

"He could not have done, because there was no point in murdering them, either or both, unless Geoffrey himself were also to be disposed of," said Mrs. Bradley. "Geoffrey was a party to the murder of his cousin, Graham; there seems no doubt about that. But he could not have visualised the rest of young Joshua's plans."

"Do you think old Mr. Joshua thought it was Graham, and not Geoffrey, who was playing chess with him that day when both were murdered?" Gillian enquired.

"He was very old, and I think it most likely that he did not distinguish the one young man from the other, as they were superficially alike, and of about the same height, build and age," Mrs. Bradley agreed. "Besides, I imagine that there was method in the madness of Geoffrey's visit here. He must have gone over to the tower and ingratiated himself with old Joshua at young Mr. Joshua's orders."

"But why, if he didn't think old Joshua had to be murdered?" asked Lesley, following the argument with knitted brow, as though she were in attendance at a lecture which was, on the whole, a bit above her head.

"Why, of course, silly! To see whether old Joshua had the map!" said Gillian.

"Old Joshua and young Graham had compared their maps, I think," said Mrs. Bradley. "I doubt, though, whether old Joshua realised what he was giving away to his eldest brother's heir. He probably hinted and chuckled, and teased young Graham, giving him bits of information and teasing him with his own surmises, for probably they were not facts but only inferences. But young Graham had brains. He pieced together the scraps, accepted the hints, joined up the tags of ballads and worked out at last the crude acrostic of *Marie Hamilton*. I agree with David's theory—it is no more—that old Joshua plotted murder just as certainly as young Joshua did."

"So that old Joshua only got his deserts in the end. I should like to think that," said Lesley.

"Geoffrey, too, come to that," said her sister. "Well, go on, Aunt Adela. What's our next move?"

"Whatever it is, I don't think we need be in any immediate hurry to make it," said Mrs. Bradley. "I see it like this : the police are bound to be much in the neighbourhood for a day or two, if not longer. They will be at the tower, because the murders took place there, and they will come here to interview David and me. I discovered the bodies, and they will suspect our poor David of the crime."

"Oh——?" said David.

"Well, obviously, my dear. You stand to gain a good deal if you become heir to a property from which good coal can be mined. It will be shown that you were from home on the day of . . ." she consulted her note-book . . . "June twenty-third——"

"Well, so I was," said David Ker, in some surprise, "but you couldn't know that! How could you?"

"Because it was the day on which the first murder took place. On June twenty-third, at just after nine o'clock in the evening, your nephew, Graham Ker, was stabbed to death outside a music-hall in Newcastle."

" But I wasn't in Newcastle ! "

" Where were you ? "

" I went to Lockerbie. I was nowhere near Newcastle."

" Which station did you travel from ? "

" Why, Biggar, of course."

" The booking clerk will remember you ? "

" Aye, I should think, maybe, he would."

" That's something. Now, may I be forgiven for asking why you went ? "

" To have a crack with William Annan."

" Did you have your crack ? "

" Well, no. You see, he'd been called away by telegram——"

" The old dodge," said Lesley, a reader of detective stories. " You've been spied on pretty closely, Mr. Ker."

" What's that, lassie ? "

" Oh, you know—the murderer always sends a bogus telegram."

" Nephew Joshua, that would be, again."

" Yes, Nephew Joshua," Mrs. Bradley responded. " Well, you see, David, the police would find enough to question you on. And I hope," she added, with a cackle, " that there's enough to arrest you on. You'd be very well out of all this for a couple of weeks."

" I'd like to see them arrest me," responded David Ker belligerently. " I'd . . ."

" Never mind what you'd do, just now, Mr. Ker,"

said Gillian. "There's a policeman coming up the path already. Shall I tell Elspat she can let him in, or do we slug him, Aunt Adela? It's really for you to say."

There was considerable police activity in the neighbourhood for a day or two, as Mrs. Bradley had predicted, but a day came when, so far as they knew, the preliminary investigation into the murders was over. David Ker had the treble advantage of being well-respected in the district and of having the booking clerk at Biggar remember not only the day on which he had travelled to Lockerbie and the train he had travelled by, but, by some extraordinary bit of luck, also the time of his return. The clerk had been in the booking hall talking to the ticket collector when David had given up his return ticket. As this time (corroborated by the ticket-collector) happened to be just before seven o'clock, it was not possible that David could have been in Newcastle at nine o'clock on the same evening unless he had chartered an aeroplane. The police did not think it necessary to find out whether or not he had done this.

His alibi for the time of death of Geoffrey and old Joshua was just as easy to establish, and here he was lucky again. The medical evidence fixed the time of death as having been not earlier than midnight. Not only was Elspat prepared to swear that her employer had not left the house during the night, but there was the fortunate coincidence that Mrs. Bradley, through fortuitous circumstances, was able to corroborate this evidence, since her car had pulled up at such a short distance from the house that she must, she said, have been aware of the fact if anybody had left the house during the night.

Although her evidence could scarcely be called conclusive, it was accepted in conjunction with what Elspat, who had been known and respected in the neighbourhood for nearly sixty years, had had to say.

The girls were sure that Mr. Joshua had gone straight in and murdered the chess players when they had set him down outside the castle at dawn.

The newspapers were inclined to call it the *Mystery of the Lone Tower*, and, for all the hope that there seemed of fixing the guilt on Mr. Joshua, a mystery it seemed likely to remain.

" But *surely*," Gillian said, " we can find *some* evidence of where he was, and what he did, and when he did it ! I mean—three murders ! And what becomes, now, of the man in the fit at the other house, the one in the marshes ? "

Mrs. Bradley herself was interested in this aspect of the subject, so much so that she installed George, armed with Gillian's revolver, as defender-in-chief of David Ker, sent a telegram to the warlike Henri, her cook, to come north with all possible speed, sent the two girls home to their mother, instructed Michael and Elspat, and then departed to look up the landlady and young Tom at the *Rising Sun*, and the cataleptic Mr. Frere at the house in the marshes.

She left David Ker on a Saturday, and, before going further south, broke her journey at Newcastle (driving herself, a practice of which George whole-heartedly disapproved) to gossip with the inspector.

"There is one thing at least which I cannot understand," she said, when she and the inspector had exchanged news and views, "and that is about the birth certificate. Didn't you tell me that the headmaster of the school at which young Graham had taught declared that he had seen the boy's birth certificate giving the surname of Graeme?"

"I did that. And that is what he said," the inspector declared. "But I'll have him sorted for ye. Maybe it was not a birth certificate, but a college certificate, or something of that nature, that he saw. He was a doddering old wife, at the best."

Mrs. Bradley readily accepted this estimate of the dominie's character, and cackled harshly.

CHAPTER XII

" ' Ye'se get a sheaf of my bread, Willy,
 And a bottle of my wine ;
 But ye'll pay me when the seas gang dry,
 For ye'll ne'er be lord o' Linne.' "

THE FUNERAL OF " MR. LANCASTER " HAD, OF COURSE,
taken place, and, conducted by young Tom, Mrs.
Bradley went to see the grave. She then returned to
the *Rising Sun* and telephoned to her son Ferdinand in
London.

" Home Office ? " said Ferdinand.

" Exhumation order ? " he enquired.

" But, mother, suppose you're wrong ? "

" But, mother. . . ."

" But, really, mother. . . ."

" Oh, well, if you say so, but . . . Oh, well, then. . . .
Yes, all right."

Satisfied, and but little wearied, Mrs. Bradley sat
down to a meal. It was six in the evening, and the
day had been perfect, although, for most people,
rather too warm. Mrs. Bradley, however, had a
lizard's love of dry heat, and had been out in the
garden all day, having arrived very late on the previous
evening.

" Haven't sacked thy chauffeur, like ? " young Tom
sympathetically enquired.

" Oh, no. George is staying in Scotland to drive

my niece, who can't be trusted with a car," Mrs. Bradley satisfactorily but mendaciously replied. She had gone to bed soon after supper, had risen early, but, except for the escorted visit to the cemetery, had lain remarkably low.

The landlady had commented on this, and had indicated possible walks and excursions in the neighbourhood which would well repay the labour and trouble of taking or making them. But Mrs. Bradley, with a mixture of truth and levity which had served many times, and upon many occasions, to disguise her intentions or views, observed that she was afraid of encountering the Dark Gentleman.

" Ah," said young Tom's mother, in immediate reaction to this, " he've been seen about again, so I do hear."

" Really ? " said Mrs. Bradley, who had hoped for this.

" Rare frit, our Tom was," Tom's mother continued, with a slight but happy laugh. " Side-stepped proper, that did, when *he* did see en over to Doubledyke Bend, t' other day."

" ' Why, our mam,' that say to me, all of a tremble, ' why, our mam,' that did say, ' if that had a white face instead of that there black un, that ud be spitting image of him that's gorn, dead and buried.'

" ' What thee do be saying, our Tom ! ' I says. ' Thee be dreaming,' I says. ' That be old Mr. Lancaster that's gorn,' I says, ' and this be Mr. Frere, come back to village after three years,' I says. But Tom, that pull at my arm, and home we have to come, and bless me and all if that didn't say, the

Q

minute we got inside door, ' Our mam,' that say, ' do
thee think the Dark Gentleman saw I ? '

" ' What thee's afraid of ?   Evil Eye ? ' I says."

Mrs. Bradley smiled, but only dutifully.   It had
occurred to her more than once that young Tom stood
in some danger.   Although the Dark Gentleman
might be prepared to brave the inspection of most of
the people in the village, there was always the chance
that, if he found out that Tom had been the person to
find him " dead," then he would conceive it part of
his duty to make it impossible for Tom to report to
the police what he had already reported to his mother.

Once the " dead " Mr. Lancaster were suspected
of being also the very much alive Mr. Frere, the
game was up.   The empty grave—and Mrs. Bradley
devoutly hoped that Ferdinand could persuade the
Home Office to dispense with a little of the red tape
which so often strangled its best efforts—would queer
Mr. Joshua's pitch, to say the least.   Immediately
enquiries began, his visit to Mrs. Bradley, Gillian's
story about Geoffrey, the reincarnation of the East
Bierley business and the singular death of Mr. Graham
Ker would bear a sinister complexion, and one as
dark as that of Mr. Frere himself.

Once the identity of Graham Ker was established—
as it could be, very readily, by his Uncle David—the
whole story would unwind itself, Mrs. Bradley surmised, like the india-rubber core of a golf ball once the
hard outer covering is removed.   But there was
plenty of time for that, and it was of no use being
fanciful with a jury.   Mrs. Bradley, who had once
written a monograph upon the psychology of juries,

sighed as she remembered cases in which the jury, confronted by evidence which it did not understand and by emotions which it did, had given a verdict not at all in conformity with the former, but wholly on the strength of the latter. The fact that, in most cases, the verdict turned out to be exactly the same as it must have been if the evidence alone had been the deciding factor, was none the less distressing to the detached, judicial and scientific mind, which, after all, she possessed.

She sent for Tom after they had returned from visiting the grave, and conferred with him upon the advisability of her sending a messenger to the North.

She felt fairly certain, from what she knew of his character, that Mr. Joshua was more likely to have followed her to the marshes than to have remained in Scotland. It was interesting and important that Gillian and Lesley had actually seen him visiting the scene of the crime, but he was not likely to remain in its neighbourhood whilst the police were still there, and he would be anxious to know what she herself was up to, for he must have realised, Mrs. Bradley sorrow-fully admitted, that by this time she could no longer be regarded as a benevolent neutral, far less as a potential ally. She was the enemy in person.

Young Tom was willing enough to be a messenger, and, his mother raising no objection, since she could easily manage the bar without his assistance, the first arrangement was that he should be hustled on to the best train of the day at the last possible minute, carrying a dispatch to the inspector at Newcastle.

The contents of the package which Mrs. Bradley had prepared for him would have surprised and disgusted the youth if he had been made aware of them, for all that they amounted to was a plea to the inspector to keep the bearer safe until Mrs. Bradley should require him.

The necessity of taking measures for Tom's safety was amply illustrated that same night. Mrs. Bradley, in the barn-like bedroom again, her revolver at hand and her consciousness only very thinly veiled in sleep, was awakened at about midnight by the sound of stealthy scramblings on the roof of the wood-shed outside.

She rose quietly (having stipulated for a bed whose springs did not creak, and, wonderful to relate, having got it) and crept to the window. Tom, she knew, had his bedroom opposite the wood-shed. Her own was at right-angles to it.

Hidden in the blackness of her room, with her gun cocked and her dressing-gown belted about her, she watched and listened. The night was extremely dark, for the moon had set earlier and cloud—the first indication of thunder—was obscuring the stars.

Mrs. Bradley breathed noiselessly. For about five or six minutes—a long time to a watcher in the darkness—there was nothing more to be heard, and certainly nothing to be seen. Then, from the wood-shed roof again came faint sounds indicative of some presence bulkier and heavier than that of a cat.

Young Tom liked fresh air by day but not by night, and Mrs. Bradley could not help wondering what the attackers, kidnappers, or whatever they had set out to be, would make of the sealed window against which their next efforts were almost bound to be directed.

She had, in this one instance, underestimated, however, the intelligence and psychological insight of the enemy. It soon became apparent that not young Tom's but her own window was to be the aperture selected by the marauders in order to gain entrance to the inn.

She was first made aware of this when an electric torch, injudiciously switched on, made a ring of light on the west wall of her chamber. There was a muffled remark, apparently on a level with her window-sill, followed by a slight scraping sound. Then the torch was switched off, or pointed in another direction, and a branch of ivy, up which, she presumed, somebody had swarmed or was swarming, began to tap against the glass.

The muffled voice joined issue with the sound, and, in a fierce undertone, insisted that it ceased. Thereupon there was the uncomfortable silence of someone attempting to maintain a noiseless but precarious balance.

Mrs. Bradley crouched low and circumambulated the room, keeping close to the wall the whole time, until she reached the side of the window.

It was open at the top and the bottom, and, reaching into the deep pocket of her dressing-gown for her torch, she waited to find out what the next move might be. She thought she could anticipate it, and her plan, simple, as befitted a great general, was quickly made.

After the interval apparently considered suitable by the housebreakers, the scraping sounds began again. They were extremely faint, and care was being taken this time, it seemed, to avoid the tapping noise occasioned by the jigging branches of the ivy.

In another moment fingers gripped the sill. Mrs. Bradley flashed her torch directly into the eyes of the intruder, then, dropping it on to the upholstered seat of a wicker-chair at hand, she slammed down the window with all her force on to the clinging fingers.

There was a shriek of agony, followed by the sound of a heavy body dropping on to the bushes below.

At the same moment both the dogs of the inn commenced to bark their loudest, another window of the inn was flung up, and the voice of the landlady announced that if anyone was there she was coming to let the dogs loose.

A scrabble of flying feet, an oath and a tumble, were the last sounds heard of the kidnappers. From a short distance down the road a car began throbbing and choking. In another half-minute it was half a mile from the inn.

There was a tap at Mrs. Bradley's door. It was Tom.

"Be thou all right, like?" he enquired. "Who was it, and what did that want?"

"That wanted thee," replied Mrs. Bradley, grinning. In her brilliantly dragon-bestrewed dressing-gown, she looked more like a witch than ever, or perhaps like a gargoyle which has gathered to itself a body and clothed it with raiment to its taste.

"Why didn't thee call I, then?" young Tom demanded. "Come to that," he added, becoming more widely awake, for the noise of the barking dogs, the shriek, and the sound of the engine of the car, had penetrated his dreams and confused him thoroughly before they aroused him from slumber, "how did that come not to be knocking at door, like proper-bred folks?"

"Ah," replied Mrs. Bradley, "thereby hangs a tale. Let us descend to the private bar, Tom, where, unless I am mistaken, we shall be completely surrounded by panelling except for one window too small to admit anything larger than a boy of ten, and when we have locked the door I will tell you all."

At this moment the landlady arrived, in curl-papers and a flannel dressing-jacket, and demanded to know what was toward.

"Go thee back to bed, our mam," said Tom. But Mrs. Bradley protested. It was time, she said, that his mother should be in their confidence.

So the three went down to the private bar, after the landlady had added a coat of many colours, in the form of a patchwork quilt, to her *ensemble*, and there Mrs. Bradley locked the door, the curtains were drawn snugly over the tiny window, from which they sat as far away as they could and not in direct line with it (for fear, Mrs. Bradley said, of draughts, when she meant for fear of shots), and, when the light was on, she began to tell her tale.

"Tom knows too much," she concluded. "But he's going away from here, so that won't matter. The only thing is that I think he ought to go now. Those who came to kidnap him to-night will go back to their masters, Mr. Joshua and Mr. Frere, and will receive, I imagine, fresh instructions. Now I find that there is a train to London at six to-morrow morning, so I suggest that Tom catches it. In the meantime, let him make his bed down here, and I will sit up and guard him."

"So will his mother," said his mother fiercely. So the two women gathered their wraps about them and sat, like two Wives of Usher's Well, guarding the sleeping boy.

But no further attempt was made that night, and at six Tom, with full instructions from Mrs. Bradley, was *en route* for London. From London he was to go north, where Mrs. Bradley promised that she would very soon join him. Newcastle, after all, was to be out of his itinerary.

Her own task, as she saw it, was to discover how many persons were likely to be available if Mr. Joshua planned a further attack on the inn. What his next move was to be in respect of his Uncle David was another question to be answered. She decided upon a bold reconnaissance.

Her first move was to telephone the young doctor to come and meet her in his car. Full of curiosity and goodwill, he arrived soon after breakfast, proposed that they should take in his round of patients (three old ladies and a child with a broken leg), on their way to the house in the marshes, and then added that she was wasting her time. The house was up for sale, and there was no one but the caretaker there.

"And who is the caretaker?" Mrs. Bradley enquired.

"Oh, the gamekeeper. He took it on."

"The sinister gamekeeper," Mrs. Bradley said, with a chuckle.

"Is he?"

"Well, he isn't a gamekeeper, and I call that sinister," Mrs. Bradley replied.

The doctor took the car round a couple of wagons which seemed determined to occupy the centre of a narrow road, and by the time he had skidded past a dyke which, even at that time of year, was brimmed almost level with its banks, he had lost the thread of the conversation. Mrs. Bradley was not sorry for this.

The doctor drove up to the iron gates, but they were locked. A side-gate was partly open, and so past the long-deserted lodge they walked, the doctor on the lodge side.

This precaution (since the doctor could be in no danger of receiving a bullet from a possible sniper hidden in the shuttered lodge) Mrs. Bradley thought it just as well to take. With the same object she took care to walk just in front of him, and lead the way to the house, since she thought it unlikely that she would be sniped from directly in front, with the doctor a material witness of her murder. Mr. Joshua, so she argued, had so many mouths to close already that he would scarcely be anxious to add one more to the list. In this, he proved later, she misjudged him.

They gained the house without incident, and rang the jangling bell. Footsteps, firmer and more rapidly-moving than the shuffling tread common to care-takers of empty houses, argued the approach of the ex-gamekeeper.

She had not calculated upon the effect which her unheralded appearance would have on him. He became chalk-white, and seemed to be going to shut the door in her face. Mrs. Bradley forestalled him, however, by smiling graciously, like a boa-constrictor after a meal before it settles down cosily to sleep off the effects, and by recalling herself (obviously unnecesarily) to his memory.

" I've come to look over the house," she added. At these words the man's mouth opened. Then it closed. Then it opened again, this time in speech.

" You can't do that without an order to view."

" Oh, nonsense," said Mrs. Bradley, elbowing her way past him without ceremony. " You know me, and the doctor will vouch for me. I am neither an incendiary, nor do I propose to commit suicide from a top-floor window."

The doctor removed his hat and followed her in, the caretaker tramping behind them. It was clear that he was feeling that a situation had arisen with which it was beyond his power to deal. Except that he followed them about all over the house, he seemed to have no plan for coping with what was obviously a move outside the scope of his instructions.

Mrs. Bradley turned suddenly on him and fired at him the unnecessary and idiotic question :

" *Pourquoi Monsieur le Noir n'est pas ici pour nous donner le clef ?* "

" Eh ? " said the caretaker, taken aback. Mrs. Bradley repeated the question slowly and with the pronunciation, she supposed, of the school of Stratford-atte-Bow.

" No compris," said the caretaker. Believing that he really did not understand her, she turned to the doctor, and said rapidly in French :

" Do you speak French ? "

"Slowly and with difficulty," said the doctor in the same language.

"Good," said Mrs. Bradley. Then she said, very slowly indeed : "We are going to fight with this man. Do you understand ?"

"Yes, I think so," the doctor answered. "We are going to fight with this man. Why ?"

"Never mind," replied Mrs. Bradley in English. "Sufficient unto the moment are the lawless deeds of self-styled civilisation. Now the view from this window is good. Caretaker, what is the house I see there, across the marshes ?"

Incautiously the caretaker placed himself between them. With the utmost gentleness they twisted his arms behind him, and, whilst the doctor held him pinioned, Mrs. Bradley secured his wrists, and then, with the doctor's assistance, his ankles, and gagged him delicately.

They stood off from the result of these labours, and the doctor then observed :

"And now, what is all this about ?"

"Help me to place him in the largest attic cupboard, where he will have air but will be out of the way," replied the organiser of the assault, "and I will explain."

So, the young male doctor taking his shoulders and the elderly female doctor his heels, the caretaker was carried up the next flight of narrow, uncarpeted stairs with an awkward bend at the top, and, the largest attic cupboard having been located, inspected and even dusted by the thoughtful Mrs. Bradley, therein he was placed with his head slightly raised upon a pillow which she went down specially to get for him, and there he was left, whilst the other two went downstairs to the hall, where Mrs. Bradley briefly explained the situation.

"But you're not going to leave him like that?" the doctor enquired. "Who's going to find him, and when?"

"What I want to know," said Mrs. Bradley, brushing aside these immaterial queries, "is why he was left here at all, and what has happened to the women."

"Oh, the girl went to her mother, and the house-keeper has taken another situation, so I heard," the doctor replied.

"And what about the niece?"

"I never saw a niece. Was there supposed to be a niece?"

"I shall be sorry if the niece is entirely fictitious," Mrs. Bradley said, seating herself on the monks' bench portion of the hatstand, and taking out her note-book. "Now, our future plans of action. First, yours: I want you to go back to your house, and go on with your duties as usual. Forget all about this little episode for, say, the next five hours. That will bring us——" she glanced at her watch, "to between three and four o'clock this afternoon. By then I shall be in possession, I hope, of the information I want, and you can come to the house and release the fellow's hands. He can get his legs free at his leisure. It shouldn't take him long."

"And what do I say when he sets the police on me?"

"He will not set the police on you, child."

"Well, I shall give you away with all the power and length of my tongue if he jolly well does."

" All right. Then that's quite settled. Good-bye.
If anything upsets my theories between now and three
o'clock I will let you know."

She watched him drive off, and then closed the front
door quietly and went upstairs to the attic cupboard
in which they had left the prisoner.

" Now," she said, addressing his furious eyes, " I
am going to take you downstairs, and into the garden.
If you remain quiet I can carry you. If you struggle
I fear that I shall be obliged to drag you downstairs
feet first, in which case you will bump—quite gently ;
I shall not hurry you—from step to step in a way which
I fear would jar your whole system. What do you
think ? "

He was not a big man nor a heavy one, but there
were four flights of stairs to come down, and in the
hall she allowed herself a short rest. Then she carried
the helpless man through to the kitchen, where, from
the appearance of the table, it seemed that he had just
concluded a meal when he let them in. There she set
him down whilst she opened the kitchen door. Then
she took him into the garden.

Not far from the door there was a wheelbarrow.
Jettisoning its load—some hedge-clippings, weeds and
a pair of gardening shears—she loaded the caretaker
on to it, and pushed her human Guy Fawkes towards
the lake.

His anguished expression when he perceived her
objective caused her to remark compassionately :

" No, no, my poor fellow. I am not going to drown
you. You were not born to be drowned."

Her opinion that he had been born to be hanged she

thought it kinder, as well as more prudent, not to express at that juncture.

Tied up under a willow there was a flat-bottomed boat which was used, Mrs. Bradley deduced, as a kind of hopper barge when weeds were cut in the lake. In this boat she placed her captive, and then went back to the house for a cushion for his head and blanket in which to wrap his feet, so that he should not be able to make a drumming sound which might later direct his friends to his retreat.

She then stepped into the punt and pushed it off, only to moor it again on the further side of the willow from where, she hoped, it was not conspicuous from the house. She stepped ashore, waddled, in the muddy boots which she had discovered in the kitchen and into which she had thrust her smaller, narrower shoes, back to the house with sufficiently masculine strides, replaced the boots, and herself went up to the attic to make sure that no tell-tale trace had been left behind by herself, the doctor and the caretaker.

She found nothing, descended to the ground floor, went up six steps and across to the long and two-storied servants' wing, and there took up her position behind lace curtains to keep what she hoped would not be a fruitless vigil.

She took out a nondescript piece of sorry-looking knitting, and, keeping her eyes on the iron gates by the lodge, commenced to knit, quickly and badly.

She was there for an hour and a quarter before there was any sign of Mr. Joshua and his party. She was glad to see him, glad to see, too, a tall man, black-avised, who was sufficiently like the Mr. Lancaster to whom she had already been introduced to give her the hopeful impression that here was the cataleptic in person. Accompanying them was one man. She supposed him to be the groom, or, rather, the man who had taken that part in Mr. Joshua's baroque, over-decorated re-staging of the East Bierley mystery.

The small cavalcade approached the front porch, and, after a short colloquy, Mr. Joshua took out a key and opened the door. This was a piece of good luck which Mrs. Bradley had scarcely expected. It disposed of her fear that he would discover, before he had a chance of entering the house, that the caretaker was not available either as servant or fellow-conspirator.

CHAPTER XIII

" ' Where be ye gaun, ye hunters keen ? '
  Quo false Sakelde ; ' come tell to me.'——
' We goe to hunt an English stag,
  Has trespass'd on the Scots countrie.' "

IN THE ENTRANCE HALL THE THREE MEN HALTED, AND
then Mr. Joshua's voice could be heard calling for
Johnson. Obtaining no reply, he called again. After
this Mrs. Bradley could hear nothing further, and so,
moving like a cat, she crossed the small room and
opened the door. Holding it ajar, she listened again.

The servants' wing, that Victorian addition to the
house, joined the main building by means of a short
corridor which ran behind the smaller ground-floor
room which faced the drive, and came out almost at
the end of the passage which joined the entrance hall
to the kitchen.

It was now possible for her to hear the rest of Mr.
Joshua's remarks as he went though into the kitchen
to rouse up the caretaker. They were principally of
an objurgatory character, particularly when he found
that the man was not to be seen.

" He'll be down at the *Rising Sun*," suggested another
voice, which, from the tone, Mrs. Bradley took to be
that of the groom. " And if he is," he added, taking, it
seemed, some sort of lugubrious pleasure in putting the
worst of the matter in front of Mr. Joshua, who was

not likely, Mrs. Bradley thought, to be a favourite with subordinates, " he'll be there till they shut, if I know him."

" It's turned two," said Mr. Joshua. " You ought to know him, if anybody does," he added savagely. " The mess the two of you made of getting hold of that boy last night."

" Forget it," returned the groom. " We can get him any time. Ten to one, he don't know the value of what he knows."

" You bet he knows the value, with that confoundedly ugly old woman putting him up to it," Mr. Joshua replied. " *She* can put two and two together, if *he* can't. Shut your mouth and find Johnson. Search the house first, and then the outside. And then you can try the pub, but make that the last place, see ? "

Grumbling, the man went off, and after he had opened and shut half a dozen doors on the ground floor, and had bellowed Johnson's name in tones of varying pitch, loudness and annoyance, he began to mount the stairs.

Since it was clear that, whatever else they were going to do, Mr. Joshua and Mr. Frere did not propose to search the grounds, Mrs. Bradley followed the groom upstairs, and, waylaying him at the door of one of the attics, thrust her gun at his waist and invited him to stand still and not to shout.

The man, in paralysed fashion, obeyed. Mrs. Bradley then suggested that he should accompany her, and took him down the stairs until they came to the passage which led to the bedrooms of the servants' wing. Along this passage they went.

R

"In here," said Mrs. Bradley, at last. It was the end room of the wing and was so far away from the main part of the house that Mrs. Bradley did not believe that any amount or degree of shouting could be heard by Mr. Joshua and his satellite.

She locked the man in, therefore, cautioned him through the keyhole about trying to leap out of the window, beneath which stood a large water-butt open at the top, and left him.

When she got back to the main building, Mr. Joshua and Mr. Frere were still talking. She located the room from which the voices were coming, went out into the garden at the back, and, re-entering the house by the french windows of what had been the library before some previous owner had sold or removed all the books, she made her way to the ante-chamber of the room in which they were conversing.

"I tell you," Mr. Frere was saying, "if we don't do it soon we'll never do it. That boy must have recognised me, and, you see, we didn't get him. That's enough to dish us. The other job will have to be done to-morrow, at the latest, and even then I don't see how we're going to pull off the rest of the doings."

"Why not?" said Mr. Joshua sourly. "Do you mean to tell me I can be kept from my own inheritance? I tell you, they can't trace me in this business. I've completely hidden my tracks."

"Oh, yes? What about the motor-cycle?" enquired the other. "And what's the good of an inheritance, if you don't even now know where it is? You don't know where the deeds are. You don't bloomin' well know anything. I'm getting sick of it."

"All we want to find will be in the house, you'll see," Mr. Joshua answered. "And, before he dies, I'll see I get it out of Uncle David."

"Well, you'll have to get it to-morrow," Mr. Frere persisted. "They're on my neck, and I can't hold them off much longer."

"You'll have to keep to the arrangement," said Mr. Joshua. "I can't help your troubles. You've been a good friend. I wouldn't wish for a better ; but . . . I'm the boss. Just get that into your head. You take your orders from me."

"Less of that," said the other, speaking sharply, and on a menacing note. "Don't you forget, my cock, I know enough to stretch your neck."

"Oh ? " said Mr. Joshua. And the monosyllable was a good deal more threatening than the other man's threatening remark. He said no more at all, and the other, giving a short laugh, said gently :

"No need for us to fall out. We've got on well enough so far. But debts are debts, and a debt is a debt."

"I get you all right," said Mr. Joshua. "You'll get enough from me to pay off old Father Abraham himself when this is over. Now, the stuff we want is in Johnson's hut in the woods. Where is the cursed fellow ! Surely Sudall must have found him by now ! "

He went out into the hall, and Mrs. Bradley could hear him calling Sudall and Johnson both. His voice echoed in the old house, and then grew quieter, as his footsteps, and those of his companion, died away.

Mrs. Bradley darted through the library and out at

the french doors again. At an amazing pace for an elderly lady she made her way through the trees to the gamekeeper's hut.

The door was shut and locked. She was so certain of what she would find there that she tore pages out of her notebook, lighted them, and tossed them on to the thatch. Waiting only until she saw that the thatch had caught fire, she turned and tore for the drive.

As she reached the gates the doctor's car came in sight. Blessing him for a most fortuitous but valuable piece of timing, she waved vigorously, hopped in, shut the door, and said, breathing rather quickly :

" Drive on. Direction doesn't matter. But get away from the house."

He obeyed none too soon. Scarcely had they covered half a mile when the blast of a loud explosion rocked the car on the road.

Lunch, at the *Rising Sun*, was cold beef, bread, cheese, stewed apples, fresh cream and beer. Mrs. Bradley, presided over by young Tom's mother, ate well, and described the morning's adventure.

Far from wishing her away, and her son at home again, the hostess took great interest in all these doings, and had, of course, heard the explosion. So had the police, she reported, but beyond the fact that the gamekeeper's cottage had been lifted and scattered, and that a few trees had suffered, they had discovered nothing helpful, and had been on the telephone (so the stationmaster had said) to the Chief Constable.

Of Mr. Frere and Mr. Joshua there was no word, so at half-past four Mrs. Bradley went on foot to the house in the marshes to set free the prisoners and to assess the amount of the damage.

As the gamekeeper-caretaker was no longer in the boat, she assumed that Mr. Joshua had found and released him. She did not fear to find either of them still on the premises, for she felt certain that neither would wish to explain to the police the presence of the dynamite, and she had no hope at all that they might have been killed in the explosion. That the devil looks after his own was a truth she had often seen exemplified. A solitary policeman had been left on guard—for what reason it was not easy to determine —over the scorched woodland where once the hut had stood, but she found it quite easy to avoid him, and, the french windows remaining unfastened, since neither Mr. Joshua nor Mr. Frere had used them as entrance or exit, she got into the house and crossed to the servants' wing.

She contented herself here by unlocking the door of the room in which she had imprisoned the groom, and then by waiting for him to come out.

When he did, he faced her revolver, and was marched out to the gates and along the road. Here Providence, in the homely combination of her own car and George driving it, took a welcome hand in the proceedings, and the prisoner was conveyed at the rate of fifty miles an hour to the inspector, and to him handed over for safe keeping.

" I can't hold him long on nothing but suspicion," said the inspector.

" You won't need to. You'll be able to hold him
upon being accessory to the fact of murder as soon as
he begins to tell you all that is in his heart," replied
Mrs. Bradley. " The murderers themselves are
probably on their way to the Border by now. I
propose to follow them. One is your precious corpse,
the ' late ' Mr. Lancaster, so if the Home Office come
along to exhume him, you won't be surprised. I
advise you to find his housekeeper and the girl who
acted as housemaid. They should be valuable witnesses. You still want to know what happened to the
former owner of the house, you know, whom Mr.
Frere, for the past three years (more or less), has
impersonated. The housekeeper should know a good
deal. Do your best with her."

She was gone, at that, leaving the inspector with
one hand stretched towards the telephone, the other
scratching his head. George, looking so like a wax-
work model of the perfect chauffeur that Mrs. Bradley
knew that he expected and was inviting reprimand,
sat at the wheel until she came down the steps from
the police station. He then came round and opened
the door of the car, still looking like a cross (as Mrs.
Bradley pointed out later) between Casabianca and
the Admirable Crichton, but was disappointed, for she
found no fault with him.

" Newcastle, George," she said. She had taken her
leave already at the *Rising Sun*, with a promise of
news by telegram of young Tom immediately she got
in touch with him.

" Very good, madam," said George.

" And why, George," went on his employer mildly,

opening the glass screen between her part of the vehicle and his own, "did you leave my poor Mr. Ker to all the assaults of his enemies, and come down here like this?"

"I found an efficient substitute, madam," replied George, "a man named James Alexander Musgrave, an old soldier, whom Mr. Ker, at the man's own suggestion, provided with a sawn-off shot-gun."

"I see," said Mrs. Bradley. "Well, George," she added handsomely, "I'm uncommonly pleased to see you."

"Thank you, madam," said George, in a disgruntled tone. He was the most skilled debater at the club of which he was a member, and it was his continually thwarted ambition to contrive a passage of arms with his employer in which he should be able to give play, courteously, of course, to his gift.

Mrs. Bradley sank back in a corner of the car, smiled gently, closed her eyes, and slept lightly until the slowing motion of the car woke her up again.

"We've got this much," said the inspector at Newcastle. "The dead man, Graeme or Ker—he gave the first name, which looks suspicious if it really wasn't his own—bought a third return week-end ticket from Edinburgh the day before he was found stabbed. That looks as though he didn't intend staying here for very long. He stayed at a common lodging-house, which looks as though he hadn't very much money——"

"Or wished to avoid meeting people who might have recognised him," said Mrs. Bradley.

"He had no luggage with him except what he

was carrying in his pockets, but that doesn't do anything to alter the fact that he might easily have been carrying the dagger tucked into his sock or hidden away somewhere else," continued the inspector.

"But still, there's the business of the gloves." Mrs. Bradley nodded. "Not conclusive. I was afraid it would turn out like that."

"The absence of any letters and papers on the body wouldn't necessarily mean anything but suicide, either, you ken," the inspector added sadly. He shook his head. "It isna that I don't believe what you say, ma'am. I believe you are right, and the man was murdered by his cousin. But, beyond this daft-like stuff about buried treasure——" he looked apologetically at her as he voiced this opinion of the Ker inheritance, but Mrs. Bradley merely waved her hand and cackled—"there isna a shadow of motive anywhere for the death. And that's where the murderer has us beaten."

He looked compassionately at her. Mrs. Bradley observed, with calmness, that she felt she owed gratitude to Mr. Joshua for giving her an interesting time.

"I am still in the dark," the inspector continued, "as to why he called you in to help him prevent the murder of his uncle."

"Oh, I think I've solved that," said Mrs. Bradley. "His cousin and accomplice, the late Mr. Geoffrey, involved him with Gillian, and Gillian brought me into it and mentioned to Geoffrey that she had. Mr. Joshua then decided to use me."

"Ah, I see. Aye, that would be it. He couldna

be held on a charge of poisoning his uncle, because no poison was to be used—not, at any rate, on *that* uncle. It was clever, in its way."

" Yes," agreed Mrs. Bradley. " It was not clever, all the same, to send his real uncle, David Ker, the caviare which contained strychnine."

" Did he do that ? "

" Again, there's no proof, but the Lanark police have the matter in hand for investigation. I think we are bound to get him. He has not used his accomplices well. His difficulty is going to be to keep them loyal to him. You see, at present he can't pay them."

" It's an interesting thing, that," remarked the inspector. " You'd suppose, if there was land, with coal under, in the family, that the family would ken where it was."

" There's a freakish strain in the Kers," Mrs. Bradley observed, " and it is more than possible that Mr. Joshua's great-uncle, who bought the land, left some hint, and nothing more, in his will, of this part of his property. He may have thought that his descendants would want to resell it if it proved to be valuable, and he may not have wanted it resold."

" He could have put that in the will," the inspector pointed out. " It might be a good idea to get hold of a copy of the will and see what the great-uncle did say," he continued, " although that would hardly come within my province."

" I have seen a copy of the will," Mrs. Bradley assured him. " David Ker had a copy. There is nothing in the will which might lead one to suspect the existence of the missing property except a couple of doggerel verses, interesting in their way, but somewhat in need of footnotes for the average reader. Mr. Joshua, so far, has proved no more than an average reader."

"And the verses?" said the inspector. Mrs. Bradley repeated them, and added the explanation she had already given to David.

"Fanciful," said the inspector.

"Too fanciful for any one of the Kers except our Mr. Joshua, who, although footnote-less, is thoroughly fanciful himself," said Mrs. Bradley. "After all, Great-uncle Ker must have had a reason for including the doggerel in his will. I still think," she added, "that a stricter search might give us the title deeds themselves, but, of course, I can't be sure."

The inspector grunted. He was too courteous to tell her what he thought, but his expression, and the grunt, were eloquent.

Mrs. Bradley strongly approved of James Alexander Musgrave the moment she saw him. He was a tall, thin, muscular Borderer with an intelligent face, grey eyes, and the carriage and long legs of a man accustomed to miles of hilly walking. He and his sawn-off shot-gun were on duty in the drive when her car drove up, and she and George were halted and inspected with military firmness before, their identity established and approved, they were permitted to proceed.

" Has anybody been seen about ? " Mrs. Bradley enquired, as soon as she gained the house.

" Not a soul, barring ourselves, and a man from Biggar with the whiskey," David Ker, now restored to health, replied confidently. " What's the news with you ? "

" Not good, and not bad," Mrs. Bradley answered. She told him about the dynamite. " I don't think they are very likely to have, or to be able to procure, any more," she added, " but we may expect them at any moment, full of fresh devilry, no doubt."

" Then this house is no place to defend," said James Alexander Musgrave, who had been relieved on duty by Elspat, and so had joined in the conference.

" But what about the police ? " enquired Gillian, appearing from the garden, where she had been keeping watch with her sister Lesley. " Surely it's their job now ? "

" Well, it might be, if we could prove that we expected an attack," Mrs. Bradley answered. " As it is, I think we should create an impression of hysteria by calling them in at this juncture. They would think we were nervous because of the murders at the tower."

" I don't see why we can't prove Mr. Joshua did those," said Gillian, eagerly. " After all, Lesley and I did see him slinking in."

" There is nothing to show who did them, child. We are against a man who is a genius in his own way. He has no idea, though, that we are abreast of his plans. He is coming with at least three men. We muster three men and four women—enough to settle their hash, I should imagine. We can call the police in afterwards to deal with the survivors. Oh, that reminds me," she added. "Hasn't young Tom turned up?"

Tom, it appeared, had not. This was worrying, since, if he had carried out his instructions, he ought to have arrived at the house before Mrs. Bradley and George turned up in the car.

"He'll have to be found," said Mrs. Bradley. "James Musgrave, you and George will have to go. George knows the lad, and can describe him. Take the car to Lanark, and see what news they have there. He should have arrived by four o'clock this afternoon, if he did exactly as I told him when he got to London."

"It will weaken the defence of the house," James Musgrave pointed out.

"It will weaken our defences so much," said Mrs. Bradley, "that I propose we leave the house and take to the tower. That we can defend against any assault. What do you say, my dear David?"

"I am against it," David Ker answered. "We have in this house food for several people for at least a fortnight. There we would have nothing but what we could put into the trap. Even your car will not be available, if the men take it to Lanark this evening."

"I don't think the siege will last long," said Mrs. Bradley. "We shall inform the police as soon as it begins, and by the time we have held off Mr. Joshua for an hour or two, the police should have arrived, and will take our assailants into their care."

David, however, proved obstinate. Therefore, perceiving that he did not intend to vacate his house, Mrs. Bradley gave in for the moment, and went round the house with Elspat to examine the possibilities of defence.

" We'll never keep them out if they mean to get in," said Elspat with what, in anybody but a Borderer, would have been the deepest pessimism, but which, in her, was a kind of gaiety, to think that the task was going to be dangerous and difficult. It was with disapproval that she had witnessed the departure of James Musgrave and George, but when their quest was explained to her she agreed readily that the poor wee laddie must be found and brought to the house.

As there was now nothing else to be done but to set watchers at top-floor windows, and then wait for the rescue party to return, or for Mr. Joshua to make his attack, Mrs. Bradley, not having the first spell of duty, set herself to work out the probable movements of the enemy, and the form the attack on the house was likely to take. With the written result she decided to go again to David Ker and urge the immediate evacuation of the house.

" We are not in a good position here," she stressed. " These men will be armed, and, judging by their conduct up to the present, will stop at nothing. I still want to leave this house and go to the tower. Once there, you and Elspat, with Michael and the two girls, can hold the fort with ease."

" And you ? "

" I want to find the deeds. I believe I was on the track of them before. I should have gone on searching then, if I had had the evidence of the will to guide me, but I did not know of the verses."

" You canna be left alone. Have Michael go with you."

" I don't want Michael. I don't think I like him very much."

" Do you not ? Perhaps you're right. I'll send him away until this business is over. Where is he now ? "

" He should be on duty on the west side of the house, looking out of the attic window."

" Aye, I'll go and find him."

He went away, and scarcely had he begun to mount the front staircase when there was a sound of clattering feet on the servants' stairs, and Lesley came bursting along the kitchen passage and through the baize-covered door.

" Oh, Aunt Adela ! " she said. " That Irishman —the groom ! He's gone ! "

" When ? "

" I don't know. Gillian just went along to give him a piece of chewing-gum, as we'd got some, and were all on duty together, and found he wasn't at his post."

Upon this, Elspat, David and Mrs. Bradley searched the house, whilst Gillian and Lesley each watched two sides of it instead of one.

Nothing was known of the groom until Lesley, gazing through field-glasses, suddenly gave a shout which brought David Ker to her window on the west of the house. He took the glasses she handed to him.

" Is that Michael ? " she asked. In the distance, and heading away from the house, was a man on a zig-zagging motor-cycle.

" It is," said David Ker. " I shall kick him harder next time I see him," he added.

" I suppose he is in the pay of Mr. Joshua," Lesley remarked. " I bet that's the way the caviare got into the house. It didn't come by post at all."

" No doubt about Michael now, I am afraid," said Mrs. Bradley, joining them. " It makes a difference of two able-bodied men, as it were, to our defences. We have lost one, and the enemy has gained one. What do you think, David ? "

" Nothing," replied David Ker. " If it seems the best thing to abandon the house, why, we'll do it. Just wait until I telephone the police."

" If Michael's had any sense he's cut the wire," said Lesley, the student of escapist literature.

" First round to Mr. Joshua," said Mrs. Bradley, when David failed to get through to the police.

" Second round, you mean," said Lesley. " What price us not spotting that a motor-bike had been left on the premises so that that beastly Michael could make his getaway ? I never did like that man. I wish George and Musgrave were still here."

So did Mrs. Bradley. She added that the motor-cycle was probably the one which Geoffrey had ridden to the tower.

" It is a nuisance about the telephone," she said.

" We should have thought of that. After all, it is
not only in fiction that a telephone wire is cut for
criminal purposes."

The exodus from the house now had to be planned
without delay. Mrs. Bradley had a last word with
David.

" Now, David," she said, " you are our trump
card, remember. As long as you are safely in our
hands we win the game. If Mr. Joshua gets hold of
you, we lose it."

" I can't owe my life to a pack of women," said
David Ker, ungratefully.

" Baby ! " said Mrs. Bradley.

" Pack of women ! " said Gillian, from her post in
the south attic.

" Isn't he the limit ? " agreed Lesley.

" It doesna seem to occur to him," said Elspat,
joining in the fray with grim thoroughness, " that
he owes his very existence to a woman."

These Amazonian tactics on the part of the despised
sex reacted strongly on David. He apologised.

" And now," said Elspat, " we are a' gaun tae dae
as Mrs. Bradley says, and that's to get oot o' here
the best way we can whiles thae limmers still dinna
ken what we are after. So up wi' you, David
Ker," she added urgently, " and get your bits o'
things, and let us a' be gaun to the tower. She's a
sensible body, yon," she added, in a loud hoarse
whisper, drawing her employer away from Mrs.
Bradley's vicinity, " and kens what tae dae, gin you
dinna."

Completely swamped, David was led away.

"And now," said Mrs. Bradley, "when you are ready, I want you two girls to go with him and Elspat, and I'll stay and search for the deeds, which may be all the time in this house."

"I'm staying with you," said both the young girls, in a breath.

"I'd like to have you," said Mrs. Bradley tactfully, "and, really, I suppose it would be far less dangerous for you if I did. But I'm afraid David will dig his toes in altogether if anybody else stays behind, and he is our first consideration. He is at once the first and last shot in our locker."

The girls agreed about this, conferred together in loud tones from their respective windows, and then, after last looks through the shared binoculars, abandoned their posts and professed themselves ready to accompany David to the tower.

"One thing, David," said Mrs. Bradley, when the party was ready to set out. "Where is the family residence? Where, for instance, did Great-uncle Gregory live?"

"Why, in the tower, of course. I bought it from Gregory's family before I leased it to old Uncle Joshua."

"I see. All right. That's all, child. Good-bye, everybody. It won't be long before I see you again."

She watched them out of the eastern attic window, and went occasionally to the other sentry-windows to look for the coming of Mr. Joshua and his adherents. The cut telephone line made any appeal for police protection impossible for some time. Mrs. Bradley

s

found herself glad of this. Mr. Joshua, with his wholesale, Renaissance disregard of life, and his, so far, brilliantly trackless trail of murder, robbery and bluff, was not only a foeman but a challenge.

It was chilly upstairs. She also saw no particular need to watch for the approach of the enemy. Her plans were made. If, by any chance, George and James Alexander should return to the house with young Tom, they could please themselves whether they remained with her or accompanied Tom to the tower. The boy must certainly be in a place of safety. Her own view was that Musgrave should take him to the tower. George, she preferred to believe, would elect to remain at her side.

The day began to darken. Mrs. Bradley made up the fire, drew the curtains, and foraged in the kitchen for food. She made China tea, and cut thin bread and butter. Then, setting this elegant English meal upon a tray, she brought it into the room where there was the fire, and set it down.

She enjoyed her solitary tea. When it was over she washed up, made a tour of the house to test door and window fastenings, and then chose a book and settled down to spend a pleasant and restful evening. She did, however, keep an ear open for the sound of the returning car, whose engine beat she thought she could recognise, and also for the sound of any other vehicle.

She had no lights on elsewhere in the house, and the curtains of the room in which she sat were so closely drawn that no chink of light could escape. In any case the night was not yet dark. The house

might have been fully inhabited, or absolutely empty :
there was nothing to show.

At nine o'clock or just after, like the trump of
doom in that it was unheralded by any preliminary
warning, there came a loud knocking at the door.

CHAPTER XIV

" Then bespake him the King againe,
  And these were the words said hee :
  ' If we stand not stiffly in this battell strong,
  We are worthy to be hang'd on a tree.' "

YOUNG TOM'S ADVENTURES HAD BEEN VARIOUS. ONCE
on the train he had fallen asleep in the corner of
the carriage for the first two hours of the journey,
and probably would not have wakened as soon as
he did, even then, but that a dining-car attendant
touched him on the shoulder, and informed him that
breakfast was ready.

Breakfast lasted young Tom until the train reached
the outskirts of London, and he returned to his
compartment with only just about enough time to
collect his cap, which he had left there, and his
waterproof, before the train drew in at the London
terminus.

Tom had received implicit instructions from Mrs.
Bradley about what to do when he reached London,
but the only clear order which remained in his head
was that he was to look out for a tall thin clergyman
who was to offer him breakfast.

" As you will already have had breakfast on the
train, Tom," Mrs. Bradley had continued, " you will
know that this is the sign."

" Sign as that be the right man, like, and not

one of t'other bloke's blokes," Tom had observed intelligently.

"That's it," said Mrs. Bradley. She had imagined that Tom would remember the bit about the clergyman and the breakfast, and probably nothing more, and so had telephoned the rest of the instructions to the Reverend Noel Wells, her friend, as well as having entrusted them to young Tom.

There was the tall clergyman, at any rate. Tom went up to him.

"Here I be," he said. "Be you a-looking, like, for I?"

"Will you have breakfast?" the clergyman enquired. Relations having been established by this simple means, Tom then broke through the careful plans by beaming, and accepting the offer. The clergyman was slightly alarmed by this, for his instructions had been to conduct the youth to Euston Station by taxi immediately he had established his identity, there to catch a train for Lanark, by way of Carlisle.

He took out his watch and made a rapid calculation.

"We'd better have it at once, then," he said. They were served quickly at the station buffet, but had cut the time rather fine. The clergyman hailed a taxi. "Come along. Jump in," he said.

At this point Fate, which entered little into the lives of either of them, decided to interfere in its usual unforeseen manner. The weather, which had been perfect when Tom left home, had turned wet. The rain was thin and light—sufficient to make the streets slippery.

At a corner the taxi-driver tried to jump the lights, decided, too late, to pull up, and skidded his cab into a lamp standard. Neither he nor the passengers were hurt, but the delay, which involved explanations with a policeman, and then the abandoning of the damaged taxi for another, which did not come along immediately, caused young Tom to miss the train.

"Oh, dear! I'm afraid that's done it!" the clergyman said, inwardly cursing young Tom's boyish appetite for breakfasts. "You'll have to get the next one, that's all."

The next train, fortunately, was not so very much later. Tom's ticket was purchased and he was seen off by the Reverend Noel Wells, and the train, a slower one, making many more stops than the one he should have taken, steamed out of Euston at thirty-six minutes past twelve instead of at twenty-nine minutes past eleven, but this did not seem too bad, thought Tom, with the country boy's placid indifference to time.

He had lunch on the train at half-past one, and made it last until a quarter to three, then he returned to his compartment and went to sleep. It must be recalled that his night's rest had been very much disturbed, and that he was a boy who needed his sleep.

He woke to find a stranger in the carriage, a very deaf gentleman who was travelling, he informed Tom, to Keswick. Conversation proved too difficult to be long sustained, but one thing Tom grasped clearly. It was that the information given him at Euston by the Reverend Noel Wells, and gleaned after exhaustive enquiry of station officials by that gentleman, was incorrect. According to this information, Tom had caught a through train to Carlisle.

" You change," said the deaf gentleman firmly, " at Leeds." As he was under the impression that Tom's destination was Redcar, he may or may not have been right. Tom, at any rate, implicitly believed him. Mrs. Bradley had forgotten, or, at any rate, had overlooked young Tom's peculiar objection to clergymen when she had made her arrangements. It was a psychological error of some magnitude, for it had become second nature to young Tom to mistrust the voice of the Church when it was applied to the discussion of earthly things. One does not have a " preached-against " mother for nothing.

He had not been at all favourably impressed, either, by the fact that the Reverend Noel Wells, although sound on the subject of breakfasts, had proved to be deficient in second sight where skidding taxi-cabs were concerned.

At Leeds, therefore, Tom alighted, and waved farewell to the deaf gentleman, who reached Keswick still happily convinced that he had assisted a fellow-traveller in making a cross-country journey.

Tom applied to a porter, and learned that the clergyman, after all, had been right, and that he should have stayed on the train. The only difference, in the end, was that whereas he had been scheduled to arrive in Lanark at some reasonable hour in the evening, he did not get out of the train there until twenty minutes past midnight. George and James Alexander Musgrave were still waiting grimly in

the car. Another watcher, lounging in the shadows
of the station with a motor-cycle, once the property
of Geoffrey Ker, propped up against the kerb, was
the groom Michael, who had been suborned by
the same Geoffrey, and bribed since by the wicked
Mr. Joshua, to lend any sort of hand that was desirable.

He had heard all about the missing country boy,
whilst he was still, ostensibly, in David Ker's service,
and had ridden off to confer with his new employer.
He had been given his commission, and, up to the
time of young Tom's arrival, had been cursing this
commission as heartily as George and James Alexander
were cursing theirs.

All things come to an end at last, however, and
when the car moved off, with the two men and the
boy aboard her, Michael started up his motor-cycle
and followed. Unfortunately for him, George, in the
long vigil, had been aware of this hidden watcher,
and although he could not manage to see the face
of the man, he recognised the make of the motor-
cycle.

"Funny," thought George; and set his sharp
Cockney wits to work, not knowing what to make
of this new factor, but convinced, in his own idiom,
that it was n.b.g. "Lead him a dance," thought
George, blessing, not for the first time, the curiosity
and pioneer spirit of the Americans who had insisted
upon so thorough an exploration of the Scottish
countryside when he had been their chauffeur.

The consequence was that from Lanark George
led the groom over hill and dale, across the moors
and over the mountains, until, striking Sanquhar,

and wondering what was happening in his absence at the Big House (as James Musgrave was inclined to call it) and feeling confident that he had shaken off pursuit, he made for home, and arrived at the iron gates just before morning.

In the meantime David Ker, the two girls and Elspat had arrived at the tower. It was a strongly-built castle, even for a Border keep, and the removal of the bodies had, as Gillian pointed out, made the place seem more homely.

"But you didn't see the bodies," said David, who had taken a great fancy, as had Elspat, to Gillian and her sister.

"I can imagine them," Gillian unanswerably replied.

It had been easy enough, following Mrs. Bradley's directions, to get in, and, once inside, they set about barricading the stronghold in all the ways that its builders had intended.

"Now," said Elspat, who was quietly and supremely enjoying herself, "let them come ben that can."

She made a fire in a small room which had probably been the solar or parlour of the keep (or possibly, said Elspat, sentimentally, the lady's bower) and, from provisions they had all helped to carry over the rough moorland road, she soon prepared a meal.

"Grand!" said Lesley. Her sister echoed this praise. David smoked his pipe. A breeze, which had got up strongly since their arrival at the sanctuary, whistled pleasingly in the chimney. Elspat employed herself in cleaning out the rooms which had been used by old Joshua. They were unexpectedly tidy, but this, Elspat announced, was due to the police. The girls did not believe this, but, such was Elspat's personality, did not dare to say so.

By nightfall David was restless, and although he was commanded by his housekeeper not to fash himself, and, later, not to be an old wife, he insisted upon going to the front door by which Mrs. Bradley had entered to find the dead men, and staring out across the moor in the direction of his house.

When it grew dark and still he could see no glimmer of light from the windows, he took comfort from the belief that Mrs. Bradley was not there, but had gone off on some wild-goose chase in search of the title-deeds, as she had said that she should. He went back into the castle, and he and Elspat, between them, made the rounds of the place to be certain that every hole by which even a mouse could enter the tower was blocked, the doors bolted, and the occupants safely blanketed away behind the three-foot thickness of the walls.

The hours passed. The girls grew sleepy, and reluctantly allowed themselves to be persuaded to go to another room and lie down. They made some attempt to go to sleep, but gave it up soon, sat up, and quietly talked together.

At midnight David himself lay back in his chair, and went heavily to sleep, but the grim woman Elspat, wrapping a rug about her gaunt, thin shoulders, made up the fire, put out the candles, and sat up, straight as a statue, her blood stirred strangely and joyously by the call to arms of an unexpected feud.

Mrs. Bradley listened. She had made her plans in expectation of just such a visit as the one which was now being paid, but she had imagined that it would come a little later, probably after it was dark.

At nine o'clock it was very far from being dark. In fact, had she looked out of the window she could, she knew, have seen and counted the visitors. Their number did not affect her plans ; neither, at that moment, did the hour at which they had chosen to call on her.

Mr. Joshua's own plans had been put into action a little sooner than he had intended, owing to the departure from the house of two of the able-bodied men. He had rejoiced to see George and James Alexander go, but the fact that he did not in the least know when to expect them back did something to mitigate his pleasure.

Mrs. Bradley continued to listen. She could hear conversation on the doorstep, but could not distinguish words. Then the voices ceased, and a second knocking thundered on the door. At this she rose, laid aside her book, glanced in a mirror at her hair, patted it (on the same principle, presumably, as that adopted by the Spartans, who combed theirs before a battle) and went to answer the door.

" Ah," she said, in a deep, rich tone of welcome.

"Come in, my dear Mr. Devizes. I have been following your case, as you asked me to do. It is so kind of you to call. We must have a chat about it."

These tactics appeared to surprise Mr. Joshua.

"I really came to see my uncle," he said.

"Another uncle? But do come in," said Mrs. Bradley. "And your friend."

There were only the two of them, then. She wondered how soon the others would make their entry, and then how soon after that the fun was due to begin. She led the way into the room from which she had come. Mr. Joshua introduced his friend.

It was not, Mrs. Bradley was interested to see, the black-avised, white-washed Mr. Frere. This short and swarthy young man was not any one of the gang that she had seen before. It looked as though reinforcements beyond what had been anticipated would shortly be brought up to the attack.

She wondered how Mr. Joshua proposed to kill his uncle in the presence of so many witnesses. But she reflected that the most surprising and interesting feature of the case was the way in which Mr. Joshua had been able to commit three murders already without leaving any clue on which he could be arrested. The all-important evidence of motive, whilst David Ker was still living, was not obtainable. The stabbing of Graham Ker in Newcastle was still mysterious, although no longer officially suicide. There was no clue at all to the identity of the tower murderer. In fact, given Mr. Joshua's boldness and the bit of luck without which all human enterprise is probably doomed to failure, there seemed no reason, Mrs. Bradley thought, why one-half of the world should not murder the other half and get away with it.

Mr. Joshua's nervousness, which had been so much a feature at their first interview, was still apparent. Neither did the friend appear at ease.

Mrs. Bradley made conversation, and produced, in old-lady fashion, madeira (which she even went so far as to refer to as canary wine) and sponge fingers. Nothing was said about David Ker, and for nearly an hour she amused herself by side-stepping the subject every time Mr. Joshua attempted to introduce it.

At last, when the clock was striking ten, she decided that the game had lasted long enough, so she glanced at her watch, and then said casually :

" I am afraid you will be disappointed at not seeing Mr. Ker this evening, but he is from home, and unlikely, now, to return. He will be staying with his friends, no doubt, now that it has become so late. He said he did not think that he should return after dark."

The two men glanced at one another, and Mr. Joshua got up.

" In that case," he said courteously, his small teeth showing in a little, foxy smile, " we mustn't detain you, Mrs. Bradley."

" Oh," said Mrs. Bradley, in a tone of disappointment. " Don't go yet. Don't you want to know what progress I am making ? "

"You can't be making any progress," said Mr. Joshua, deliberately. He looked her in the eye for the first time. "You know what's what, I reckon."

"I guess that's so," said the friend. From his waistband, which, Mrs. Bradley noted with fascinated interest, was a cummerbund of vivid red and yellow (a stealing of Jove's thunder of which he was unaware), he had taken a small revolver. He tapped the muzzle of it on to the palm of his hand with the movement a man might use to remove a loose dottle of tobacco from a pipe.

"Come on. Come clean. Where is he?" said Mr. Joshua.

"Where is Mr. Ker?" Mrs. Bradley enquired. "Well, now, I'm willing to tell you on one condition. But, my dear Mr. Devizes," she added, with deep horror, "you are unprovided! Look at your friend!"

Mr. Joshua, against what would have been his better judgment had he been given time to think, did look at his friend—only for the fraction of a second, it is true—and at that instant Mrs. Bradley flicked out her little gun. The first bullet went through the friend's wrist, and he dropped his revolver involuntarily upon the floor, where it chose to fall near enough to Mrs. Bradley's foot to be kicked neatly backwards underneath her chair. The second bullet parted Mr. Joshua's sandy hair in a new and unbecoming furrow which was soon red with blood from the scraped skin.

"My condition——" began Mrs. Bradley; but her condition was not even heard, much less con-

sidered, by the two gentlemen. They both dived
out of the room.

Mrs. Bradley encouraged their flight with another
couple of bullets, one of which broke a vase on a
bracket, the pieces descending, film-fashion, on to
Mr. Joshua's head, and the other of which entered
in behind the left ear of a stag, where Mrs. Bradley
hoped it would remain unnoticed by David Ker,
who was particularly proud of the trophy.

The front door slammed. The footsteps continued to run. Mrs. Bradley remained in cover.
Bullets, presumably from a gun carried by Mr. Joshua,
rattled against the house, and one, at least, broke
a window.

Mrs. Bradley continued to listen. Then she bolted
the door, and locked the door of the room with the
broken window. She could hear no sound of a motor-
cycle or a car. That meant that the two men had
no immediate intention of leaving the neighbourhood.
She went back to the room which the three of them
had so lately and dramatically vacated, and, seating
herself out of the range of the windows, she took
out her notebook.

She then looked at the clock again. By the time
she had finished it was nearly ten minutes to eleven.
Even by the most liberal computation, young Tom
should have been met long before this at Lanark,
and she had been expecting, at any moment during
the time that she had spent in making up her notes,
to hear the sound of the car.

Eleven o'clock came, and then half-past eleven.
Something, clearly, had gone wrong. She supposed

that young Tom had lost the train, or had failed to get his connection at Carlisle. Of the two courses which would have been open to her if she had had the assistance of George and James Alexander Musgrave, only one was now possible to follow, especially since she could not even telephone. She must vacate the house and contrive to make her way to the tower without being discovered by the enemy.

She thought the position out carefully. It was necessary to let George know that nobody was at the house, so, watching the clock creep to midnight, she decided, at a minute to twelve, to risk capture, walk along the moorland road in the opposite direction from the tower, and flag the car with her torch. If she mistook the sound of its approach, and pulled up a car filled with Mr. Joshua's thugs and myrmidons, so much the worse for her, she thought, with some amusement of a grim but genuine kind.

Gillian was seriously perturbed. She would not have denied, if anyone had asked her such a question, that she felt very considerable affection for her odd and witch-like aunt-by-adoption, and the fact remained that their friendship was strong and that there was a pronounced feeling of mutual sympathy between them. Gillian felt acutely responsible, on the present occasio , for Mrs. Bradley's personal safety, for, as she had admitted to Lesley, she had been the means of Mrs. Bradley's entry into the affair of Mr. Joshua.

When, therefore, the night darkened, and still Mrs. Bradley did not join them at the tower, the girl became anxious. She did not know what to expect in the way of an attack on the tower by Mr. Joshua; but, if things or people were going, in Lesley's expression, to get tough, she wanted to be certain that Mrs. Bradley was safe; at any rate, not alone in her danger.

"I'll tell you what," said Lesley. "We're in no danger. Nobody wants to kill *us*. Suppose we trek back to the house, and get her to come back here with us?"

"Not much good, I'm afraid," answered Gillian. "Ten to one she wouldn't come; and, ten to one, from what she said to Mr. Ker, she isn't there. She's gone off treasure hunting on her own. We'd never trace her in the darkness."

"Well, if she's left the house, she's probably safe enough," her sister argued. "Now I've got another idea. I think we ought to get some notion of the geography of this place. I've only the very foggiest idea of how it's built, and which part leads to where."

"We can't begin exploring at this time of night," expostulated Gillian. "How can we? We should only wake everybody up."

"Oh, well, let's go to sleep, then. That's what we're here for, I suppose."

"But what about Aunt Adela?"

"I don't know; but if we can't get at her, I don't see what you're worrying about."

"I'm not worrying about anything. I just thought —keep absolutely still!"

T

Lesley was well-disciplined and had strong nerves, but she needed all her training and all her phlegm and will-power to do exactly as she was told.

" I just thought," Gillian continued, speaking as naturally as a wildly-beating heart and a feeling of faintness would allow her to do, " that perhaps it would be a good plan if we went to the kitchen, or whatever they call it in this place, and foraged for food. Fall sideways, it doesn't matter which way."

Lesley flung herself flat on the ground to her left, and rolled right over. There was a slight thud and then the click of a closing aperture.

" Keep your locks well oiled, don't you ? " said Gillian. Before her, in his stockinged feet, stood Mr. Joshua. Above his head the picture which had concealed an aperture had settled once more into place. It displayed, to the untutored eyes of those who did not know what lay behind it, an insincere and vacuous-looking portrait of the late Prince Consort.

Mr. Joshua made no reply to Gillian's ironical question, but stood there looking at Lesley, who had now picked herself up and was standing beside the picture. He allowed them to inspect the gun he carried.

" So what ? " said Lesley, managing to catch his eye.

" Oh, yes," said Mr. Joshua. " Now I'll tell you what it is. Mrs. Bradley knows where to find what I'm after, doesn't she ? "

" Yes she does," said Lesley.

" Has she spilt it ? "

" Has she what ? "

" Has she told you where it is ? "

" Oh, yes."

" Well, where is it, then ? "

" Somewhere along the banks of the River Clyde. That's all she knows. She's gone to-night to find out the rest," said Lesley solemnly.

" Oh, Lesley ! Don't tell him that ! " cried Gillian. Mr. Joshua looked from one to the other of them. Then he seated himself upon the floor.

" Take a seat, won't you ? " he said. " We shall be here some time, and I shouldn't really like you to feel tired. Would you mind telling me how many people are in your party, and where they are all to be found at this hour of the night—or rather, morning ?'

He moved the gun ever so slightly, but the movement was significant enough. Lesley stirred as she sat. Mr. Joshua smiled. Gillian said :

" Well, we're expecting the others to join us at any moment, but, so far, there are only ourselves, old Elspat the housekeeper, and Mr. Ker."

" Very nice ; very nice," said Mr. Joshua. He glanced down at the gun, waggled it a little, and then added : " Very, very nice."

" You might tell me one thing, before we go any further," said Gillian, striving to maintain an unforced note. " *Was* it you who sat next to me in the music-hall in Newcastle, the night you killed your cousin Graham and shot at Mrs. Bradley across his body ? "

"It was," said Mr. Joshua, with a smirk.

"Thanks. I've won my bet, then, Lesley," said Gillian, turning to her sister. "You remember I said so, that time you tried to smother me with the rug and kick my wrist?"

"Oh, yes, I remember," Lesley replied. "Nothing doing." She looked up confidingly at Mr. Joshua, hoping that he had not followed her sister's hint and her own repudiation of it. "Wouldn't you have thought it a pretty safe bet?" she enquired.

"Oh, I don't know," said Mr. Joshua, squatting down on his haunches, but not attempting to lay aside the gun. "After all, it might not have been me."

"You were seen in Newcastle, you know, with poor Geoffrey," Gillian went on.

"Why do you say 'poor' Geoffrey?" Mr. Joshua enquired.

"I say poor Geoffrey because he's dead," answered Gillian, unable to restrain a slight shiver at the recollection that it was in that very house that Geoffrey's body had been found, and that she was looking upon his murderer.

"Dead!" said Mr. Joshua, contriving to look astounded. "How? Dead?"

Gillian stared at him in astonishment. His shocked amazement seemed entirely genuine. She realised, then, for the first time, to what extent the sandy little man was a villain.

"He was found dead here," she said unwillingly.

"Poor Geoffrey," said Mr. Joshua. There was a slight pause. Gillian, terrified of having to sit in silence, made an effort to resurrect the conversation, and wished that Mrs. Bradley were at hand.

At the end of three-quarters of an hour, Mrs. Bradley began to wonder whether she had done wisely in deciding to leave David's house.

The night was dark and not particularly warm, and she reflected that if something had happened to delay seriously young Tom's arrival at Lanark station, she might easily wait about all night for the car, and, even then, in the end, be disappointed.

She wondered, also, whether she was at fault in her diagnosis of Mr. Joshua's movements. He would, she thought, reconnoitre at the tower, and he would probably make some attempt to find out how many people were likely to be in occupation of the keep. But she still could not make up her mind how the murder would be committed.

She had just decided to make her way to the keep to join the others when she was aware of a lantern which bobbed and danced above the heather about thirty yards, as nearly as she could judge the distance, in front and to the left of where she was standing.

She walked towards it, secure in the protection of the black night and the quietness of her footfalls on the heather, and then, as it moved onward in front of her in the direction in which she herself had elected to travel, she followed it, shortening the distance between herself and the light to about half, she thought, of what it had been at first.

The bearer of the lantern moved rapidly, but seemed to have no clear idea of the way. Over humps and tussocks Mrs. Bradley followed him, and was saved from stepping into a little burn by the fact that he did so first. He must have dropped the lantern, for the light, which had been dashed suddenly from her view, did not appear again, and she could hear the man floundering and cursing. She recognised the voice of Mr. Joshua. He seemed to be alone.

She herself had in her head a bird's-eye map of the journey between the house and the tower, so, making a slight detour, she found the culvert which carried a small, unwilling, skittishly-winding track across the water. Then she waited for Mr. Joshua and tailed behind him again, this time not five yards away.

So they made their way to the castle, and there Mrs. Bradley received a considerable shock. At one moment, it seemed, Mr. Joshua *was*, for she heard a faint scraping sound against the wall of the castle, but the next moment, most certainly, *he was not*. She took out her gun, and switched on her torch. Of Mr. Joshua there was no sign.

She waited, listened, and then walked all round the keep. It was very small ; a shell, in fact, of what it had been when it was built. It was open to the wild moor on the side by which they had approached it, but on the other three sides were remains, in fair condition, of a thick stone wall, which, as late as the early eighteenth century, had enclosed the bailey of the keep. Unless Mr. Joshua had climbed this wall —a pointless proceeding, and one which the evidence

of her own acute sense of hearing informed her he had
not followed—she could not think where he could have
gone, except inside the keep itself.

She had never under-rated Mr. Joshua. The
mistakes which had been made in his wild elimination
of everyone who stood between him and the family
inheritance had been the result of his collaboration
with lesser intellects. He himself had made no
mistakes, so far as Mrs. Bradley could tell, except
the capital error of entrusting his plans to con-
federates, especially to the unfortunate Geoffrey
who, through Gillian, had brought her into the
case.

She waited for a quarter of an hour—an endless
vigil it seemed in the silent darkness—and then
switched on her torch again and began to take stock
of the keep into which, it seemed certain, Mr. Joshua
had contrived to disappear.

She tried to judge at what part of the wall she had
heard the scraping sound which was the last she knew
of him, but it was difficult to do this, for noise by
night is deceptive.

The wall which she was inspecting had no opening
below the first-floor window of what she supposed
must be the great hall of the keep. Opening off the
hall was a small chamber probably used in medieval
times as a solar. The window which she could see
was no more than a slit. Even supposing that Mr.
Joshua could climb like a cat (and even that Mrs.
Bradley did not regard as impossible in a man so
obviously talented) she did not believe that he could
possibly have squeezed his body through it.

She shone the torch up at the window, but its beam did not penetrate, or else there was no one there, or else the occupants were asleep, for no response came, although she held the light steady whilst she counted slowly to a hundred.

CHAPTER XV

" ' O I hae lost my gowden knife ;
  I rather had lost my ain sweet life !
  And I hae lost a far better thing,
  The gilded sheath that it was in. ' "

Failing, so far, of her object, Mrs. Bradley walked
up to the front entrance of the keep and was about to
secure admission by a special rhythm of knocking
which had been arranged previously between herself and Elspat, when she was aware that the keep
was again the object of a person carrying a
lantern.

She withdrew strategically below the level of the
castle floor, and suddenly, as she descended the
mound towards the burn which ran at the foot of it
like a moat, she solved the problem of Mr. Joshua's
interesting disappearance.

She remembered that below the hill on which it
was built the castle had a water-gate. Mr. Joshua,
with an animal sixth sense, must have been aware
that he was being followed, or, more likely, had
merely felt the nearness of some undefinable danger,
and had done the one thing which at first she believed
he could not have done, that is, climbed the bailey
wall and dropped over on to the moor behind the
castle.

From here all he had to do was to run, behind

cover of the wall, around two sides of the tower to reach the water-gate.

The course of the burn had altered during the centuries. Where once had been an entry for little boats there was nothing now but the steep dry bank on which the tower was built. The burn was some six yards away.

Mrs. Bradley wondered what the approaching stranger had seen of her torch, but it was too late to worry about anything of the sort, and so she concentrated upon slipping away and making her way to the water-gate to discover by what means Mr. Joshua had used it to get inside the castle.

It then occurred to her that possibly Mr. Joshua was not inside the keep, but merely in hiding in the archway formed by the water-gate. She approached it carefully and suddenly switched on her torch. The water-gate hid no one. On the other hand, it appeared to be bricked up. She advanced to it, switched off her torch and listened.

There was no sound of footsteps, but if the new-comer—she thought that the man approaching the keep was most probably Mr. Frere or another of Mr. Joshua's gangsters—was aware of a secret entrance, she had no time to lose.

Risking discovery, she switched on her torch again, but the archway appeared to offer no possible means of entry to the castle. She put away her torch, and began to feel carefully all over the new, tight brickwork.

The unknown man was now approaching. Mrs. Bradley crept out from under the archway, lay in the heather, and waited. She could hear the man slipping and slithering as he descended the steep bank, and she could hear him cursing as he lost his footing, regained it, lost it once more, and finished up by rolling down the last six or seven feet of the mound.

Mrs. Bradley moved quickly and with characteristic dash and determination. It was the action of a couple of seconds with her to leap on the man, push her gun into his ribs and order him, in a horrid whisper, to remain absolutely still.

The man obeyed without a word.

" Now," said Mrs. Bradley, " in with you." She switched on her torch again, kept the gun pressed against his body for a moment, and then removed it whilst he got up, but kept a spotlight on him.

The man had no option but to obey her. He crawled into the archway.

Gillian, racking her brains, had hit upon a subject of conversation which seemed to amuse Mr. Joshua. It was an account of the trouble she had been at to find out where Geoffrey had gone when he had left her in her seat at the music hall.

That the account itself was exaggerated and mis-leading was not appreciated by Mr. Joshua, who, although he did not in the least under-rate Mrs. Bradley and her powers, thought the girls vapid and absurd, and this in spite of his experience of Gillian as a rugby football player.

Mr. Joshua, the girls soon realised, was willing to be amused, for he was waiting for something or somebody. The hints which had been passed from sister to sister could not be put into practice, as Lesley had immediately foreseen. Mr. Joshua might despise the girls for a couple of unintelligent hoydens, but his little green eyes were watchful, and, of course, he was armed.

So, in point of fact, was Gillian, but she doubted her ability to shoot Mr. Joshua before he shot her. In any case, she could not face the thought of firing at him unless he commenced the attack.

About a quarter of an hour passed, and then followed a curious scraping. Mr. Joshua turned to look up at the picture through which he had gained entrance to the room. The instant's hiatus in his watchfulness and preparedness was sufficient for both the girls. Gillian snatched up her coat and fell on him with it. Lesley, with the movement of a dancer, neatly kicked the revolver out of his hand.

There was a Kiplingesque mêlée of a sumptuous kind, during which the candles went out. At the end of it, Gillian, with the beginnings of a black eye, and Lesley, with two badly bruised, stamped-upon fingers, sat up, as the candle-light sputtered into being again, to find Mr. Joshua gone, the picture disappeared in favour of a yawning gap in the wall, and Mrs. Bradley, metaphorically licking her whiskers, grinning in the midst of the débris.

Lesley, holding her crushed fingers tenderly in the palm of her other hand, looked at Mrs. Bradley without surprise.

"My dear girls," said Mrs. Bradley, "you are wounded." She rose and looked at the hole where the picture had been. She clicked her tongue before she turned away. Then she said : "Our friend's hasty departure has ruined the mechanism, I fear. Gillian, point your revolver at that hole, and if anyone enters, or even shows his face, shoot, and do not hesitate. Lesley, you come with me."

She took Lesley down the stone staircase to the guard-room on the ground floor in which the bodies had been found. Here she produced a first-aid outfit and dealt tenderly and skilfully with the crushed fingers.

"Badly bruised, and hurt, I know," she said. "But the bones are all right. More comfortable?"

"Yes, thanks," said Lesley, in the gruff voice of one who suffers very considerable pain and hopes that she does not show it. Mrs. Bradley patted her kindly upon the shoulder. They returned to Gillian, and Mrs. Bradley did what she could (without raw beef) to a rapidly darkening eye.

"And now, what happened?" asked Lesley. Mrs. Bradley described her dramatic entry by means of the water-gate in the wake of Mr. Frere.

"Some people have luck," said Gillian. Mrs. Bradley acknowledged this back-handed compliment with a cackle.

"I thought Mr. Joshua must have some scheme for entering the tower," said Mrs. Bradley. "But it was necessary for us to leave the house. We never could have defended it."

"Bit of a risk, though, if he knew he could get in

here," said Lesley critically. Mrs. Bradley agreed
but Gillian suddenly broke in.

"What I'm most anxious to know," she said, with
some vehemence, "is how we get the tabs on Mr.
Joshua. I mean, how long is he going to be able
to make himself such a pest, and go on murdering his
relations ? "

"He will not murder David Ker," said Mrs.
Bradley, "and because he doesn't, he will give himself
away, I rather fancy. Our Mr. Joshua is not only
a clever criminal. He is a monomaniac."

"Certifiable ? " asked Gillian.

"Certainly not. But, all the same, a man of only
idea, and that one dangerous."

"Then you mean we've no more evidence against
him than we had before Geoffrey's death ? "

"We have no more evidence that we could offer
a jury," Mrs. Bradley agreed, "but, all the same,
we make progress. One end of the very long string
which we have to unravel is at the house in the marshes
I feel strongly—and have left the inspector there to
carry on his investigation along the lines I have
indicated to him—that we still have a corpse to
discover."

"Oh, no, Aunt Adela ! Who ? "

"The original Mr. Lancaster. I think that pressure
brought to bear upon Mr. Frere, who has been im-
personating Mr. Lancaster for about three years
may have a strange and, to us, a satisfactory result
Even Mr. Frere may not be the original Mr. Frere
but another impersonation."

With this the girls had to be content, for Mrs.

Bradley insisted upon going into the great hall of the keep and waking David Ker. Elspat had never even dozed. She had made a great fire of logs in the centre fireplace, and then had retired to her original seat, and was there, bolt upright still, her strong hands clasped, her petticoats up to her knees—a habit she had from being accustomed to a chimney corner —and her calm face passionless and at peace.

She looked up as Mrs. Bradley entered. She recognised the brisk, light footfall.

" Aye, ye're here," she remarked. " I ken na how ye came ben, but I'm glad to see ye."

" Thank you," said Mrs. Bradley. " I came in by way of the water-gate, if that's what it is."

Elspat shook her head.

" I dinna ken. Whaur's your man George and whaur's James Alexander Musgrave ? "

" I don't know. I wish I did. They've the boy with them, too—or so I hope. We've to block the secret entrance from the water-gate. I must wake David. He'll know more about it, likely, than anyone else."

David knew nothing about the water-gate. He did not believe it had ever been a water-gate. Most likely it would be the entrance to the cellars.

Conducted by Mrs. Bradley and the two girls he inspected the hole in the wall. Gillian and Lesley volunteered to explore it, and did so. The mechanism behind the picture could not be located, but the short steep ramp which had been built up from a flight of steps above the water-gate to this first-floor room formed a ready means of ingress.

To block it up seemed impossible until Elspat, called into consultation, suggested filling the opening with coal and coke.

A fatigue party, consisting of the two girls, Elspat and David, thereupon carried up coal and coke from well-stocked cellars opening out of the guard-room used by old Joshua as a kitchen and living-room, and shot it through the picture-hole down the ramp which was shut off from the flight of outer steps by a stout door. It was clear that the whole formed one of the original entrances of the keep, for the door was three inches thick, nail-studded, and capable of withstanding any shock short of an explosion.

The coal and coke were brought up in pails, an old zinc bath, cooking pots, David's hat, and in bags formed by loading the fuel on to thick table-covers and blankets and dragging them upstairs by the four corners.

Fortunately old Joshua seemed to have found warmth a necessity, for there were about two tons of coal and half a ton (according to Elspat's computation) of coke. By the time they had cleared out all this and shot it down, the entrance was satisfactorily blocked, and nothing but dynamite would have blasted open the door against which the long heap was piled.

" Still plenty of room," said David, putting his head in at the aperture which remained. He was as black as though he had been coaling ship, and so were the two girls. Elspat, although she had worked harder than anybody, was reasonably free from grime, and retained her usual dignified appearance.

"They'll no force an entry that way," she observed with satisfaction. "I have the copper heated," she continued, "and when I will have scoured a bucket, the lassies and all of ye can wash."

"What about the outside doors?" asked Mrs. Bradley.

"There's na but twa," Elspat responded, "and they'll not break them down in a hurry."

Mrs. Bradley went with her to inspect them. It appeared that she was right. The keep had taken on its original aspect of fortress.

The time was now three in the morning. It would be light in a couple of hours.

"They must attack us to-day, and soon, if they're going to, surely," said Gillian. "They daren't wait very much longer. Surely we've got a case against Mr. Joshua now?"

"I don't know, I'm sure," said Mrs. Bradley. "And, in any case, we're in a state of siege. Nobody is likely to come by here. We are not on the telephone, and even if we could get back to David's house, the wires there are cut. As for having a case against Mr. Joshua, what has he done? Certainly he broke into this place to-night, but he did no damage, he brought nobody with him (so far as we could prove) and, after all, he is related to the owner of the building."

"But aren't we ever going to be able to get him arrested?" asked Gillian.

"Time will show," Mrs. Bradley replied, "and probably that time will condense itself into the next

U

two hours. Before we go into further details, however, I have something here to show David."

She drew out a bulky document, stiff, crackling, and ornamented with the decorations of that romantic institution, the law.

"Those are the missing deeds, I think, David," she said. "You remember the hint about good Saint Rosalie ? Well, when we discovered the entrance from the water-gate, thanks to Mr. Joshua and Mr. Frere, it seemed to me that the hole behind the picture made quite a good crevice in itself. As for our burn, above which this castle is built, the Ordnance map indicates that it joins a tributary of the Clyde."

David examined the deeds.

"I'll have to let Braid see these. Meanwhile, Beatrice, I'll be obliged if you will keep them in your possession," he said.

"I shall be very glad of the opportunity," said Mrs. Bradley, "to examine them at my leisure."

Her leisure, to the amazement of the girls who were waiting in feverish excitement now for the promised attack on the keep, seemed to commence at once. She settled herself comfortably in the solar, now swept clean of coal dust by the indefatigable Elspat, and examined the deeds with every appearance of absorption.

At the churchyard where the coffin of Mr. Lancaster-Frere had been interred with the usual ceremonies some time previously, there was mild, restrained, but genuine, interest and excitement. The coffin, taken up from the grave by order of the Home Secretary, had been opened, and Mrs. Bradley's hints and prophecies had proved true. The coffin was nothing but an ,empty, silk-lined husk.

What followed next day is historic, for it appeared in all the newspapers and was absorbed, along with Sunday breakfast, in greater detail, by most of the British public three days later.

The house in the marshes was searched, and the garden was quartered and dug over by the police. The search went on for two days. At the end of the second day the remains were found of an elderly man and of a woman. This discovery was made at about the time that David Ker, the two girls and Elspat were leaving David's house for the castle, so that by three o'clock next morning, when Mrs. Bradley had settled herself to peruse the deeds of the Clydesdale property under which, presumably, there was a deposit of coal, the news was not known to anybody but the police. The besieged party in the castle did not even know what must have been known by that time throughout the length and breadth of England, that is, of the discovery of the empty coffin. As Mrs. Bradley, however, had deduced that both discoveries must be made, it was the same to her as if she had been in direct receipt of the information, and made no difference at all to her plans.

She was not troubled, either, as to what would be the ultimate fate of Mr. Joshua, for it was logical to suppose that the mystery of the empty coffin must soon involve Mr. Frere, who, according to evidence which could be produced from young Tom, should have been lying in it.

The solving of this little problem of the corpse which was not, would be bound to lead to the discovery of the corpse (or corpses, if the late Mr. Lancaster had had a servant or servants) which was. It was this corpse which would arise, as it were, from its grave, to confront Mr. Frere, its impersonator, and it was at this point, thought Mrs. Bradley (truly, as it turned out shortly afterwards), that Mr. Frere would break down. His breaking down would at once involve Mr. Joshua, and that would be, for Mr. Joshua, the beginning of the end. From corpse to corpse, as it were, the police would pipe, advancing, and step by step, inevitably, Mr. Joshua would be compelled to follow, dancing.

Mrs. Bradley grinned mirthlessly as she rustled the stiff pages of the title-deeds. Mr. Joshua's ultimate fate would not cause her, she thought, to shed a tear.

The grandfather clock in the guardroom where Elspat sat, knitting now, ticked on, with aged insistence upon the passing of time. At four o'clock Elspat got up, put away her knitting, went to the great door shaped like the archway leading into an Early English church, and listened carefully. Then she lay down on the cold stone flags, laid an ear to the ground and listened again.

She got up and ascended the stone staircase to the solar.

" I hear them coming," she said. " They're dragging something. Likely they'll burn us out."

Mrs. Bradley had already considered this possibility, but had rejected it because such a proceeding was likely to fire the heather, and a heath fire, even in that remote district, would soon attract attention. She mentioned this to Elspat, but the housekeeper shook her head.

"They'll not set fire to the house before dawn," she said. "A fire doesna show up in daylight the same as it would in the dark. I'm thinking they could burn us out in a twa-three hours, and help wouldna be likely to come to us much before that."

Mrs. Bradley considered this lugubrious opinion and felt bound to admit that, although they were pessimistic, the housekeeper's words were probably none the less true.

"What do you advise, then, Elspat?" she enquired.

"I would say a sortie. Dinna ye see, they'll no expect anything of the kind. A pity your mon George and James Alexander Musgrave are no here to help us. Then we wad ding them fine."

Mrs. Bradley was not certain that the bold plan advanced by the housekeeper would succeed. All the same, she and Gillian were armed,

"We maun surprise them, ye ken," said Elspat. "It wouldna do to wait too long, for they think to frighten us into rinnin' awa'. But gin we cam' oot at them and themselves no thinkin' aboot it, it wad be a grand battle, ye ken."

Mrs. Bradley grinned, and went off to work out a plan. The first thing to do, she felt, was to reconnoitre. This reconnaissance would be best carried out by Elspat or herself. With the modern instinct against exposing other people to danger, she went

to the second door of the keep, unbarred it and slipped
out, leaving the door ajar and Gillian, with her
gun, on guard at the entrance.

The night was preparing to give place to day.
There was already a greying in the east. She crouched
by the wall of the keep and listened. Then, keeping
low, she made a complete circuit of the castle. At
the water-gate she hid, and listened long, for she
thought she heard stealthy movement.

As she came round the angle of the wall towards
the pointed arch of the main entrance to the keep,
she discovered that movement certainly was going
on, for a sheaf of brushwood seemed suddenly to
make a rush at her, and it was only by a hasty with-
drawal that she literally saved her face, which must
otherwise have been lacerated by the twigs.

She withdrew rapidly to the open door, slipped
in, with a whispered word to Gillian, who had received
orders not to fire unless the entrance was rushed,
and pushed the door to, but did not close it for fear
of giving the alarm.

She then took over the guardianship of the door,
and sent the girl on the rounds with a message.

In a short time Lesley, David and Elspat were
with them, and had received the simple instructions
which would lead to the evacuation of the keep.

One by one the besieged slipped out and crept
round the outer wall away from the side at which
Mr. Joshua's men were piling up the brushwood.

There was only one danger. The brushwood
was being dragged in through the wide gap on the
burn side, where there was no longer a wall round

what had been the courtyard of the castle. On every other side the wall enclosed the castle ground. This meant that the evacuating party would need to climb the wall on the opposite side of the courtyard, and the now rapidly lightening east made anyone climbing a wall a mark for a shot.

Mrs. Bradley sent the two girls over first, then she and Elspat helped David up, and he, lying flat, pulled up Elspat. Mrs. Bradley heaved herself up, and all three dropped to the heather, whose springy stems broke their fall.

The plan was to regain David's house, and then trust to luck that George, James Musgrave and young Tom would return in time to be of some assistance.

This trust was soon repaid. By the time they reached the house the east was primrose instead of pale grey, and, bumping over the moorland track which turned off the road from Biggar, came the car. Lesley and Gillian ran forward. Lesley tripped and came down, but was soon up again, and the young girls cantered, stumbling, towards the now stationary headlamps.

" Miss ? " said George, addressing them collectively.

" Oh, George, wait a minute. Aunt Adela's just coming," panted Gillian. " Is James Musgrave there ? "

" Yes, miss, at the back. And the boy madam was after. A nice dance he's led himself and us," said George, in vengeful accents.

James Musgrave and young Tom got out. Mrs. Bradley and Elspat came up, the one with brisk, the other with lengthy strides. David, slower and stiffer, followed at his own pace.

"Now, George," said Mrs. Bradley, "bring a spanner. A nice large one would be best. James Musgrave, can you fight?"

James Musgrave grunted. There was a humorous undertone in the sound.

"And what about you, Tom?" Mrs. Bradley enquired.

"Aye. I'm a right fighter, like," Tom answered modestly. "I'd be best hammering stones on their yeads."

"You show an intelligent grasp of the situation," said Mrs. Bradley. "It does you credit, Tom. I say nothing of the hour at which you choose to arrive, nor my anxiety concerning your welfare. We can discuss those things later, at our leisure. All the same, though, I am not at all sure you ought to be allowed to fight. You happen to be a material witness. You'll be needed to swear to Mr. Frere."

"Havers," said David. "Let the lad have his fun."

So it was settled that all should take part in the battle. It was still uncertain how many people were with Mr. Joshua in his attack on the tower, and of the proposed victims only two, in the popular conception, were capable of bearing arms. On the other hand, Mrs. Bradley was, in the popular phrase, a host in herself, David and young Tom were what the Scots are apt to call bonny fighters, and as for the two girls, they had the modern Amazonian streak, and were capable of proving themselves, if not as muscularly strong, as determined, brave and resistant as the men.

Mrs. Bradley, however, considered them doubtfully, when counting heads for the counter-attack on the besiegers still urged by the militant Elspat. She was old-fashioned enough to feel she owed a duty to their mother.

" I think you two had better go back to the house and get some food ready. It will be needed," she said in persuasive tones.

" Elspat's job," said Lesley, engaged, out of range of the headlights, in delicate female preparations for battle. These condensed themselves into taking off her stays, and rolling down her stockings to the ankles.

" And suppose we got kidnapped or something, stuck there in the house alone ? " demanded Gillian, with unreasonable but forceful pessimism. " We're coming with you, while we're safe. George, got a spanner with a knob on it ? If you have, you can take my gun."

" Spanners don't take knobs, miss. They are more apt to end in a kind of what's-it," said George.

" Gimme," said Lesley, putting out her hand for one of the neat, heavy implements. " Gillian, keep your gun. George doesn't want it. He likes a hand-to-hand."

As there was no time to be lost, if the counter-attack were not to fail, Mrs. Bradley thereupon gave the whole enterprise her blessing in a cackle of hideous mirth, and, under her direction, the oddly-assorted but resolute band set out.

As they approached the castle, absolute silence was enjoined. This proved to be scarcely necessary, however, as, apart from the crackling of the piles of brushwood to which Mr. Joshua and his party had already set fire, he and they were shouting at the tops of their voices to the supposed inmates of the tower to come out and to surrender.

This scene was enjoyed for a moment or two by the advancing band, before they charged in to the attack.

The surprise assault succeeded beyond all hopes except those of the valiant Elspat. By the time the incendiaries had realised that the tables were turned, both George and James Alexander Musgrave, shedding their civilised prejudices like bathers shedding garments on the banks of a limpid stream, had waded into the thick of the fray and were laying about them with so much hearty goodwill that Mrs. Bradley, leaping after them, stumbled over the unconscious form of one of their victims and came down full length among the heather. Mr. Joshua's bullet, which should have taken her in the body, ploughed a furrow, as she fell forward, in the ancient felt hat she was wearing, but did no other damage. At the same instant Elspat, a torch of flaring pinewood (picked up out of the very heap which was nearest to firing the building) gripped in her left hand and a heavy little axe in her right, caught Mr. Joshua on the end of a vicious swing with the back of the axe, and knocked him senseless into one of his crackling bonfires.

She dropped her torch on the blazing heap, let

go the axe, and, plunging both arms in, as she might have plunged them into the suds of a wash-tub, plucked him forth and, literally flinging him to earth, stamped out the flames from his clothes.

Gillian and Lesley had picked out Mr. Frere. He, however, bolted like a runaway horse as soon as he heard the sounds of battle. The fleet-footed girls pursued him, and brought him down. In supremely business-like fashion Lesley then sat on his head, whilst Gillian tied his ankles and wrists with his own handkerchief and one of her stockings, and rolled him further off from the rapidly encroaching flames.

The morning was now full day. The rest of Mr. Joshua's people, pursued, yelping, by George and James Musgrave, both of whom were obviously in their element, made ff, and, since they would not repay pursuit, were permitted to go.

Water from the burn, scooped up in buckets—the door of the keep from which the party had escaped was still open—was used to put out the fires. Fortunately the flames were still consuming the brushwood piles, and had scarcely reached the heather.

"Dirty swine," said George, as, smoke-blackened, tired, and somewhat disgruntled at having been baulked of his prey so soon, he returned, with James Musgrave, to the house.

"It was a bonny wee fight, yon," said James Musgrave, with moderate enthusiasm, wiping the end of his spanner with a handful of heather he had gathered. "Will I be coming back wi' ye in the car?"

"You better. Those blokes may have to be lifted in, and the ladies and the old gentleman have had enough, I should reckon."

"Well, Elspat," said Mrs. Bradley, as the tall and militant housekeeper stalked beside her.

"Aye," the Borderer replied, with a slight, tight smile. Mrs. Bradley cackled, but her first task, when they were all assembled at the house, complete with prisoners of war, was to examine everybody's hurts and dress them. Casualties were few. Elspat's burnt hands and Mr. Joshua's scorch-marks were the most serious, but were derided by both the victims. Mr. Joshua, in fact, literally spat with annoyance when Mrs. Bradley deftly attended to his burns, and Elspat pettishly exclaimed that it was all a lot of nonsense.

"In fact," said Gillian to Lesley, "if she hoots and havers any more, I shall go into screeching hysterics, especially if I hear Aunt Adela repeating the words and trying to get the intonation right."

"Ah, but Aunt Adela thinks she's got Scots blood herself," said Lesley, in extenuation of Mrs. Bradley's behaviour, which, north of the Border, sometimes embarrassed her friends.

Mr. Joshua was hanged on the twelfth of December, after a trial which lasted three days. As Mrs. Bradley had expected, Mr. Frere, whose name turned out to be Hill (and who had served seven years for black-mail before he met Mr. Joshua), supplied the police with details of his partner's exploits for which evidence was otherwise lacking, and received a sentence commensurate with this courtesy.

Besides digging up the bodies of the poor, mad Mr. Lancaster and of the woman who was identified as his housekeeper, the police also discovered, under the ground on which the gamekeeper's hut had been built, the body of the real Mr. Frere, a dark gentleman whose negroid experience had included (according to evidence gathered in his empty house) an extensive and messy acquaintance with the Voodoo cult.

The housekeeper upon whom Mrs. Bradley had forced her society ; the pseudo-Mr. Lancaster's groom, gamekeeper and garrulous housemaid, had all been in the employment of Mr. Frere, and were thankful (they said) to obtain Christian work after his disappearance, which they had (they said) attributed to Satan his master. (This opinion Mrs. Bradley found was also current in the village.)

There was little doubt of their complicity in the plot, and the housekeeper and the gamekeeper were known to the police, but proof did not materialise and they were merely called as witnesses for the prosecution.

The mysterious niece Phyllis (or Madeleine) turned out to be Mr. Joshua's wife. She was not, of course, called upon to give evidence against her husband, and it was not clear what part, if any, she had played in his schemes.

David Ker did not take advantage of the fact that there was a seam of coal beneath the land he had inherited, and as, in his will, he has left the whole of his property to Mrs. Bradley, it is likely

that his few acres of Scottish moorland will retain
their larger usefulness, and that to-morrow, and
for many years to come, it will still be possible to say :

> " La y Isobel sits in her bower sewing,
>   Aye as the gowans grow gay—
>   She heard an elf-knight his horn blowing,
>   The first morning in May."

MORE VINTAGE MURDER MYSTERIES